As Much as I Ever Could

Brandy Woods Snow

Filles Vertes Publishing

COEUR D'ALENE, ID

To my children, Maddox, Hayden, and Colton:
Be Fearless. Live Fully.

"Death is not the greatest loss in life. The greatest loss is what dies inside us while we live."

— Norman Cousins,
American journalist, author, professor, and world peace advocate

As Much as I
Ever Could

Brandy Woods Snow

Chapter One

A summer away at Memaw's can't rectify everything that fell apart in a single minute, but that won't stop my dad from forcing it on me.

My fingers wrench tighter around the handle grip of Dad's Ford Explorer as he hugs the center line, tires thumping over golden reflectors in waves and shooting vibrations through my seat. I glance over my shoulder to make sure the door lock is crammed to its neck into the tan vinyl interior. Not that it'd make a difference if he were to flip this thing head-over-end into the muddy goop of tidal flats along either side of the road. If a body's going to exit a car in a hurry, it sure as hell won't wait for an unlocked door.

These kinds of thoughts never shoved their way into my brain before the accident. Now they circulate like a washing machine stuck on the spin cycle.

I sigh and yank my phone off the dashboard. 4:15 p.m. Only ten more minutes to get my summer of hell underway.

A notification blinks on the home screen. One new email from Trent Casey and all I can see of it is, "CJ, things have changed so much this last year that I think..." Inbox preview cruelty at its finest. A little sneak peek of my on-again, off-again boyfriend kicking me to the curb because I've been too screwed up to screw him the past year. Not that I'd screwed him before, or anyone else for that matter.

I toss the phone in the cup holder and stare over at my dad in the driver's seat, his eyes fixed and hooded as if in a trance. He hasn't spoken in over a hundred miles, but I've strategically coughed from time to time to make sure there's at least a reaction to the noise, and he's not comatose or something. Plus, it's easier than actually talking, and it warrants no response from him. Win-win.

Dad flips on the blinker, its *dink-doonk, dink-doonk, dink-doonk* signaling a right turn. Into where I have no idea, and unless Memaw has taken up living in a dilapidated open-air shack, he's seriously misguided. He pulls into one of the ten open parking slots, demarcated by rows of conch shells instead of actual painted-on lines. How beachy of them.

Dad lets the engine idle, sliding his phone from the pocket of his polo and pecking out a text message without so much as a word or glance in my direction. I unlatch my seatbelt and open the door, easing out onto the hot, gritty sand, which creeps into my sandals and scratches at the skin.

"Where are we?" When he doesn't respond, I step beside the open door, banging my hand on the window. "Dad, where are we?"

"Edisto Island, of course," he mumbles, never looking up from his phone, his fingers still moving furiously over the screen.

I point to the rectangular banner draped atop the entrance with what looks like a hand-stenciled *Welcome to Edisto Beach, SC!* in blue paint. "No shit. I mean, what is this place?"

"Watch your mouth, CJ. I'm still your father." He finally looks up long enough to glare across his steering wheel at the banner, squinting as if it's written in some foreign language before looking back at me. He waves his hand around. "We're obviously at the market."

The entrance isn't a single open-close door, but one of those garage-style deals that pulls down from the ceiling. Oyster shell wind chimes tinkle in the breeze. I take a deep breath, the briny air expanding in my lungs and coating my skin, and somehow start imagining myself as one of those slugs we used to find on the back porch at home and pour salt over. Almost immediately, their slimy little bodies would foam up and implode, turning into a dried-up crispie we'd flick off into the grass the next day. Maybe that'll happen to me, and I can simply shrivel up and disappear.

Dad gets out and lifts the back hatch, and I walk to meet him, giving an extra foot shake on each step to loosen the stowaway sand from my sandals.

"But why are we here?"

"This is where Memaw's picking you up." He hauls out my two large suitcases and sets them under the overhang. "She's running late, but she'll be here within the next twenty minutes."

"And you're just gonna leave me here?" I thumb over my shoulder.

He stares at me as if I've just asked for an explanation on the meaning of life, standing like a statue except for the front flip of his thinning auburn hair that tousles with the breeze. That hair, along with his chocolate brown eyes and freckles, are the only things we even share anymore. Everything else is gone. Evaporated.

"Don't be dramatic, CJ. I have a long drive home." He slams the hatch, walks to his still-open driver door and slides in behind the wheel. The passenger window rolls down part-way. "I'll see you at the end of summer. Bye." The words scarcely exit his lips before the window's rolled up and he's peeling out of the parking lot on two wheels as if he's off to a five-alarm fire.

Wow. Truly heartfelt. I think he might miss me. I lock my jaw, forcing my quivering stomach back in its rightful place. Part of me loathes him for just dumping me here. The other part understands, though. He hates me for what happened and wants me gone too.

I can't blame him for that.

"Bye Dad," I whisper in the wind, staring down at my bags before glancing out across the surrounding marsh.

What am I supposed to do for twenty minutes? Lotus pose? Stare out over the grasses and become one with my new home-away-from-home? Not likely.

I force out an audible breath and bend down to grab my wallet from the suitcase, folding out the side flap to check myself in the tiny mirror. The jagged tip-top edge of my scar peeks out from the neckline, so I inch my white T-shirt straight on my shoulders, making sure it's hidden. Not like I need another reason for the people in this market to look at me like a freakshow. I secure the magnetic clasp on my wallet with a click and walk inside.

The floor is packed dirt and sand, the shelves nothing more than overturned crates and stacked-up pallets brimming with rainbow-hued mounds of fresh fruits and vegetables. I trudge to the refrigerator cases, their motors humming in a monotonous chorus, swing open the door, and grab a bottled ginger ale from the rack. Glass bottles, huh? This place is *all* about modern ambiance.

At the cash register—the only thing in the whole place that doesn't look like it got dropped off of Noah's Ark or dug out of some grungy guy's truck—a girl about my age stands behind the counter, power grin spread wide, lips stretched around both rows of teeth. The top ones have braces with little purple bands.

"Hey there! Will this be all for you today?" She takes the bottle, punches in the barcode numbers by hand, then slides it back across the counter, tilting her head just enough that the honey-blond ponytail poked through the back of her baseball cap waggles from side to side.

"Yeah, thanks." I pull out my debit card and hand it to her. She slides it and then pushes the handheld electronic device in front of me. While I type in my pin, she flicks my card in her fingers, staring at the front of it.

"Wait...Ainsworth? Are you Bessie's granddaughter, CJ?" She leans across the counter on her elbows, blue eyes wide like polished sapphires.

"Uh, yeah. That's me." I pluck my card from her fingers and shove it back inside my wallet. "How do you know Memaw?"

"Everyone knows your Memaw! She's like a grandma to all of us." She looks over her shoulder and yells, "Bo, get in here!" before turning back and sticking her hand out to shake. "I'm Ginny Lee, by the way. You can call me Gin." I reach out and take her hand. A stocky, chocolate-haired guy with the same eyes as Gin jogs to the counter and waves. He's cute in a boy band-meets-rugged-farmhand kind of way.

"I'm Beauregard Johnson, Gin's brother."

"That's some name there, Beauregard."

"My mama loves historical family names. My great-great-great-great grandfather was also a Beauregard."

That's a lot of greats. I give him a thumbs-up. "Ah, then her name choice stands completely validated." I smirk and pick up my bottle, wrestling with the stubborn-ass metal cap.

"You can call me Bo. Everybody else does." He offers a dazzling white, if somewhat crooked, smile. His curly hair, longer on top with shaved-close sides, flops lazily over his brow. "Did I hear you say you're Ms. Bessie's granddaughter?"

"In the flesh. By the way," I turn back to Gin, "when you said Memaw's a grandma to 'all of us,' who exactly is us?"

"Pretty much the whole town. She's a legend around here. Volunteers like crazy." She narrows her eyes. The question marks practically float in speech bubbles above her head. "You didn't know that?"

I bite at a piece of dry skin on my lip. "I don't know much about her. I haven't seen her since I was eight."

The two of them glance sideways at each other. "Oh. Well, we live right next door to her." Gin hesitates, then reaches out over the counter to touch my arm, her fingers barely brushing my skin. "She told us about what happened…"

My heart catapults to my toes as a familiar frenzied vibration courses through my veins. Not here. That was never supposed to follow me here. "No." I point the longneck of the bottle between the two of them. They both step back, hands up. "I don't want to talk about that. Everyone over the last eight months has steered clear of me because…" I open my mouth wide, willing the oxygen to saturate me. "I can't believe Memaw would tell." I slam the bottle on the counter and wrench my hands over my face.

"CJ?" I glance at Gin from between my fingers. "Only Bo and I know, and we won't tell." She stares at Bo, who nods in agreement.

"Ms. Bessie wanted you to have some friends here who understood if…it took you a while to open up. We won't mention it again." Bo shifts from leg to leg, rubbing his hands together.

Somewhere down deep, my backbone relinquishes its grip on my stomach, and I swallow hard. "Thanks, y'all."

He ducks around the corner of the counter and walks over to me, holding out his clenched fist. "Bump 'em." I stare at his knuckles, then follow the ridges over the top of his hand and up his arm. He widens his eyes and shakes his fist a bit, still waiting.

"C'mon CJ. I know we're all gonna be great friends." Gin's syrupy drawl makes me almost believe it's possible. I force a smile and reach forward to bump my fist into Bo's, but we're interrupted by the squealing of tires and the gritty pitter-patter of displaced sand raining down in the parking lot.

A bright orange Dodge Challenger with parallel black racing stripes pulls in front of the entrance and revs its engine, the thunderous growl rattling the walls. Bo looks at his watch, and a grin creeps across his lips. "Aw hell, here comes trouble."

He walks halfway to the front and stands with his hands on his hips while Gin begins fidgeting with her hair, sticking loose wisps under the cap's brim, and running her tongue over her lips time and again until they glisten with wetness. Damn, these two must have a major yen for trouble. I smirk and shake my head, but find myself leaning forward on tiptoes to see just who's creating all the commotion.

He gets out and slams the door, twirling the keys on his finger. Taller and thinner than Bo, his arms and legs look a bit too long for his body, but it doesn't affect his stride. He glides in, heavy on the heels of his sneakers, almost as if he's somehow reclining on an invisible cushion while walking. Bo high-fives him as he saunters to the counter across from me and hops onto it in one seamless motion. Gin's at his side almost immediately, arms folded underneath her boobs, creating a vertical line of cleavage above the scoop neck of her tank.

"Hey kid." He flicks the brim of her cap, and she giggles, swatting his hand. But he's not looking at her. His jade eyes pierce me like daggers as he nods in my direction. "Who's the chick?"

Oh God. One of those.

I roll my eyes and grab the ginger ale from the counter, renewing my fight against the stubborn bottle cap. "Someone who doesn't appreciate being called chick," I say through the grunts as I twist raw ridges into my palm.

Bo steps in between us. "CJ, this is my best friend Jarrett Ramsey. Jett for short. And Jett, this is CJ Ainsworth, Ms. Bessie's granddaughter. She's here for the summer."

He runs his eyes up and down me in a way that makes my bones shiver and my blood boil. My body wars within itself. "I didn't know Ms. Bessie had a granddaughter. We've never seen you here before."

I purse my lips and shrug my shoulders. "Can't say that now."

"You don't look like a CJ." Jett stops and runs his tongue across the front of his teeth, and as it swipes from right to left, a metallic flash catches my eye. A gold-capped tooth. Odd.

"What does that stand for, anyway?" he asks.

"Camelia Jayne."

Jett smiles, but Bo slaps his hand over his mouth, laughing. "And you made fun of Beauregard! I'm sorry my name seems too old-fashioned for you, *Camelia*."

"Quit being an ass, Bo." Gin sashays around the counter and inserts herself between us. Jett jumps down and walks beside me, tugging my French braid between his fingers. I flick my eyes toward Gin who frowns and looks at her flip-flops.

"I think I'm gonna call you Cami." He drops my hair and folds his arms across his chest. "Yeah, Cami. That's better."

"You can call me what you want. Doesn't mean I'll answer." I snort then pick up the edge of my T-shirt, protecting my hand as I try again to open my drink.

The edges of his lips crinkle into a grin. He yanks the bottle from my hand, leans back, and pops the top off in the metal bottle opener hidden on the side of the counter. The top drops with a *clink* into a white bucket with about a million others. He holds the bottle up to his eyes, scanning the label, then tucks his bottom lip between his teeth, nodding. "Blenheim Hot. A bold choice."

"You even have commentary for ginger ale?" I yank the bottle from his hand, the jostle creating a thin, foamy line in the bottle neck. That's when I notice they're all staring at me like I'm some three-headed goat, and I dart my eyes down to make sure my scar's not showing. It isn't. Whatever. If watching me drink this is so damn interesting, I can't wait to see what the next three and half months bring. I wrap my lips around the smooth bottle edge and take a substantial gulp. Their smiles widen, eyes huge.

Suddenly I know why. The liquid sloshes down my throat like a river of fire, the flames sucking back into my nostrils, robbing my breath. My nose runs and eyes water. "What in the hell?" The words squeak out as I fan my open mouth. "I think I just swallowed a firecracker!"

"Told ya it was a bold choice," Jett says as they all circle around me, laughing. "That's the real deal. The famous southern tradition."

"It's a southern tradition to burn holes in your esophagus?"

"A little bit of fire is good for the soul. Where's your fire? What's your passion, Cami? Gotta let it out. Put the pedal to the metal." He leans back, sticking out his leg like it's on a gas pedal, his right hand shifting imaginary gears.

I shudder. "No thanks. I'm good."

He thumps his fingernail against my bottle. "We'll see."

I glance up. Jett stares at me, gaze like stone, with a slight upturn to the corner of his lips. He wrenches his arm toward his face, clicking the side button on his watch, then turns to Bo. "You ready to go, man? We gotta be there in ten."

"Yep, I'm done here today." Bo nods and waves at me. "Nice meeting you, CJ. I'll catch you later at home."

"Bye kid." Jett side-hugs Gin who clamps her eyes closed and nestles into his side like a faithful puppy. He walks toward his car but pauses at the pallet of cantaloupes, looking back at me over his shoulder. "See you around...Cami."

I break eye contact, whipping my head sideways to the stacked containers of pimento cheese and crab dip on my left. He laughs, and seconds later, two doors slam and the engine roars to life in a deep rumble. I look back as Jett accelerates out the drive onto the blacktop, tires squealing and smoke rising in the air behind him.

Gin sighs and rubs her fingertips down the length of her neck. "He's trouble, all right. The good kind."

I shake my head. "There is no good kind. Trouble's trouble, and I don't need any more of that in my life."

Chapter Two

G in ducks behind the counter and re-emerges with a crate of bottled sodas. "Keep me company while I re-stock?"

I glance at the empty parking lot. "Captive audience," I say and draw in a much smaller sip of my ginger ale. "So, I'm guessing you have a thing for what's-his-name?"

"Jett?" She giggles, double-fisting Cheerwines to load into the freezer. "He and Bo have been friends forever. We were all raised together. He's gorgeous—I mean, you saw him—but it'll never be like that between us." She pulls the door open with her foot, steps in front and lets it bump on her hip, continuing to talk as she refills the shelves. "Jett thinks of me as a kid sister. Always has." She steps toward me, and the door slams, the bottles clinking together inside. "But he seemed to like you."

I roll my eyes with a throaty snort. "Hardly."

"Trust me. Jett's hyper-focused on his racing." She picks up the empty crate and props it on her hip under one arm before walking back to the counter. "If it ain't got wheels and a motor, he usually ain't interested."

I narrow my eyes, every muscle rigid. "His racing? Like illegal street racing?" That explains the hot dogging in the parking lot. Just some punk trying to prove his manhood with a flashy car and a disrespect for anyone in his way.

"Heck no!" Gin tosses the crate on the ground behind the register then turns to me, eyes wide, head shaking back and forth at light speed. "He's the real deal. Gonna be on the NASCAR circuit one day. His daddy was years ago, but then he retired young and stayed here to run shrimpin' boats." She presses her lips together and releases them with a pop. "They say Jett's better than he ever was."

"Well there goes your theory." I shoot her a thumbs-down. "No way would a hotshot racer ever be interested in a professed car hater who doesn't drive."

Her nose crinkles as she frowns. "I saw your license in your wallet."

"I said I *don't* drive, not that I *can't*."

A knowing glint lights her eyes. "Oh…because of…" I jerk my head in her direction, wilting her under my glare. "Right." She drops her head, walks behind the counter, and leans forward on her hands, her fingers rat-a-tat-tatting the wood. "What are your plans for the summer?"

Quick change of topic. Good. She's getting the point.

"Lay low. Forget everything. Maybe get a job. Anything to make this summer go by faster." I chuck the empty bottle into the glass recycling bin by the front door, then weave back through the pallets to the counter. "Hey, do you know anyone hiring?"

Her smile returns as she triggers her finger at me. "Beachin' Books at the marina is looking for a part-time cashier." She thumbs over her shoulder as if the bookstore is visible from the back window. I shuffle sideways and peer out the screen-covered hole. Nope. Nothing but swamp grass and mud. Gin stops talking and follows me with her eyes. "It's that way," she points her finger in the opposite direction. "On the other end of the island. But only a mile from Ms. Bessie's house."

I nod. A mile is perfectly walkable. "Cool. So, books, huh? Sounds easy."

"Yeah. New and used books, souvenirs, drinks, and live bait."

I stop-sign my hand. "Live bait?"

She laughs, explaining that I won't have to touch it. Apparently, it's scooped out downstairs on the dock. My only responsibility would be taking the cash.

"Plus, the place has awesome windows overlooking the water. Best views in town."

"Of the beach?"

She winks. "Among other things."

"Wait. If the job's so good, why don't you want it?"

"I don't get a choice. This market is my dad's. Family business means everybody in the family works here."

"Gotcha." Making spending money in an obscure little shop while watching the ocean all day? I think I can swing it. "In that case, it sounds perfect."

Gin claps her hands together, the huge power grin returning. "I'll text the owner right now with your information." She slides her phone from her pocket and begins pecking at the screen, looking up every so often to smile at me. Her friendliness is tough to swallow after dealing with the shitstorm of people walking on eggshells around me for the last eight months. We've known each other all of twenty minutes, and here she is putting her own neck on the line to recommend me for a job. Such hopeful naiveté reminds me of Emmalyn, my best friend back home. The only person who didn't treat me like a fragile flower. The only one who kept trying when I balled up and pushed everyone away.

I should call her, but I probably won't.

The gravel crunches out front. An older model blue Cabriolet convertible pulls in the space in front of my suitcases, inching so close, one topples over on its side. The driver lumbers out and slams the door with a foot-shove. She drops the keys in the sand, then reaches for them with a few cuss words to boot.

"Sounds like Ms. Bessie's here." Gin chuckles under her breath.

My eyelids sink backwards in my head. No way is this Memaw. Standing about five-foot-nothing, her stature doesn't match her boobage, which hangs long and low in her black tank top. I'd swear she isn't wearing a bra, but the cheetah-print straps peeking out the side prove me wrong. *Cheetah-print? Really?* She slides her hands over her ripped denim capris, perhaps knocking off the ever-present grittiness I've determined is inevitable here, then strolls inside.

Pausing by the zucchini, she steeples her hands against her mouth. "This cannot be my little CJ! You've grown a foot since I've seen you!" Before I can respond, her arms circle me, yanking my head into her chest. A puddle of her sweat dribbles onto my nose and cheek, and I jerk back, swiping the remnants away with the hem of my sleeve.

"That kind of thing happens in nine years."

Her shoulders snap backwards as if I've scorched her with a branding iron, lips curled in a grotesque scowl. "That wasn't my doin'. I've always loved you and wanted to see you. And I did. Your mother," she stops and makes the sign of the cross, "emailed me pictures and videos of you girls quite often."

My mouth drops open the same way it did last week when Dad called me into the living room, ran his hand through his hair, then spontaneously announced I'd spend my summer in Edisto. This doesn't make any sense. I was always under the impression we didn't visit Memaw because there'd been some huge falling out between her and Dad after Grandpa's death. I remember the night I snuck out in the hallway after bedtime and heard him telling Mama that Memaw should be committed and was an embarrassment to the family.

After that, no one ever really spoke of her again, though my sister and I used to wonder about her late at night when we had sleepovers in my room. She'd ask me all sorts of questions, and sometimes I knew the answers, and sometimes I didn't. But if I didn't, I made it up because it made her happy. She was four years younger than me, so she had no memories of Memaw and Grandpa, and I figured my made-up stories were better than nothing.

"But I thought...so Mama sent you...I didn't..." I stammer, rubbing my hand across the back of my neck.

She shakes her head. "You didn't know. No one did."

"And Dad?"

"We talked for the first time about a month ago. My son...your father..." She sighs, replacing her frown with a toothy grin. "Never mind. That's nothing to worry about right now. Point is you're here, and we're gonna have a terrific summer!"

I stare at her, unsure of what to say. How can it be I've only just met her again and I'm more confused than ever? She seems genuinely concerned, not at all the aloof and uncaring woman

Dad insinuated. Eccentric, quirky? Yes. Self-absorbed? No. Why did they start talking again a month ago? And why did Mama feel the need to go behind Daddy's back to keep Memaw in the loop?

Gin taps me on the shoulder and thrusts a piece of paper into my face. I pinch the note between my fingers and survey the words written on it.

Mrs. Baxter. Beachin' Books on the Marina. 2PM.

"You have an interview this week. If she likes you—which she will—the job is yours." She clasps her hands together against her chest, her full cheeks smooshed up like some overly-eager cherub. Something about it makes me want to slap her and hug her all at once.

Memaw plucks the note from my fingers. "Edith Baxter's a dear friend! I'll call her and..."

"No. I don't want any special favors. If I get it, I get it. If I don't, I don't."

She tucks the paper into the pocket of my cut-off shorts, then pretends to twist a key into her puckered lips.

"Thank you," I say to Memaw, then turn to Gin, her blue eyes shining. "And thank you."

She nods and touches my arm. I shrink backwards; it's involuntary now.

"Once you're settled, we'll hang out. It'll be nice to have another girl around," Gin says.

I smile and nod as Memaw reaches out and cups Gin's chin in her hand. "Such a sweet girl. I know you and CJ are gonna be quick friends. Now, come on." She turns toward me, hoists her purse higher on her shoulder, and fans herself with one hand. "Let's get your bags and get to the house. I'm hotter than a hooker in Sunday church."

Chapter Three

I pry my right eye open about a millimeter. My hand death-grips the beige passenger seat of Memaw's convertible. Hasn't she heard of the "ten-and-two" rule? If it wasn't an actual thing, I doubt cars would have those ergonomic steering grips to clue everybody in.

But then again, Memaw's not everybody.

Obviously.

She steers the car with her knee (*her knee!*) and rifles through her purse, mumbling something about her Chapstick. The speedometer needle holds steady at 58 mph, her right foot jammed onto the accelerator.

Put your hands on the wheel, Memaw! For the love of all things holy, put your hands on the damn wheel! Inside I'm screaming. Yelling. Outwardly, I fidget, checking then rechecking my door lock. Tugging the seatbelt just in case.

I roll my head to the right, looking out over the mangle of swamp grass and inlets, and beyond, a cluster of houses and civilization. The wind whips through the topless car, my nose burning from the wafts of rotten-egg stench forced up my nostrils, my forehead stinging from the assault of a few loose tendrils of hair. I turn back toward the windshield and clamp my eyes shut. The glow of the late afternoon sun filters to the backs of my eyelids, splashing orange swirls through the darkness, and spreads out like hot fingers over my skin. Beads of sweat squish between my back and the cotton material of my shirt.

The car jerks as she slows, leaning into a tight curve. High-pitched squawks overhead, the steady rhythm of crashing waves, and the saltiness on my lips mean one thing. I peek again through slits as multiple shapes—houses in row after row—carve through the graininess. The greenish-blue waters of the Atlantic whitecap in the distance.

The brakes squeal as Memaw stomps hard, swerves onto a packed dirt road, then whirls into a driveway. The continuous twisty motion throws me side to side, then forward toward the dash. The seatbelt strap digs into my chest. Once stopped, I struggle to unlatch the belt, stepping out of the car on Jell-O legs.

Memaw gets out and runs to my side, throwing her arm over my shoulder. "What d'ya think?" She pans her hand wide.

The house is not much different than the countless others around it, maybe a little smaller than most, though the twelve-foot stilts give it a faux-mansion curbside appeal. Its moss-green planked siding and white wraparound porch organically fade into the palm-shaded lot, and the staircase going to the front door has about a gazillion steps. At least my butt will be in good shape by summer's end.

"It's great."

She squeezes my shoulder. "Right there is where the Johnsons live." She points to a large, two-story, cobalt blue home studded with hanging flower baskets. The ocean breeze tousles the monogrammed flag on the porch, friendly and welcoming like the kids who live there. "You met Gin already. Did you meet Bo?" She nudges me with her hip and licks her lips. "Now that boy's a looker."

Awkward.

"I did meet him. And his friend."

"Friend?"

"Some guy named Jett. Drives this really loud car."

She nods and pushes her sunglasses back onto her head. "Jett Ramsey. Good boy…good family. He's pretty fine-lookin' too, huh?" Her eyebrows waggle up and down.

Again, awkward, but not totally off base. There was something about the way his green eyes pierced me, simultaneously infuriating and exhilarating, as though he looked through me instead of at me. Like he knew exactly which buttons to push.

I wipe his image from my mind. I didn't lie when I told Gin I'm not looking for trouble this summer. I'm not looking for anything.

"If you say so, Memaw."

She huffs out a stiff breath, walks to the car, and grabs my bags from the backseat, handing me one, then nods toward the house. Halfway up the stairs, she stops and stares back at me. "Are you that resistant to fun? What are you here for if it's not to cut loose a little?"

I follow her to the landing, waiting behind while she slides the key from underneath the garden gnome by the door. With a click, the door swings wide, and she steps inside. I step in beside her. "The point of all this is to 'get away.' I want to forget everything for a while, and then, after I testify in August, I never want to think about it again."

She slams the door with her foot. "Sounds like an impossibility to me." She reaches out and grabs my arm, her fingers melding through the folds of the shirt into my skin, forceful. "You're gonna think about it. Always. Except in time, you'll focus more on the positive, realize how much——"

"Please don't give me that 'better to have loved and lost than never loved at all' bullshit, Memaw. I've heard it a million times—from Daddy, the pastor, my therapist, Dr. Phil." I tick off each name on my fingers. "Forgetting is the only way to move on."

"I think you're wrong, but then again, what do I know? I'm just an old lady." She grabs my chin and gives it a shake. "Hell, I'm glad to see some passion in your eyes. The way your Daddy talked, I thought I'd have to keep you from drowning yourself with the swamp gators."

"I'm not *that* bad." I leave my bag at the foot of the stairs and trudge behind her to the kitchen. One entire wall of windows overlooks a lagoon sprinkled with crooked palmettos. Globs of greenish, curly moss trickle from the branches.

"You're not that good either." Memaw pulls out the first of three metal barstools at the island and pats the seat, motioning me over with a head tilt. "That's why you're here."

I snort. "No, I'm here because Daddy doesn't want to deal with me anymore." My therapist mentioned a few sessions ago that I might benefit from some time away. Dad's eyes whirled in their sockets and a month later, bada boom, hello Memaw.

"You're here because your Daddy asked for my advice, and I told him your ol' half-cocked Memaw might be able to get through to you. That, and the ocean." She snaps her fingers and sways back and forth. "Heartaches are healed by the sea." She smiles and cuts her eyes at me. "I think it's the salt."

I pick up her near-empty bottle of Jack Daniels. "I think it's the whiskey."

She rips the bottle from my hand and clutches it between her droopy boobs. "Everything in moderation, my dear." She plunks the bottle on the counter and gives it a rough shove. It slides neatly back to its place. Obviously, she's done that more than once. "Which brings up another important topic. House rules."

I palm each side of my face, propping my elbows on the counter, and blow out a loud breath. Of course there'll be rules. Not that I need any sort of lecture since I've basically been living as a nun who took all the big vows—silence, sobriety, chastity. Pretty hard to cause trouble when your life is as bland as a saltine cracker.

Memaw wallops the butcher-block in front of me. The unexpected thwack nearly sends me backpedaling right off the stool. "Don't start. I ain't trying to run your life."

I steady myself and trace a small group of linear gashes on the island top with my fingertip. "I don't have a life, remember? I sulk alone in my room with my journal and my music."

Her eyes bore into me as she stands, hands planted on her hips. "Self-imposed exile, from what I hear, which brings me to rule number one." She walks to a framed chalkboard on the kitchen wall where last week's shopping list is scribbled.

Bacon. Avocados. Wine. Soap. Drill Bit. Duct tape. Nope, not an ordinary grandmother.

She swipes the black eraser across the surface, words disappearing into a haze of white dust, then grabs a chunky stick of chalk from the metal ledge. *Tink, tink, tink.* She stands back and stabs her finger beside the new verbiage.

1. Get a life

I flick my eyes between her and the board. "Can we narrow that down a bit?"

She smirks, arching her sparse eyebrows into the midst of her forehead wrinkles, then steps back to the board again. *Tink, tink, tink.* Shortly afterwards, a small subset appears underneath.

1. Get a life
   - Try everything at least once
   - Fall in love—with yourself, someone else, or your situation
   - Fear nothing
   - Be present

She turns toward me. Two white circular smudges mar her black tank top where she leaned in a little too close. "Better?"

"Much."

"Good. Two more to go." She moves back to the board. *Tink, tink, tink.*

2. Have fun
   - It's that thing that makes you smile and laugh. A lot.
3. Be safe
   - If you drink, don't drive. If you drive, don't drink. Always use protection.

She steps back and waves her hand in front of the board. "I took the liberty of giving you a few helpful notes before you had to ask."

I squint at the words. Surely I'm misreading. No way she's condoning going out, getting drunk, and having sex. I shake my head. "Number three isn't applicable to me."

"You're seventeen. Situations arise, circumstances change, and I'd rather you be prepared than not. Too many ostrich parents out there nowadays." She jabs her thumb against her chest. "Memaw keeps it real."

Real? Memaw single-handedly just gave me the longest talk on drinking and sex I've ever received outside the public-school system. I moved to Edisto Island and somehow entered an alternate universe. That's the only explanation.

She drops the chalk on the ledge with a clink. "Questions?"

My brain may have exploded. Or liquefied. Other grandmas are out there baking cookies and knitting, and mine just green-lighted sex and booze. Talk about your freak flag. I have the Memaw that doesn't just wave hers, she hoists that bitch on a flagpole.

When I don't respond, she says, "Good. Let's go see your room."

When Dad was pushing this whole idea on me, he kept saying Memaw's house was beautiful and comfortable—general bullshit terms because he's never even seen it. She and Grandpa used to live in Charleston, but she picked up and moved here less than a week after his funeral, which coincidentally *was* the last time we'd seen her.

At least his guesswork is on point.

This house is nice. In addition to the large kitchen, there's a spacious living room with comfy recliners and a full entertainment package, as well as three bedrooms and two baths upstairs. The décor is beachy—the slightly predictable shell paintings and nautical maps against blue, green, and sand-hued walls—freckled with flashes of vibrant-colored wooden signs with slightly inappropriate beach sayings. The more I survey the house, the more I find.

Mermaids Smoke Seaweed.

Got Crabs?

Size Does Matter (featuring a fish holding a ruler in its fins).

Eat, Ship & Dive.

Toes in the Water. Ass in the Sand.

I grab my suitcase and put my foot on the first step when Memaw shakes her head. "I thought you might be more comfortable down here. Have your own space away from the old lady." She grabs my other bag and walks down a short hall on the other side of the staircase to a white door in the far corner. I follow her in.

It's twice as big as my room back home and sunny. Light pours in between the blue-and-white striped sheer curtains hanging floor to ceiling on each side of five large windows in the room, three of which overlook the Johnsons' house. The other two flank a glass French door that leads out onto a sun deck. The white down comforter on the iron bed is covered in fuzzy chenille throw pillows and a matching blue blanket. Above the bed is a framed quote.

Everything I need to know in life, I learned at Memaw's.

Words to live by, she says, but what I can't tear my eyes away from is a pink-and-green floral print fabric doll. It matches nothing else in the room. That, and I don't play with dolls. Haven't in a whole bunch of years now.

She must catch me staring because she walks over and picks it up. "I got this for you."

I take it and flip it over in my hands. Its arms, legs, and head are all rectangular, with X's for eyes and yarn strings for hair. "Thanks, but I don't play with dolls anymore."

"This ain't just any doll. It's a DAMMIT! Doll." She grabs its legs in her fists and swings it hard against the bedpost. "You beat him against the wall when you're pissed off or stressed out. Here, try it."

She tosses the doll back to me, and I give it a half-hearted swing against the shiplap wall.

She frowns. "Well that's so weak it wasn't worth a daggum, much less a dammit. We're gonna work on that."

I toss it back on the comforter and cross my arms in front of me. "I'm not a project, Memaw." Why do I get the feeling I'll be reminding her of this all summer?

She leans close and wags her finger in my face. "Of course you are. We're all projects. Just a collection of messy weirdness

31

walking around in skin suits. Gotta embrace that weirdness. Grab your passion."

Grab my passion—the sentiment Jett threw in my face earlier. A low rumble echoes against the windowpanes and interrupts the memory. Next door, the familiar orange and black car idles in the Johnsons' drive. Bo stands outside the passenger door, half leaning in the window, but Mr. Cool himself is nowhere to be seen, probably somewhere behind those dark tinted windows. The twinge of disappointment is quickly extinguished by the furious heat that boils in my stomach as I remember our conversation.

How could Jett make such assumptions when he didn't even know me? And why was Memaw saying the same thing now? I've got passion.

Somewhere.

"You're the second person who's told me that today."

She pulses her finger toward the ceiling. "Maybe *somebody's* sending you a message?"

"Maybe." I shrug my shoulders and finagle with the end cap on the iron bed post, the metal hard and cold against my finger. It's obvious she's waiting on me to look up so she can challenge me, but I twirl my nails over the rails like they're the most fascinating thing I've ever seen.

"I'm gonna let you get acclimated." She sighs and walks to the desk. "Your TV remote and Wi-Fi password are here," then swings open the door beside it, "and your closet." A sapphire blue dress hangs on the middle of the wire rack. "I almost forgot. I also got you this." She snatches it out and holds it up to the daylight.

I run my fingers across the gauzy fabric to the scoop neckline and teeny-tiny straps. It's stunning in its simplicity and is exactly what I would've picked out for myself.

Before.

"It's beautiful Memaw, but...I can't wear it."

"How come?" She holds the dress to me, pressing the hanger hard into my shoulders to correct my posture. "It looks like the right size. Your Daddy said a six, right?"

I chew my lower lip. "It has spaghetti straps."

"And you don't have a strapless bra?" She shakes her head, then stops and smiles. "Just go braless!"

My jaw drops open. A ludicrous idea, especially since it's obvious now I inherited "the girls" from Memaw. I flick my finger back and forth between our matching chests. "Neither of us should ever, *ever* be braless. But..."

"But what?"

Silence drops like a heavy curtain between us. I swallow hard. "My scar. I have to wear sleeves to at least my elbow. And higher necklines."

Her eyes blaze as she wags her head. "You don't *have* to do nothing."

"I kinda do, unless I want people gawking at me."

Truthfully, no one except Dad has seen my scar. No one. Not even Emmalyn or Trent, who are supposed to be my closest friends. I slip my finger into the collar's edge and pull it off my shoulder. The pinkish-silver chasm snakes its way from the top of my left breast into the hollow of my armpit then out across my bicep, its jagged journey pin-pricked by dots of white puckers where the stitches had laced me back together. "Tell me you don't see that."

I expect her eyes to pop from their sockets, her tongue to loll out. But nothing happens. She's a statue, her face flat-lined.

"Oh, I see it, all right. There's no denying it."

I throw my free hand in the air. "Exactly! That's why I—"

"I see courage. Strength. Survival. Purpose." She points her finger at my scar with each word. "If people don't see that, then their eyes don't deserve to look at you."

I snort and look at my sandals. The big boobs must be the limit of our genetic similarities. Our minds sure do operate on opposite wavelengths.

She grips my chin, bringing my eyes to hers. "Let me tell you something. There ain't a person in this world who doesn't have scars. Some people have them on their skin. Some people have them on their hearts. Some have both. You hide yours because

33

you're afraid. Afraid to love. Afraid to lose. It's in your hands to turn something you call ugly into something beautiful."

I glance down at my skin. Time healed the flesh in its own crude, primal way, but the wound is still raw. Gaping and oozing where only I can see. "This will never be beautiful."

Without warning, she jerks up her shirt and pulls down the waistband of her capris, exposing a wrinkled, stretch-marked expanse of lower belly. Across the southern boundary and scarily close to her thank-you-Lord-they're-still-covered privates, a curved stripe winds itself from one hip to the other. She rams her fingers into the mark. "See this?"

I nod. Frankly it's all I can see at the moment, the way she's thrusting her pelvis toward me with each finger jab. I'll probably keep seeing it long after this moment. Maybe even in my dreams. A deep shudder courses through me as she continues.

"I was a real looker back in the day. Trim body, big boobs, long legs. Honey, I was hot. But after this scar, I quit wearing my bikinis on the beach, scared people were gonna look at me, judge me."

Memaw in a bikini? Oh God, I can't even.

She continues, "But then I got over myself. Decided to ignore the stares because this scar was more than an imperfection. It's my badge of strength in enduring an emergency C-section. And I love it more now than I did then. Know why?"

I shake my head. How could anyone love a scar? A reminder of the pain.

"Because if this," she runs her finger along the scar, "didn't exist, then you wouldn't exist. And the world sure would have missed out. Think about that."

Chapter Four

A loud clanging rings through the darkness, pulling me out of a dreamless sleep, and a nutty sweetness filters under my closed door. What is that? Coffee? And pancakes? My stomach growls its response, but no matter the gnawing inside, I don't feel like getting up yet. I push my head further into the pillow, the sides fluffing around me. The cotton sheets are too soft, the comforter too cozy, to even consider putting my bare feet on that cold hardwood floor.

I pick up my phone and swipe right. 7:04 a.m. It's surprising Memaw hasn't zipped in here already, ripping the covers off, singing some chirpy, weirded-out morning song. She used to do that when we were kids. It was cute then. I'd hate it now.

It'd taken an act of congress to escape her last night, and I hope I didn't offend when I mumbled something about a headache and being super tired then darted to my room, slamming the door. That probably could have been taken as a slight. I needed some space, and from the looks of the six board games she had stacked on the coffee table, that obviously hadn't been part of her evening plans.

I burrow further under the covers, the comforter's hem pulled so high it tickles my nose. The familiar haze of sleep creeps back in, my eyelids turning to lead curtains.

Raaaaawr, Raaaawr, Raaaawr.

The deep revs shoot ice through my veins as I bolt upright, and the wall, which borders my bed on the left side, vibrates. What the hell is that? The loud bursts give way to a deep, gravelly hum. I crawl out from the covers to the iron footboard, pulling back the sheer curtains.

Jett.

The sun glints off the front windshield as the engine silences, and the door pushes open partway, revealing glimpses of him. His flaxen hair is erratically tousled in one of those rebel-without-a-cause styles. He steps to the side and slams the door, twirling his keys a few times around his finger before plunging them into his pocket. The same black sneakers and frayed jeans from yesterday hit the sandy drive.

I swallow hard and readjust my stance closer to the window, my nose leaving a greasy mark on the pane. There's something about him that pisses me off, but I can't quit watching, and I don't know if it's a residual reaction from Bo and Gin's obvious hero worship yesterday or from the way my lungs wilted in on themselves when his eyes bored into me.

Jett yawns, fisting his hands and extending them wide overhead. His black V-neck T-shirt pulls up enough to show tanned skin melting into the black elastic waistline of his boxers, which sit an inch above his jeans. He doesn't have the rippled washboard abs from the magazines, but they're firm, lean.

He straightens his shirt and bends down, checking his hair in the side mirror. I inch closer, lifting slightly to press even further over the edge of my bed. My left knee tangles in the bedsheet, and I slip, inadvertently smacking the window with my hand as I scramble to brace myself. The curtain swishes back to the side.

I'm a statue. No breathing. No blinking. *Surely, he couldn't hear that, right? He's all the way next door.* I ease my eyes above the sill.

Jett's staring at my window, eyes locked, lips curled on each edge. He steps backwards and relaxes onto the fender. Propping his weight on the car, his long legs extend out in front of him and cross at the ankles. Without moving his eyes, he slides his phone from his pocket, pausing only a moment to wave at me with his free hand before dropping his head to concentrate on the screen.

I duck out of sight, slinking backwards to collapse into my sheets and yank the comforter to my chin. Maybe he thought it was Memaw. Yeah, that makes sense. He knows her and she knows him, and he's probably already forgotten about me being in town anyway. I sigh. The oxygen washing through me quiets the terrible thumping in my chest. The last thing I need is some idiot guy thinking I'm hot for him.

My phone buzzes on the pillow beside me. One new notification—a friend request from Jett Ramsey.

Oh my God.

My phone is a bungee cord, pulling me back to it each and every time I wander away. At this rate, it's going to take me all day to get dressed, braid my hair, and dab on some make-up. A little powder on my face in the en-suite bathroom mirror. A quick phone check. A smidge of gloss. Run back for another quick peek. The finishing touches on my French braid. Did my phone make a noise? Swipe. Nothing. Just the friend request hanging out there in cyberspace, Jett's profile picture taunting me. Why? Why do I feel like everything to do with this boy is a challenge? And why is it affecting me?

Okay, so I'd done some perusing last night. It'd started innocent enough. I only wanted to see if Gin and Bo had a page, but somehow the nagging need to see if Jett had one took over. Just a peek. That's what I'd told myself before I stalked through all of his social media pictures over the course of two hours. Most of it was restricted to friends-only content, but internet keyword searches came to the rescue with info dumps of his racing career stats and a gazillion pictures of him in those racing jumpsuits that zip up the front.

What the hell, CJ? I don't even like this guy, so who gives a crap about a friend request? "You're a dumbass," I mumble to myself, clicking Accept.

Ding. You are now friends with Jett Ramsey.

Big whoop. So we're friends, huh? Just like magic. I snort, pushing back the stupid girly giggles circulating inside and shake my head. Not like he's going to show up at my door anytime soon.

Memaw hunches over the stove, arm whisking furiously. The frying pan beside her sizzles, little oil pellets popping above the bacon strips. A stack of pancakes, swimming in melted butter, sits on the butcher block island.

She glances over her shoulder. "Morning. Grab those pancakes and put 'em on the table." She nods toward the whitewashed farmhouse table in the breakfast nook. I grab the plate, my forearm screaming under the weight, and have to use two hands to carry it over.

"You know, I don't have much of a morning appetite. I hope you have room for all this." I set the plate on the table, stopping to scan the place settings. One, two, three, four, five. "Why are there so many plates?"

"You never know when company might pop by." She winks at me and begins humming as she shovels scrambled eggs into her china bowl.

"Memaw..."

A loud clunking echoes from the front porch. The doorbell rings.

"Now, who could that be?" She doesn't turn around from where she's forking bacon strips out onto a paper towel-lined plate, her curiosity *obviously* piqued. I shake my head. I've traded in Dad the Ignorer for Memaw the Instigator.

"Funny how guests magically show up."

She spins around from the stove, bacon plate in one hand, egg bowl in the other, a Miss America grin on her face. "Aren't you going to get that?"

"Do I have a choice?" We both know the answer is a resounding no.

She bites her bottom lip and pretends to look at the ceiling before catching my eyes once more. "Uh-uh."

"Didn't think so."

I turn and plod through the den to the foyer, my bare feet slapping the hardwood floor. I stomp a little bit harder and glance over my shoulder, but Memaw's ignoring me, bent over the table, piling food on each plate.

The door's cut glass utilizes both clear and frosted panels, pieced into a mosaic through which three distinct forms take shape. I pull the door open wide, the chattering outside ceasing as six eyes turn toward me.

"Come on in." I pan my hand beside me. Gin bounces through the door first, wearing a happy yellow tank top and jean shorts and wiggling her fingers hello.

"Morning, CJ." Her voice has more sugar than the pancake syrup, but I smile back at her anyway. Bo reaches around from behind for a fist bump. As my knuckles meet his, Jett strolls in, the corner of his top lip curled slightly, holding his fist out toward me as well.

I stare at him, unyielding, pulling my hand into my chest.

"What's this? I've known you as long as they have," he points toward Bo and Gin, "and we're online official."

Gin's eyes dart between the two of us. "Online official?"

"Jett sent me a friend request."

"I figured it'd be okay since you about broke your neck watching me out the window this morning."

Caught, dammit! Three sets of eyes float back to me, two of them wide and eager, one pinched at the corners in a cocky smile. My heart skips a beat (or three) as a fiery wave floods over my cheeks and neck, and I'm acutely aware of them staring at me as the roaring silence rips through my head. "Wasn't me." I slam the front door and walk toward the kitchen. The others follow. "Maybe it was Memaw?"

"Yeah. Maybe." His smug grin translates through the air. I don't even have to look at him.

Memaw looks up from pouring coffee into a mismatched collection of mugs. "Maybe *what* was Memaw?"

"Nothing." I open the refrigerator door and rifle through the top-shelf containers, searching for the glass carafe with the painted dancing oranges circling the rim.

"Why, Jett Ramsey, you get cuter each time I see you!" Memaw clicks her tongue a few times. "You're all grown up and filling out nice. So handsome. Isn't he, CJ?"

It's improper to tell your grandmother to shut up, right? I kick the door shut, walk over, and slam the glass jug down so hard the plates and forks rattle against each other. All the while, Memaw's pinching his jaw in her palm, wagging it back and forth. I glare at her, trying to hide that shrinking feeling gripping my insides, like all my organs are huddled in a little ball somewhere south of my pounding heart.

"Shouldn't we eat before it gets cold?" I ask, pulling out the closest chair. Memaw drops Jett's face and barrels toward me, sliding it from my grip.

"No dear, over there. And Jett, you're beside CJ." She motions us to the back of the table, and he falls in line behind me as I walk around to my assigned seat.

Memaw plops in her place at the head of the table, Bo takes the opposite end, Gin sits facing us, and suddenly it's all crystal clear. Memaw's coerced them into her matchmaking game, and they're corralling me and Jett into the alcove of windows, cornering us like cattle on the way to the slaughter.

I sigh and glance over at Jett, who's rearranging the pancakes and bacon on his plate, acting oblivious, but I can't help thinking this slick scheme has his name written all over it, too.

"The food's awesome, Ms. Bessie," Jett says as he cuts his pancake into small triangles, which he spears onto his fork. A short golden trail of stickiness dribbles from the corner of his lips. "Thanks for inviting me. I owe you one."

Invited, huh? Memaw glances in my direction, lips pressed into a thin line. She shrugs and dabs the corners of her mouth with a napkin, her smile peeking out from behind the paisley paper square.

Gin plows a forkful of eggs into her mouth, stifling a giggle, while Bo stares at his plate and gnaws a bacon strip. Now everyone wants to suddenly clam up? I shift my eyes to Jett. He looks up and shrugs. Five minutes lapse without a word, just a combination of slurps, lip-smacks, and clangs of silverware on plates.

Gin finally breaks the lull and asks me if I'd like to plan a sleepover at her house sometime in the next couple weeks. She sips her orange juice as I mull it over, swirling a spoon around the inside of my coffee mug. It's been almost a year since I've had a sleepover, and that was with Emmalyn. It was always with Emmalyn. The thought of going over to Gin's almost feels like cheating on my best friend, except I'm not totally sure she's my best friend anymore or if she'll even want to talk to me. A twinge of longing circulates in my belly, mixing with the syrup and pancakes.

"Please?" she asks, her doe eyes springing wide in anticipation as she thumbs over at the boys. "It'll be nice to have someone besides them around."

Gin's an innocent, totally unaware of the suckiness life can bring. The worst thing she's probably encountered is a flaming pimple on the first day of school. But her sincerity is endearing, and the way she's looking at me, I can't imagine anyone being able to tell her no. Even cynical old me. "Let me get acclimated, and we'll plan it."

"Yay!" She giggles, clapping her hands together.

Bo mocks her in a high-pitched sing-song voice. "We're gonna have a slumber party and talk boys and do our make-up!"

Not to be outdone, Jett joins in, fluttering his fingers in Bo's direction. "Oh my gosh, and then we'll do our nails and our hair, and we'll spy on Bo!"

I roll my eyes, but Gin's smile drops as she leans over to swat Bo's arm. "And what exactly are we going to spy on? My stupid brother with his collection of girly mags, or him chatting online with his internet girlfriend?"

Bo's cheeks bloom like pink carnations as he squirms in his chair. "Quit making it sound bad. She's not some random internet girl. She comes here every year with her family, and we...keep in touch."

"All that work for one week a year," Jett mumbles.

I elbow Jett's ribs, and he recoils. "Don't listen to him. It's sweet. Any girl would appreciate that kind of effort."

Bo nods a silent thank you as Memaw pounds her fist on the table, demanding our attention. "So...what's everyone's plans for the day?"

41

What can be so exciting in a sleepy little town like this? My room is already unpacked, but a few interesting-looking books on the hallway shelf caught my attention—ones I wouldn't mind checking out before visiting Beachin' Books later. I shrug. "Not much. My interview this afternoon."

"Dad needs help at the docks," Jett volunteers, scraping up the last of his syrup along the fork's edge. "It gets a lot busier once the weather gets warm."

"Bo and I have to work at the market later. Dad says there's a big shipment of—" Gin begins, but Bo interrupts, waving his phone in her face.

"Actually, we need to go now. Just got a text. The shipment arrived early."

They jump from their seats in unison, juggling empty plates and cups in their arms.

"Drop those in the sink. I'll tend to those." Memaw looks at her watch then bolts up, too. "Later. I've got to get going myself. Promised to help at the charity flower show over at the State Park."

The three of them rush toward the door in a coordinated flurry, Gin glancing over her shoulder to quickly wish me good luck on the interview. Memaw stops and backpedals into the kitchen, her hand on the doorway molding. "Jett, remember that whole 'you owe me one?'"

He nods.

"I ordered a patio set and a swing for the yard. It comes in to the hardware store on Thursday. What time Friday should I expect you to assemble it?"

Jett combs his fingers through his erratic hair. "I could be here around eleven, I guess."

And Memaw strikes again. What she lacks in discretion, she makes up for in tenacity. I grab my dishes from the table and walk them to the sink. "But Memaw, isn't Friday your volunteer day at the animal shelter? You mentioned it last night, remember?"

"So it is." She shrugs, a smile creeping over her face. "I guess you'll have to keep Jett company and bring his lemonade." She waggles her fingers at us. "Ok, bye now!"

The door slams. We're alone.

His chair scrapes across the tiles and heavy footsteps echo in the kitchen. I keep my back turned, rinsing the plates under a stream of water, then loading them in the dishwasher.

He stacks his dirty dishes on the counter and reaches for the one in my hand. "Let me help."

"I got it."

He grabs hold anyway, pulling it from my grasp, and secures it in the rack. "You told Bo a girl appreciates a little effort, right?"

I hand him two more plates. "Sincere effort."

He clangs them into place, then grabs for another. His fingertips miss and land on my hand, shooting warm spirals of electricity pulsing across my wet skin. "You don't think I'm sincere?"

"I don't know what you are, Jett. I haven't figured you out yet." I pull my hand away, then wash out a few mugs and pass them his way.

He drops them into place on the top rack. "Why are you resistant to me and not the others? I've known you, like, a day, and you won't give me a chance."

Because the others are safe, but he's trouble. Because I hate the way his eyes microscope in on me, as if he sees below the surface. Because I hate his self-assured swagger. Because I hate how something about him makes me want to like him. Like, really, truly like him. And I can't have that. "Why should I?"

"Because everyone deserves a chance. Because they all see something apparently you don't."

I pop a detergent pack in the holder and slam the dishwasher door. With a push of a button, it whirs to action. "What does that mean?"

I slip past him, walking toward the foyer.

He snatches his phone off the table and follows. "Come on. You do realize this, and me coming over Friday, is a set-up, right?"

I shake my head, slack-jawed. "And you had absolutely no idea about what was going on?"

I swing open the front door, and Jett walks out onto the porch, turning back with a three-finger Scout salute. "I didn't. Swear."

His eyes zero in on mine, no looking to the left like liars do, and without a shadow of that world-on-a-string ego he wears like a mask.

I offer a thin smile. "Well, in that case, I'm sorry."

His gold tooth glints against his extra-white teeth. "I'm not. See ya, Cami."

A flurry of emotions swirls inside, a whirl of excitement with a twinge of fury. "CJ!" I yell out behind him, but he doesn't turn around.

Chapter Five

The last person I expect to see at my job interview is Jett, but there he is, a 10-foot-tall decal plastered to the side of a monstrous racing trailer parked in the lot next to the bookstore. His image stands against a checkered-flag background with orange and red flames shooting up from under his feet beside an orange and black Dodge with the number 17 on the door. I guess it's a picture of his racecar. A smattering of logos, probably his sponsors, lines the top edge. The largest belong to an energy drink and an auto supply store. They must pay the most.

I shake my head. Memaw, Bo, and Gin all trying to force us together when we're the two least likely to make a match. I want to disappear, fly under the radar, and here he is driving around with his big mug on the side of a trailer.

A large wooden sign with *Beachin' Books* painted across it stands at the far end of the next paved walkway. The cement, cracked and stained, is swept clean, and a hedge of white petunias line each side up to a set of wooden stairs. A neon sign flashes *OPEN* in the second-floor window.

"Cami!"

His voice cuts through the humid air, and I turn my head toward the trailer. Damn. I swore I'd never respond to that name, and here I am looking for him like a lost puppy the moment I hear it. Jett runs across the sparse lawn, more sand than Bermuda grass, from the ramshackle gray building next door. He wears the same clothes from earlier except for the knee-high rubber boots. "Wanted to tell you good luck on your interview."

"You came all this way to tell me that?"

He points over his shoulder to the building. Part of the bottom floor is an open breezeway leading to a long, wood-planked boardwalk. A row of faded, painted-on letters runs across the side: *The Shrimp Shack / Fresh & Local Edisto, SC Seafood.*

"This is my dad's shrimping business. See those big masts out there on the inlet?" He points beyond the structure where two massive white boats sit on the water, each with two large metal arms stretching to the sky.

"Oh..." I mumble, ducking my head to hide my rosy cheeks while wishing for the ability to swallow my tongue for saying stupid stuff.

"But I would've."

"Would've what?"

"Come all this way to wish you luck." He grins as I run my fingers along my brow, swiping away the sweat freckling my skin, partly from the mile-long walk, partly from the way my anxiety skyrockets when he's within spitting distance.

"Nice trailer." I thumb over to it. "People never have to guess who they're driving beside with that 10-foot twin over there."

"I make it look good, right? My racing team's idea. Speaking of which..." He turns and yells toward the trailer where two figures lean against the back, watching us. "Hey guys! Come over here."

They saunter toward us, a girl and a guy about our age or maybe a couple years older. His black hair, dark eyes and russet brown skin contrast her ultra-pale complexion and cotton-candy pink hair. "This is Trévon and Rachel. We race together."

"What's up?" Trévon's voice is gruff. He hinges his fingers in the belt loops of his jeans and stubs the toe of his black boot in the sand. Taller and more muscular than Jett, his prominent brow shadows his deep, almond eyes.

"Hi," I mutter, forging a small smile, but never take my eyes off the girl.

Rachel walks behind Jett and wraps her arms around him, resting her chin on his shoulder while she smacks her gum. Stacks of silver and black bangles line her wrists, complementing the small rings in her nose and eyebrow, as well as a black arrow daith piercing. Pretty, in a punk sort of way. From the way she touches him, I automatically wonder if there's more to their relationship. My stomach churns as the thought crawls deep into my spine.

"You must be Callie?" She squints. "No, Candi? Cami!" She extends one arm in my direction, snapping her fingers. "Jett says you're here for the summer?"

"It's CJ, and yeah, until August."

"And you're staying with your Memaw? How sweet." She cocks her head to the side with a condescending smile that implies I'm some sort of immature child. "I should warn you, though. Don't get used to this face being around too much." She pinches Jett's chin and gives it a shake. "He's gonna be workin' his butt off to be in top racing form."

"Jett's already a beast on the track." Trévon waves her off and high-fives Jett as Rachel shoots icy daggers in his direction.

"What I mean is he can't get distracted. The team comes first. Especially this summer. Everything's riding on it."

Jett's face stonewalls as he yanks from her grasp. "Funny, you're making it sound more like a cult. And by the way, I have a manager, and it ain't you."

She narrows her eyes, hands planted on her hips. "Well, I'm sure your Dad...I mean, our manager...would agree."

"My dad would tell you to concentrate on your own racing. Finishing in the last half of two races in the past season isn't exactly prime." He crosses his arms with a taunting grin. She sticks her tongue out at him, then playfully pushes into his chest. He stumbles back a few steps, laughing.

A wave of nausea slinks through me every time she touches him. Every time he flirts back. There's a battle between the green-eyed monster and the red-eyed devil boiling inside me, and the only clear explanation is I'm sick of the race talk and this would-be lovers' spat, or whatever this is. But the questions bouncing around in my brain are the worst. Why hadn't he mentioned her before, and why would he flirt with me? More than that—why do I even care?

"I'm the last thing you need to worry about," I volunteer, both hands in the air. "I'm not here to crash your racing practice or whatever, just interviewing for a summer job." I pull my phone from my pocket, backing away from the group. "And I'm late. Gotta go."

Jett opens his mouth to respond, but I turn and dart toward the bookstore before anyone can issue a rebuttal.

An hour later, along with Mrs. Baxter's full-frontal, needle-down-my-spine-inducing hug and a smiling, "See you on Monday!" I walk out as the new cashier/stocker/live bait money-taker for Beachin' Books. She subjected me to no grueling, complex questions, other than a few things like *How are you liking Edisto?* and *How's your Memaw doing?* There was no interview, just Mrs. Baxter showing me proper cash register operation, the pile of new stock that needed shelving, and her signature answer-the-phone greeting.

You've reached Beachin' Books, where every day is a beachin' good day! How can I help you?

There's not enough honey in the world to make that flow off my tongue just right, but my lackluster attempts didn't seem to constitute a problem for her.

Outside, heavy purple-bottomed clouds build in the South, the same direction from which a salty gale is blowing in. What I remember most about visiting Memaw in Charleston are the typical late afternoon thunderstorms, marked by loads of streaked lightning and heavy downpours. I sniff the air. The musky odor of rain floats on the breeze, and I pick up the pace. It's a twenty-minute walk back to Memaw's, but by the looks of it, I'll have to make it in ten or get wet trying.

I cut through The Shrimp Shack's parking lot. The racing trailer is gone, and the closed sign hangs crooked on the glass storm door. I cross the grass median to the paved walking path that circles the entire island as a few fat raindrops dot my blue long-sleeve blouse. My sandals pinch my toes as I hit double-time.

A golf cart whizzes by me, followed by a rusty green Jeep, and when the hum of another engine approaches, I instinctively glance toward the traffic. Jett's orange Challenger rolls into my vision, stalking beside me at a snail's pace. The tinted passenger window slides down into the door.

"Need a ride?" Jett steers with his left hand while he leans across the center console.

When I stop walking, he stops rolling.

"Where's your girlfriend?" The words simmer with unintentional venom. I bite my tongue, holding back any other spontaneous outbursts waiting to strike.

He jerks his head backward like I've spit on him. "You mean Rachel? She's *not* my girlfriend. She's my teammate. And besides, she's with Trévon." He pauses, a mischievous spark lighting his face, teasing the corners of his mouth. "Wait—are you jealous?"

I'm fifty-percent jealous. And fifty-percent pissed about being jealous. I want to whack myself in the skull until I remember my "summer of no trouble" policy. "No! I just…she didn't seem too happy to see me."

He shakes his head. "Rachel's not in charge around here. I am. Well, my dad is…so technically, it's me." He stares at me, not blinking. "Get in before you get soaked."

I hold out my palm and gaze upward at the clouds rolling in. "Thanks, but I'm fine. That storm's probably still a good fifteen minutes away."

The words no sooner leave my mouth than the lightning flashes and a crack of thunder rumbles across the sky. "I didn't even get to one-Mississippi on that count." Jett deadpans. "Storm's here. Get in already." He leans across the passenger seat, pulls the handle and pushes the door open toward me.

I slide in—the black leather butter-soft against my bare thighs—and slam the door behind me. The clicking of the seatbelt into place only increases my nerves, which crackle like a handful of sparklers under my skin. I inhale through my nose for four counts and blow it out through my mouth for seven, a breathing technique my therapist says diffuses anxiety in record time.

Jett eyes my ritual and laughs. "Don't worry. I won't kill you."

I cringe and stare straight out the windshield, white-knuck-ling the armrest and kneading my feet into the mat as he pulls away from the curb. Another bolt of lightning snakes through the clouds and a torrent of rain unleashes, pounding the roof of the car and flooding the windshield so that even the wipers on the highest level barely make a difference. My heart slams in my ears, the big vein in my neck on the brink of sure implosion, while Jett reclines back in the driver's seat, still with only one hand on the wheel.

"So…you gonna get a car while you're here?"

"No. I don't drive."

He leans forward, whipping his head in my direction. "What? No way! I don't know anybody our age who doesn't have a li-cense." He relaxes back into the leather seat. "Your parents make you wait or something?"

I shake my head quickly. "I *have* my license. I *don't* drive. By choice."

After a quiet beat, I glance over at him. His face is scrunched, nose crinkled, and mouth slightly open. I instantly turn back to the windshield, hating how his expression implies I'm some kind of weirdo.

"Why would you make a choice like—"

Ahead, a pick-up truck runs the light and swerves in front of us at full-speed. "Watch out!" I yank my legs up in the seat, cir-cling my arms around them.

"What the—" Jett flicks his eyes back to the road and the tailgate of the truck that fills the front glass. He stomps the brake, which saves us from impact but causes the back tires to spin on the wet asphalt. The seatbelt bites into my skin as the car fishtails to the left, then jerks right before the tires grip and straighten out in the lane. "Asshole!" Jett screams.

My lungs refuse to expand. The rain and the taillights swirl together, and bile burns the back of my throat. I sink my head into my knees, wrapping my arms around my head, the same way they taught us in school to do for tornado drills.

"Cami? What's wrong? Cami!" His words get harder, his tone frenzied. The tips of his fingers press into my arm, and I jerk away.

"That...idiot...almost...hit us!" My screams sputter out through gasps. My lungs remain wilted flowers, limp in my chest.

"Calm down. It's okay. It wasn't even that close." His tone steadies as he pulls the car into an open space on a beach access and shifts to neutral. That's when he laughs. "Remember, I'm a professional. There's no shame in a little bumpin' and rubbin' if necessary. I got this."

An inferno ignites in my stomach and explodes upwards into my chest. I stomp both feet to the mat and slap the dashboard in front of me. "No! You don't! You can't control what happens if some maniac sideswipes you!"

"Please. I've been involved in scrapes way worse than that would've been. How d'you think I got this gold tooth, anyway?" He inches up the corner of his mouth and points to the bling on the top row, right beside his pointy canine, like it's a trophy. "Besides, I would've been more pissed about the jackass wrecking my car." He strokes his hand back and forth on the steering wheel, laughing.

"Laugh it up! It's all a big game to you, isn't it?" My control slips as I stab an accusatory finger at him, threatening to wring his neck as the rush builds momentum like a bowling ball rolling down a hill. It sizzles, frantic energy pinballing against my insides. "With your fast cars and your big ego and your devil-may-care attitude. You *really* don't get it. You think these cars are your play toys? They're weapons. Killers!"

Jett's eyes saucer. "That's pretty melodramatic, don't you think? Killers?" He pans his hand in front of the windshield. "We braked hard. We fishtailed. Nobody died."

I sink back to the seat, the invisible punch to my chest robbing my breath. He has no way of knowing how his words slice through me like a knife, but I want to hate him for it, for bringing back all those horrible images I've tried so hard to forget.

He unbuckles his seatbelt and leans closer, leaning in low to try and intercept my gaze. "Cami?"

"My mama and sister died!"

Jett grabs both my arms. I try to wrench free, but his fingers press harder. "Wait. What?"

I shift my eyes away. Why did I let it slip out? Between Me-maw's big mouth and my outbursts, I might as well hire a freaking skywriter to make sure all of Edisto knows.

"You can't blurt out something like that and then ignore me!" He shakes me a little. "Please...tell me..."

I turn, meeting his eyes head-on, our faces mere inches apart. "Last year. They were killed because some selfish jerk couldn't stay in his own lane."

His eyes are red-rimmed with a hint of moisture along the lashes. It's surreal to see in his what's eerily been missing from my own for months. I haven't cried since the memorial service. It's like I've run out of my lifetime allotment of tears, and my body's dry. My therapist says it's proof I'm hiding from my grief, hiding from my recovery. Daddy agrees.

It's all part of the reason I'm in Edisto.

I sigh, giving in to tell him a partial truth. I couldn't bear the judgement in his eyes if he knew everything. The whole truth. "Eight months ago, some guy ran our car off the road. It flipped and hit a tree, killing my mama and sister instantly."

"Oh my God." He repeats it over and over through the fingers clamped over his mouth. "I made all those stupid jokes. I'm so sorry. I..." He flounces back in his seat, mouth hanging wide.

The look on his face, somewhere between shock and pity, is exactly what I don't want to see. People tiptoeing around me, afraid to say something to set me off. That's why I never wanted anyone here to know about it. That's why I should never have let it slip.

I slouch back into the soft leather. "I just want to be normal this summer. Forget it ever happened. At least until August."

"What's in August?" he whispers.

Hell. Absolute Hell, that's what.

"I have to testify at the guy's trial. He's been charged with vehicular homicide."

Jett rakes his fingers through his hair then grips the back of his neck. "My God, I had no idea. Was he drinking?"

"Texting."

He clasps his hand over his mouth, once again talking through his fingers. "Shit, I'm so sorry. What can I do?"

I roll my head against the headrest, looking over at him. He stares back.

"Don't treat me like some fragile freak. And never mention it again. Ever."

"I promise." The look in his eyes tells me he's being honest. And there's a hint of something else there too. Understanding? Empathy? I don't know.

We hold each other's gaze, and for the briefest minute, a connection, a magnetic pull, ignites between us. A chill ripples through my veins, and I shiver, pulling my arms in tight to my chest.

The walls renew. The moment vanishes.

"Can you take me home? I'm exhausted."

Jett nods without a word, revs the engine, and pulls into traffic. His silence is a typical response. People either clam up or succumb to diarrhea of the mouth, unable to shut up, rambling about anything and everything in some supreme effort to avoid the subject at all costs.

By the time we pull into Memaw's drive, the heavy blanket of clouds has pulled back to reveal crystal blue slivers overhead. Jett parks and leaves the car running while he jumps out and walks around to open my door. He trails me up the front steps, and when we get to the door, I stop before walking in.

"Thanks for the ride. For everything."

"Anytime." He turns to walk away but pivots on his heel, steps forward, and wraps his arms around me. Hints of coconut, car exhaust, and shrimp whirl around us as his heart pounds against my chest, the warmth of his body encapsulating me.

I clamp my eyes and wait for the involuntary flinch.

It never comes.

Chapter Six

Two days pass at a snail's pace, yet the memory of his arms, the pressure of his hug, still lingers on my skin. When I close my eyes, it intensifies, like fiery swirls below the surface, burned into the nerve endings. Since the accident, the faintest of human contact has crawled over my skin like angry scorpions.

Not his.

But I didn't hug him back. Instead, I planted my arms flat against my sides, waiting for the knee-jerk reaction that never came.

Or maybe I was willing it to come, because that'd be easier than the alternative.

What if I could *like* this boy?

I shake my head. No. Hell no. Not going to happen.

Letting anyone in is dangerous. That whole "loved and lost" crap really loses its sting if you never love in the first place. Can't lose something you never had, so I've made it my life's mission to keep everyone at arm's length, cordial enough to not be considered a loner freak with hidden terroristic plans but far enough away so no one can make me lose my balance. It's why I can agree to a sleepover with Gin but not call my best friend in the whole world. Gin is a new face, and our relationship is superficial and will probably remain that way. How close can you actually get to someone over a summer? Besides, I never asked to be exiled here anyway, so I might as well slap on the happy face and play along.

But Jett. One look in my direction, one twinkle in those green eyes, one infuriating smirk, and my barriers breech. I hate him for having that power, but I hate myself most for wanting more—more of his time, more of his attention, more of him.

It confirms what I already know. Jett Ramsey is trouble.

The good kind. That's what Gin said.

I flip the book I'm reading closed and whack it against the deck railing. "Nope. There's never a good kind."

"Never a good kind of what?"

I lurch forward on the folding chair, dropping my book to the wooden floor with a thud. Drowning in my obsessive thoughts, I didn't hear anyone approach, and now I can't help wondering how long he's been standing there. I grab my book and jump to my feet, turning around. Jett's at the top of the stairs, arms folded across his chest, smiling with his gold-toothed glint.

"Uh...spider. No good kind of spiders. I just squished one." I pretend to flick guts from the back cover.

He pinches his shoulders up with a little shiver. "Yeah, I don't like 'em either."

My eyes rove over him, from his white muscle shirt to the frayed ends of his jeans. A rip across the thigh exposes a tiny portion of his bronzed skin. So, he does wear something besides jeans all the time. An image of Jett in swim trunks skips through my mind, and my breath catches in my throat as heat circulates in my cheeks. I glance at him, his head cocked in my direction, brows furrowed like he's reading my thoughts.

"Where'd you even come from?" I mumble.

"My house."

"I mean, I didn't expect you'd come to the back door when there's a perfectly good front door that way." I point toward the house.

"I knocked on your front door. Rang the bell, even. Turns out *you* can't hear it back here. So, I walked around. I know— genius level stuff. I'm good like that."

I laugh in spite of myself, shaking my head. "You're such a jackass."

"My parents think so, too." He plants his thumb in his chest. "That's my middle name."

"Jett Jackass Ramsey? What great foresight they had."

"Exactly. That's where I get the genius stuff from." He walks past me to my bedroom's glass French door and peers in. "So, this is your room? Miss Bessie said something the other morning about giving you your own space on the first floor."

"Yeah, at least for the summer." I join him and lean against the siding. "So, what is it really?"

He looks over at me, eyebrows furrowed. "What?"

"Your middle name?"

"Why? You gonna run a background check on me or something? It'll be clean..." He pauses and looks skyward, clicking his fingers. "Except for that one incident about a year ago..."

I give him a playful shove on the arm. "Shut up. You brought up middle names. I was making small talk."

"It's Dodge."

"Like your car?"

"Exactly like." He presses his nose back into the glass, shielding his eyes from the sun's glare. "Nice décor, by the way."

"It's not mine. Memaw gets all the credit."

The edge of his lips curl. "Well, nice panties then."

"What?" I squash my nose to the glass as Jett points to a stack of my freshly washed laundry laying on my desk, waiting to be put away. Shit. I meant to do that earlier.

He pulls back and nudges me on the shoulder. "Just playing. I'm gonna get started downstairs. You gonna bring me some of that lemonade Ms. Bessie promised?"

I smirk, heading toward the kitchen's sliding door. "I'll see what I can come up with. I make no promises."

By the time I pour a glass and head down the steps, the cement pad under the house resembles an accident scene, the big brown boxes of the swing, two Adirondack chairs, and side table scattered in a crumpled pile of cardboard. The wood and metal pieces, all singularly wrapped in cellophane, lay grouped together in specific areas as Jett kneels in front of a battered red toolbox, scrutinizing the page of directions and laying out appropriate tools. He glances up, screwdriver in hand, as I walk down.

"Looks like a big job," I say, eyeballing the mess.

He tucks the instructions in his back pocket and shrugs. "Nah, it won't be too bad. Hour and a half, tops."

"No way. I bet it'll take you longer than that."

"You bet? Now you're speaking my language." He shoves the screwdriver under his armpit and rubs his palms together. "How 'bout a little wager?"

"A wager?"

"Why not? Let's make this interesting." He slides his watch off his wrist and dangles it in the air. "I'll put 90 minutes on the timer."

"Okay. So, what are the stakes?"

"How about we each set our own?"

This could be my opportunity to get rid of Jett—to purge him from my thoughts and my life—before all these puppy-eyed feelings get out of control and in my way. "I'm down. If the whole thing isn't assembled in ninety minutes—and I'm talking whole, entire thing down to the last bolt—you, Jett Ramsey, have to quit partaking in this whole 'set up' business everyone has going on. No more following me in your car while I'm walking. No more spontaneous breakfasts. Nothing."

He squints his eyes and twiddles his fingers on his chin as he considers it. "Fair enough. But if I win—and I will—you agree to let me teach you to drive again. I promise you'll be behind the wheel by the end of summer." He pulls the screwdriver from underneath his armpit, twirls it in the air and catches it again. "And you'll get the awesome side-perk of spending all that quality time with me." He leans in close to my ear, his breath tickling the skin. My heart flutters as he whispers, "Once you quit trying to fight it and realize what a great guy I am."

I smile at the thought but disguise it as sarcasm. "Awful confidant, aren't you?"

He winks and holds up the screwdriver like a trophy. "Always."

"Fine. I'm game, so you better go set that watch. Time starts on my count." I set his lemonade on a plastic plant stand, and while he's turned around finagling his watch, I swipe a large eye-bolt from the swing pile and slip it into the pocket of my yellow shorts.

"Ready. Tell me when to press start."

"Three, two, one, go!" I yell, then turn, walking back to the steps. He stops me on the third one.

"You're not gonna keep me company?"

The way his eyes stretch out, wide and innocent like a child, makes me want to run back and plant myself on the concrete beside him. But surely that'd be counterintuitive to The Plan. The one that answers to the nagging voice inside, that insists alone is better. Easier and safer.

"You have a lot of work to do and not long to do it, so I'm going to finish my book on the deck." I walk up another step, then stop to add, "And don't even think about cheating. I can see your watch from up there."

He crosses his arms and cocks his head to the side. "I don't have to cheat. I always win."

"We'll see."

On the deck, I pull out a beach towel from the brown storage cube and spread it out next to the railing. With book and phone in hand, I lay belly-down and prop on my elbows to read. Except there's no finishing a sentence, because every time Jett moves, it flashes in my periphery, compelling me to watch the way his biceps flex when he lifts the larger wooden pieces or how his jeans hug his butt when he leans forward on his knees to grab tools from the toolbox. The way—

No. Nothing's going to happen between us anyway. I have the insurance in my pocket, the silver bolt nudging through the cotton into my hip. I roll over onto my back and pull the book to my nose, blocking out anything and everything except the words on the page.

It works for a while, until he starts singing, so low at first, I mistake it for a radio playing somewhere. But as it gets louder, his distinctive tone shines through. A low country drawl, southern like mine but strung out a little more. Slower. Throatier, with a smidgen of gravel.

Still holding the book overhead, I roll my head to the side and cut my eyes to where I can see him bolting together the second chair, singing to himself, wagging his head to the tune. When he tightens the last bolt, he drops the wrench, stands up, and pulls his shirt over his head. Sweat glistens across his back.

A thousand fireworks go off, working their way up from my toes.

So not fair.

He twists his head suddenly over his shoulder, catching me mid-stare. I fumble my book, and it falls on my face, knocking my head into the wooden floor with a thump. My cheeks burn hotter than all my skin exposed to the blistering afternoon sun as I lay there silent and still, praying to be absorbed into the wooden deck boards.

After a few minutes, I slide the book from my eyes and peek over the edge. He bends over, hammering the side table's leg, so I slink sideways off the towel, get up, and tiptoe toward the house, phone and book clenched in my hand, going extra slowly to make no noise. At the sliding glass door, I stop, easing down to a seated position.

Humiliating. I lay my book beside me and wipe the residue of salt air from my phone screen with the long sleeve of my T-shirt.

Twenty more minutes and then it's over, CJ. You won't have to worry about him—or yourself—anymore.

The self-coaching session falls flat. No matter how much I reason "what's for the best," I can't smile at the thought of not having him around. My jaw locks tight, forbidding it. I'll miss him, which is crazy since I've only known him a measly week.

My phone buzzes, and I swipe my finger over the screen.

<Memaw> *Are you taking care of Jett? Be nice*

<Memaw> *Don't do anything I wouldn't do!*

Typical Memaw. Always pushing.

Instead of replying, I scour social media, accepting friend requests from both Gin and Bo and cyberstalking some of my old friends from back home. Trent's relationship status still says "it's complicated," but his latest posts show him happy and smiling on the field in his baseball uniform. Emmalyn's in the background of several of them, and I wonder if she's dating someone on the team. I used to know everything about her. Now we're more strangers than best friends.

Her page is a mishmash of the usual dance recitals, selfies in her bedroom, and even a few at the baseball field. Definitely a new boy in her life. Sad I don't know who. Sadder I won't have the gumption to ask. Scrolling farther down the page, a photo of Emmalyn, me, and my sister Noli-Belle flashes on the screen and stops me cold.

That night from last summer plays in my mind as clear as if it were yesterday. Emmalyn spent the night at my house, and my sister demanded to be included.

Mama came in, wagging her finger in the air. "Magnolia Belle Ainsworth, you let these girls have some privacy!"

But with all the ferocity of her 12-year-old firecracker self, she stood up, hands on her hips, feet planted firm. "Mama, I hate being called Magnolia. It sounds like an old lady. Besides, they said I could stay!"

Just a few weeks later, our entire world crumbled, and I lost every one of those people. Two never made it out of the mangled wreckage; one was collateral damage. A bone-deep shiver, defying the blazing overhead sun, creeps down my spine.

What the hell am I doing? How could everything good in my life be gone, vanished like it never even existed? How do I get over something like that?

I tilt my head toward the sky, sending up a silent plea to my mama and sister for guidance. For wisdom. For some sort of sign on how to move forward without them.

Clanging echoes below, and I glance down at my phone. Ten minutes left on the countdown. I creep forward on my knees, peering over the deck's side. Jett rushes from box to box, shaking out cellophane, patting his pockets. To his right, both Adirondack chairs and the side table are completed, and on his left, the swing is completely assembled minus one arm.

"Where is it?" he grumbles, kicking a box across the cement. "It's gotta be here somewhere." He checks the watch, slams it down, then renews the search, his frenzied eyes sweeping over the mass of cardboard and plastic. As I lean farther toward the edge, the bolt in my pocket pokes into my thigh, and a swirling sensation kicks up in my gut, like mama is whispering her advice to my heart from the great beyond.

You can't move on by standing still.

My breath catches in my throat. It's as if her voice is audible, a strange blend of the wind through the palm fronds and distant roar of the waves. It reminds me how much I miss her; how much I need her here. How much she'd hate what I've let myself become. And suddenly, I know what I want to do—what I have to do—even though it's everything I've railed against.

Darting inside to grab the lemonade jug, I then head downstairs. Jett's still rummaging through the debris and doesn't glance up, his attention focused on one goal. After filling his glass, I discreetly drop the bolt beside the Adirondack chair's front leg then walk over and pick up his watch from the railing.

"Tick-tock, tick-tock."

He narrows his eyes at me, then continues sweeping his hands across the cement, edging closer and closer to the chair. The minutes tick away.

Come on. Come on. Open your eyes, for the love of God! My stomach knots.

"Aha! I knew it was here!" His fingers wrap around the bolt, and he jumps to action, holding the arm in place as he twists the screwdriver.

"T-minus thirty seconds and counting…"

He glances at me, beads of sweat dotting his forehead. *Come on, come on.*

"Ten seconds…nine…eight…seven…six…"

"Done!" Jett jumps to his feet and throws down the screwdriver, which clangs against the toolbox lid. It's the first time I've seen him bare-chested this close, and my breath catches in my throat at the sight of his long, lean muscles and how his coppery skin smooths over them.

He connects the swing's chains to hooks installed in one of the wooden supports underneath the house, then stands back with arms folded across his chest, admiring his work.

"It's only right to give her a trial run." He nods his head toward the swing then grabs my hand and pulls me to sitting beside him on the wooden slats. With a rough shove from his feet, we sail backwards then forwards, and instinctively, I grab his arm, squeezing in close.

He leans in, sweaty and hot, and the only thing running through my mind is why this isn't grossing me out. But it isn't. In fact, the more the heat rises between us, the harder my heart thumps against my ribs.

"Aren't you gonna congratulate the winner?" he asks with his signature cocky smirk.

"Congratulations," I say straight-faced, then turn my head in the opposite direction to conceal my grin. From the way his arm slides against mine, it's evident we're both winners.

Chapter Seven

Amber rays flood over my desk from the brass lamp, the only light in the room since the moonless midnight outside is black as pitch. Sleep's elusive. Every time I close my eyes, I think of Jett, our wager from the other day, and how much I want to tell Emmalyn all about it.

The nerves. The happiness. The fear. The anger. Only a best friend can help sort out all those mixed-up emotions somersaulting in my stomach.

But would she even care at this point?

I open my laptop. The blue screen comes to life, so bright it mars my vision, and I wince as my eyes adjust. I click open the email browser, the cursor flashing in the text box. Blip...blip...blip...blip. It tells me to get off my stubborn butt and contact her already.

To: <Emmalyn Henderson>
From: <CJ Ainsworth>
Date: May 15
Subject: Long Time, No Talk

Hey Em. It's CJ, but I guess you already know that. How are you?

Ok, that sounds like small talk, but I do want to know. I hate not knowing things about you when I used to know everything. Things have been...weird.

I saw a picture of you, me, and Noli-Belle online the other day, and I remembered last summer when we spent the night at each other's houses like four times a week. I miss those days. I miss us.

I know you prefer texting, but I can't muster the courage to do it. If I text you and you don't respond right away, I'll know how angry you are. If I email and don't get a response, at least I can pretend this got lost in SPAM and had nothing to do with you ignoring me.

I haven't said it yet, so I'll say it now: I'm sorry. There's no reason to turn your back on your best friend, but I did. It's just…you reminded me of how great my life was before. I can never get that life back now. Talking to you was too hard, because it reminded me of that.

I don't know if any of that even makes sense. It does in my mind, but that's probably not the most reliable measurement of sanity these days. (That was a joke by the way. Go ahead and laugh. I want you to.)

Please forgive me. For the first time in almost a year, there's hope things are going to get better. It's a faint glimmer, but it's there when it never was before. I want to tell you all about it, but I realize it might be too late for all that now. I was depressed and took my friendship away. You didn't deserve that, but I'm hoping somewhere down deep, you still want me around.

I miss you, Em.

<3, CJ

I flounce backward, my shoulder blades digging into the wooden chair. There it is in black and white. All my heartfelt emotion, devoid of the usual cynicism, laid bare, exposing my vulnerability. A brand of honesty so dangerous, it forces me out there, unprotected, unguarded and with no control over the outcome.

The flashing cursor morphs into a hand, its digital finger pointing at Send. I sigh, slide the mouse over the icon, and click. The email disappears from the screen, replaced by a pop-up message. Saved to Drafts.

Chapter Eight

Well, this is boring. The bookstore has been quiet for well over an hour now, but Mrs. Baxter assures me that'll change once the official tourist season kicks off on Memorial Day. Right now, the island's population is still mostly locals who don't give a flying fig about beach reads and "I heart Edisto" postcards. So, other than the two orders of live bait I rang up this morning for a few grungy-looking fishermen and the obligatory first-day-of-work-courtesy-visits from Me-maw, Gin, and Bo, the time has lagged.

Mrs. Baxter doesn't even stick around. She retreats to her sweet setup on the lower level, half back-stock and supplies for the shop and half private lounge with a full leather reclining sofa and big screen TV, disappearing down the back stairs with a, "Give me a holler if you need anything. I'll be watching my soap operas."

A stack of hardback books sit catty-cornered on the counter's edge, ready to be shelved. I load them in my arms and carry them over to the metal shelves against the wall, sliding each into its alphabetical home and sending poofs of dust spiraling into my face. I swipe my finger across the metal ledge and pull back a black smudge. *Dust much, Mrs. Baxter?* Now I know why the white feathers on that duster hanging on the peg beside the cash register are, in fact, still white.

I'm on my way back to the counter to grab it when the chimes on the door sound.

"Welcome to Beachin' Books where every day is a beachin' good day. I'll be right with you," I call over my shoulder.

"No rush."

Her voice is immediately recognizable—Rachel, the pink-haired girl from Jett's racing team. I walk to the register and

peek at her around the metal shelf. She saunters to the refrigerator case in the back and bends over to grab a Cherry Coke from
the bottom row. In her short shorts and cropped purple tank
top, she moves toward me like a panther—stealthy and fluid
with just the smallest hint of cunning.

"So, how's your first day?" She twirls one of her cotton-candy
pigtails around her finger while I ring up her purchase.

I hand her the change, and she shoves it in her itty-bitty pockets. "Not bad. A little slow."

"Any visitors? You know how people like to get all stupid
about first days." She rolls her eyes.

I nod. "Memaw came in, of course, and Gin and Bo? You
know them, right?"

"Are those the kids Jett's known forever?" She pauses and
takes a sip. "They're okay. Not really my crowd."

Imagining sweet, innocent Gin hanging out with this girl is
comical. And I'm sort of confused as to why she and I are even
having this conversation. She didn't seem too interested in getting to know me before.

"So...you and Jett have become friends?"

And there it is—fishing for details. He told me she was with
Trévon, but the way she acted the other day was "extra." Obviously, she wants something more from Jett than friendship. "I
wouldn't say friends. We've hung out a little. I barely know
him, really."

"That's an understatement."

My lips crimp together. "What do you mean?"

She sighs and slams her drink so hard on the counter, the
brown fizz crackles around the bottle's rim. "Look, Carlie..."

"Cami...I mean, CJ."

"Sorry...Cami, CJ whatever...I'm going to be honest with
you. Jett can draw you in. He's hot, lots of natural charm. He's
like a freakin' magnet. But magnets don't attract just one object
at a time. Get what I mean?"

"Not really." I shake my head, grab the duster from the peg,
and head toward the shelves.

She follows behind. "Look, I saw how you puppy-dog-eyed him the other day." I whip my head toward her, starting to protest, but she waves me off. "You aren't the first girl to get that look, and Lord knows you won't be the last. Girls flock to him. You should see him work the rooms at our promo events. Smiling, flirting, hugging for selfies with all the chicks in line drooling, pawing, and showing him their boobs."

The words and the images running through my imagination sucker-punch me in the gut. I blow out a deep breath and attack the book dusting with a vengeance, spewing minute particles into a frenzied haze around us. This. This is the reason I wanted no part of this romance shit this summer. This summer of relaxation is turning into a hellacious stress-pit already.

Rachel winces as the dust storm attacks her face, stepping back a minute to sneeze a couple times before reigniting her argument. "I don't mean to be crude. It's just..." She grabs my shoulder, spilling icy-cold droplets across my skin as I jerk away from her touch. "Anyone can see you're an old-fashioned sort of girl, and, well, Jett appreciates the fast and wild. He's a racer, first and foremost. Girls are just a diversion, and that's something he doesn't need right now."

"Girls?" I repeat. Plural. Like multiple girls. My chest wrenches in a vice grip.

She shrugs. "How else do you explain his disappearing acts every time we go on our promo trips?"

"Disappearing acts?" I repeat again over my shoulder as I walk back to the register. Having a counter between us is ideal. Too bad it isn't a brick wall with razor-wire across the top.

She leans across it on her elbows, lowering her voice to barely a whisper. "He denies it, but every time we're gone, the girls will line up and fawn all over him. Then two hours later, he's gone. MIA. He'll finally show up again around midnight or later. You connect the dots." She raises her eyebrows higher on her forehead and reaches out to touch my hand. Seeing it coming, I jerk it from the counter and shove it in my pocket. Rachel smirks at the slight and continues, "I'm not trying to ruin anything for you. I mean, you *are* only here for the summer, so if a

69

fast and crazy months-long fling is what you're looking for, you're probably in luck. But, honestly, you picked the wrong summer for that. He doesn't have time this year for playing around. He'll be training or on the road because we have a hectic schedule this summer before his big race in August."

"Big race?" I cringe, wanting to punch myself in the face. I'm like her ventriloquist dummy stuck on repeat.

"He didn't tell you? Weird. He hasn't shut up about it to everyone else." She pauses and waits for my reaction, searching my face, eyes wide. I don't give her the satisfaction; my stone façade won't crack. I'm mad enough at myself for the emotions raging inside right now. No way I'm giving Rachel a reason to enjoy it at my expense. She sighs. "It'll be the race that makes or breaks his career. If he wins, he's going to the big time, and he's taking us with him. The sponsorship dollars will *really* roll in then." She rubs her first two fingers against her thumb, making the "cash" sign. "Maybe then—and only then—he'll slow down enough to have an actual girlfriend. I know that's what Dani's waiting on."

"Dani?"

She slaps her hand over her mouth, giggling through her fingers. "She's part of the racing promotional team we've worked with on and off again for the past three years. They hit it off when they first met. You know, so much in common with the racing and all. We'll be working with her all summer on promotions."

Maybe this Dani girl will get her wish. Maybe she'll work with Jett, so freaking close she can fulfill her every fantasy. Fine with me.

Only that's a lie.

It isn't anywhere close to being fine with me, and I can't believe how stupid I was to believe for even a moment there was something between us. But even as I'm thinking it, even as my resolve says to forget him completely, my heart rages in protest. There *was* something there. A spark.

Wasn't there?

My bullshit-o-meter is pretty astute. At least, it always was before.

Maybe the wreck took that away from me too.

The door chimes again as Jett strolls in, smile stretched wide. I drop my head and inspect the ragged cuticles on my nails. He walks forward and raps on the counter, and when I glance up, he points to his ear.

"What?" I fold my arms across my chest, careful to keep the stone-face intact.

"A true Beachin' Books cashier needs to give me the traditional welcome. I'm waiting."

"Welcome to Beachin' Books where every day is a beachin' good day." My voice lacks any inflection, almost robotic in measured beats.

Jett studies my face, while I strangle the gnawing desire to simultaneously hug him and ring his neck. He swallows hard and cuts his eyes back and forth between me and Rachel.

"What are you doing here, Rach?"

She smiles and pushes her soda in Jett's face. "Getting a drink."

Silence envelopes us. Not one of those peaceful lulls, but a negatively-charged cloud. Everyone begins fidgeting. Jett pops his knuckles while I tap-tap-tap a red pen against the side of the register.

His green eyes burn through me, the same way they have every time we've been together. But now I'm more confused than ever. I'd mistakenly taken it as his interest in me—who I was—but if Rachel's right, he's only interested in a conquest, some no-strings summertime fling that'll die way too soon, like everything else in my life. It's not like I expect us to fall in love or anything, but I am not someone to be used.

"Is there anything you're needing to check out, or can I be excused to go wash these filthy windows?" I reach beneath the counter to grab a bottle of glass cleaner and shove a roll of paper towels under my arm.

"I came by to chat if—"

"Sorry. I'm on the clock," I say, pointing to the digital display on the wall.

Jett pulls his shoulders back as if I've taken a swing at him. "Seriously?"

71

"I take everything seriously. I don't have time for playing around or players." I walk around the counter, smooshing between the two of them and a shelving unit on my way to the plate-glass windows. "Oh, and have a beachin' good day!" I holler over my shoulder without looking back.

Without another word, Jett and Rachel leave, the electronic chimes followed by the door slam and their staccato steps on the staircase. I stand, nose nearly touching the glass, and watch the sailboats, their happy fabric sails like Skittles thrown out against the blue sky. Something catches my eye from the dock. Jett stands there, looking up at me with his shoulders shrugged and palms in the air.

Ask Rachel.

I concentrate my energy into the thought as if somehow it'll reach him through telepathy. But he still stands there, pretending he's Mr. Innocent.

I raise the bottle of cleaner and pull the trigger. Blue liquid sprays across the glass and runs down in streaks, warping and puddling his image. I wad a few paper towels and swipe the glass in circles, never meeting his eyes. After a minute, he drops his hands and walks away, disappearing into the back door of The Shrimp Shack.

I pull my phone from my pocket and tap out a quick text message to Memaw.

<Me> *Might be a little late for supper.*

Chapter Nine

A warm breeze blows in off the ocean, but my arms still prickle with chill bumps. The beach lays empty, proba- bly because most everyone is at home having supper. I should be—undoubtedly Memaw is waiting on me despite my earlier text—but a moment of solitude was calling my name, some time to collect my thoughts before being subjected to her full-scale interrogation of my first day.

I wiggle deeper in the sand, stretching my legs out in front of me where my toes can tease the white foam left behind from the outgoing tide. Beside me, an oval depression with a tiny hole in the middle sends bubbles to the surface from somewhere below. I grab a sliver of broken oyster shell, digging deep at the hole, creating a small mountain of sand behind me. Salty water fills in from the bottom, flushing out a small hermit crab that circles around in the pool and then attacks the side wall, burying himself away from daylight. Before he can get away, I gather him in my palms and bring him closer to my face. His wiry legs nip at my skin as he tries to burrow into my flesh.

"Hey there, buddy," I say, poking my finger at his antennae. He shrinks back into his shell. I capture him between two fingers and hold him in front of my eyeballs. "It feels safe in that shell, doesn't it?"

I get it, little crab. I so get it.

I lower him into the damp hole, and he scoots away, vanish- ing underneath a layer of sand.

Too bad I can't follow.

Loud squawking from a line of pelicans passing overhead draws my attention skyward. I relax, laying back with my arms curled behind my head, and stare at the clouds. Noli-Belle and I used to lay on the trampoline in the backyard and make cloud pictures. Elephants and dragons and rabbits. Now they look formless, uninspired. I close my eyes, blocking them behind a wall of darkness.

One week down. One week closer to going home. At least what's left of it.

If there's anything left at all.

My story is the stuff of those urban legends—a dire warning to selfish teenagers to be grateful for what you have in case you lose it all in the blink of an eye. I did lose it all, and it sucks. Majorly.

The loss gutted me, and then I made it worse, tucking myself away in a shell like that damn crab, ignoring Dad, Em, Trent, and anyone else who crossed my path. Being alone forever seemed like the best choice. Alone is good. Easy. Safe.

But then Stupid Me lets my heart flip-flop over the first cute guy who catches my eye in Edisto. I poke my head out of my safe shell, and *bam!* His phony, playboy reputation smacks me right across the face. I'm pissed at Jett for being that way. I'm pissed at Pepto-Bismol Hair for rubbing it in my face. I'm pissed at myself for the nagging doubts that he's really capable of everything Rachel suggests.

"CJ?" Her shadow darkens my face, breath heavy and coming out in spurts. "I've been calling you...the whole time I was...running out here. Didn't you... hear me?"

I slit open my eyes. The setting sun's light dances around Gin's blond hair like a luminescent halo as she bends over me, hands on her knees.

"What? No, I...I didn't. Sorry."

"So? How was your first day?"

I sit up, pinching the shoulders of my T-shirt and shaking it to loosen sand from my back. "Boring, other than my visitors." I visor my hand over my eyes as I look at her, still standing over me, eyes wide. "You gonna sit down or stand there all day?"

Gin giggles, using her foot to rake the sand smooth over the once-exposed hermit crab hole, and flounces beside me. "Visitors?"

She wiggles her butt back and forth in the sand, so hard her whole body shakes. Always eager. Always optimistic.

"You're hopeless, know that?" Gin reminds me of myself not so many months ago, how I used to bite at the bit when Emmalyn would come over with some juicy gossip. Our circle had been large, but no one was closer than me and Em. Watching Gin rub her hands in anticipation of my story, I can't help thinking she'd have been a welcome addition to our duo. "You, Bo, and Memaw, of course, then Jett and his racing partner, Rachel."

She cocks her head to the side, scrunching her nose. "That pink-haired girl?"

"Yep."

"What'd she want?"

"To make a point."

Gin's eyebrows practically shift into question marks. "What did she say to you?"

I ignore her question. "So, you've known Jett your whole life?"

Her shoulders loosen, and a smile creeps back across her face. "Forever. Jett and Bo have been friends since they were toddlers. He's pretty much been a brother to me. A very hot brother, but still…a brother." She puckers her lips, a mischievous glint dances across her sapphire eyes. "Why do you want to know about Jett all of the sudden? Are you two—?" She nudges me repeatedly in the side.

My cheeks warm. "No…it's just…"

"Because I know he likes you. It's obvious from the way he looks at you."

"From what I hear, he looks that way at a lot of people." My knee-jerk response stuns me, and I clamp my mouth shut, turning away from Gin to scan up-shore. Damn my ever-present foot-in-mouth disease.

She clears her throat. "Is this about something Rachel said?" When I don't say anything, she takes a deep breath and starts again. "Jett's my friend, CJ. If someone's talking junk about him, I need to know."

I pivot on the sand to face her, relaying Rachel's comments about Jett's flighty hook-ups with random girls at his racing events.

"She said that?" Gin narrows her eyes again, the smile completely wiped from her face and replaced with a deep scowl.

"Yeah, and that he's too busy for me and only being nice because I'm a summertime fling."

Gin balls her fists and slams them into the sand, spraying a few grains against my legs. They sparkle like glitter in the golden sunlight, and a few sandpipers near us take flight. "That's total crap!"

As she seethes, I muster up the nerve to ask more. "Have you gone to any of these promo events?"

I want her to tell me yes. That she's first-hand witnessed his upstanding-ness.

She shakes her head. "No, but...come on, you know Jett's not how she says he is."

Do I? He waltzed into my life a short week ago and has already created this much havoc. Still, I can't shake the inkling in my gut there's something inherently good about him.

"I don't know. I don't really know him at all."

"Trust me. Jett's a good guy."

"But how do you know for sure if you don't go to his racing promos?"

She sighs. "I guess I don't, but..." she grabs my hand. "That doesn't sound like Jett. Besides, he'd tell Bo. They're best friends. You tell your best friend everything."

Not everything. My current relationship with Em is a testament to that. I swirl patterns in the sand with my finger. "I don't know what to believe."

Gin pouts her lips and folds her arms tight across her chest. "Don't let her pettiness ruin your *thing* with Jett."

I snort. "I don't have a *thing* with Jett."

"If you say so." Her sing-song tone proves her imagination's running wild.

I roll my eyes and check my phone. Supper is probably cold by now. "It's time to be getting back to Memaw's. She's probably been waiting on me." I stand up, sweeping my hands from shoulders to shins, the sand gritty against my palms. "You heading back now or staying out here a while?"

"I'm gonna hang out. Watch the sunset."

I nod and trudge a few steps toward the beach access, pausing to look back over my shoulder. Gin brushes a few wisps of hair from her face and stares back.

"Don't mention what we talked about to Bo or Jett, okay?"

She smiles, the metal braces stretching across her teeth reflect a glint from the sun. "Sure. What are friends for?"

I return the smile and muddle through the sand drifts toward the sidewalk. She's right. We're becoming friends, and for the first time in months, I don't want to run from it.

A few yawns and some well-placed stretches throughout dinner score me a pass on chores for the night. Memaw says I've earned it after a long first day on the job. So, I mop up the last of my fajita chicken on a scrap of tortilla, shove it in my mouth, tell Memaw goodnight, and escape to my room for a hot shower and a tortuous game of *Who the Hell is Jett Ramsey?*

I hand-squeeze the extra water from my hair and comb out the tangles. The auburn ends stretch all the way to mid back, much longer than I've had it since late elementary school. Mama used to take me to the fancy salon downtown to get it cut and styled on Girls' Day, but there haven't been any of those since last summer, and consequently, no haircuts either. I stare into the mirror, french braiding my hair. The braids sort of showed up a couple months after the accident. I never wore them before, but when my hair started to become unmanageable, it was an easy solution to keep it all tamed. That, and the fat end of the braid tossed in front of my left shoulder is a terrific cover-up for any would-be scar sneak peeks.

I flip off the bathroom light and sit in front of my laptop. The saved draft of my email to Em waits in the folder. Pressing Send would be so simple, but for some reason, I can't. Instead, I open a new search tab and type in "Jett Ramsey" and "racing" in the white box. More than 1,000 entries pop up, mostly highlights from past races. Under the Images tab, a slew of the pictures I saw before—the ones with Jett in those zip-up racing outfits—fill the screen, but toward the bottom are a few shots of him sitting at a long table, smiling and signing autographs.

I enlarge them on the screen, scouring each picture for proof of Rachel's insinuations. A middle-aged man, Jett's father Jeff Ramsey as noted in the caption, sits beside him at the table in every shot, and there's even a few with Trévon and Rachel and another guy I've never met. Girls, lots of them, crowd each picture as well. Fangirls with Jett's number smeared across their big chests and barely-there T-shirts. These must be the girls Rachel's referring to, but in the pictures, Jett's not leering at them, ogling their bodies, or even touching them. He's signing autographs. Unless it's not autographs, but secret messages with hook-up details for later.

My heart beats triple time, and I slam the laptop closed. *Get a grip, CJ. You're freaking losing it.*

My phone vibrates against the wooden desk, the light from its screen reflecting a greenish-glow against the painted surface. I pick it up but don't recognize the number. Everyone I usually text is entered in my Contacts, but this number features a local 843 area code. I tap the notification and the message appears on-screen.

Hey. It's Jett.

How did he get my number?

<Me> *Hey. How did you get my number?*

Waiting on his answer, I plug his information into my Contacts. Stupid, since this *cannot* become a habit. The least I can do is give myself a friendly reminder of the futility of our relationship with every text. The phone buzzes again, and I smile as his name appears.

<Jett "Jackass"> *Gin gave it to me. We need to talk.*

Great. Gin went flapping her jaws to Jett after our talk, when I specifically asked her not to. A fire rises from my belly.

<Me> *About what*

<Jett "Jackass"> *Why you were pissed at me today*

<Me> *I wasn't*

<Jett "Jackass"> *Try again*

<Me> *If you've already talked to Gin, why ask me?*

<Jett "Jackass"> *Because Gin won't spill.*

The fire subsides. Gin kept her promise. I shouldn't have doubted her. Suddenly, I want to walk next door and high-five the crap out of her.

<Me> *It's nothing. I was busy. First day and all...*

<Jett "Jackass"> *Come on, Cami. I know it has something to do with Rachel.*

<Me> *Why do you say that?*

<Jett "Jackass"> *I'd have to be an idiot not to catch all those weird vibes between y'all. What did she say?*

<Me> *Why don't you ask her?*

<Jett "Jackass"> *I did. She says I'm crazy*

<Me> *Maybe she's right about that one*

<Jett "Jackass"> *Rachel's only right in her own mind. She said something about me, didn't she?*

<Me> *It's nothing*

<Jett "Jackass"> *If it's about me, I deserve the right to defend myself*

I tap out the reply, re-read it fifty times, then press send. I drop the phone and clasp my hands over my mouth. Did I really just say that? I turn the phone over and read my words once again.

<Me> *She warned me about your shady reputation with fangirls at your racing events*

Buzz! An immediate response.

<Jett "Jackass"> *What reputation?*

<Me> *It doesn't matter. I told her we're just friends*

<Jett "Jackass"> *Oh*

<Jett "Jackass"> *You really shouldn't believe everything you hear*

<Me> *You don't have to explain anything to me. It's cool*

<Jett "Jackass"> *Why do you believe Rachel so easily but not me?*

Because it's easier.

<Me> *I don't know. Doesn't matter.*

I lay the phone face-up on the desk and stare at the glass orb I keep on my bedside table; its aqua color swirls around a tornado of crystalline flecks forever suspended in the middle. Mama and Noli-Belle's ashes, the only physical part remaining of them, are preserved in an art piece to carry with me forever. There was nothing I couldn't confess to Mama, nothing we couldn't talk about. What I wouldn't give to have her opinion now. No sooner do I think it than her voice whispers as a faint memory in my brain. *Always follow your heart. It feels the things we're not yet prepared to see.* Something about her nuggets of wisdom always seemed risky. Even more so now.

My phone buzzes again.

<Jett "Jackass"> *What can I do to make you trust me?*

The million-dollar question, and I have the answer, uncomfortable as it may be. It's not so much about trusting Jett as it is being able to trust myself when he's around.

Chapter Ten

Me> *Actions. Not words.*

The reply I sent to Jett before crawling under my covers last night is still on the screen when I wake up. And nothing else. No response. No virtual thumbs-up. Not even an emoticon. Worse still, I'm not scheduled to work again until tomorrow, so I have the whole day to contemplate the hidden meanings behind his silence.

Sitting around this house is not an option, and one thing keeps swimming in my mind. Memaw swears heartaches are healed by the sea. And while I think Jim Beam is the one really doing the heavy lifting where she's concerned, my getting drunk in the kitchen is out of the question, so I might as well see if her theory holds water. Of course, I won't tell her this and subject myself to the lengthy discussion on how I should make some sort of bold move on Jett. Or worse yet, have her call him and arrange another "chance meeting."

I stumble to my bureau and slide open the top drawer, looking at the bland selection of post-scar bathing suits. This time last year, I sported a sweet two-piece halter number, yellow with pink polka dots. Every time I wore it, Dad sang the "Itsy Bitsy Teenie Weenie Yellow Polka-dot Bikini" song. I'd cover my ears and talk over him, but now I'd give anything to go back. To have his attention. That bathing suit. That body.

Those days are long gone, like everything else normal in my life. I snatch the first suit on top of the jumbled pile and then slam the drawer. Holding it in my hands makes me grimace. The stringy black bottoms, leftover from last year, still look cute, but the long-sleeved, hide-everything, gray rash guard sucks. I get that there's a totally legit function for these. Surfers and boogie boarders swear by them, and now, so do I. They do wonders for covering my scar under a layer of dry-weave fabric without inspiring too many questions, though people probably get the wrong impression. I'm so not sporty, and I've never ever been on a boogie board.

Once dressed, I head to the kitchen where Memaw sits at the table, cup of coffee in one hand and pen in the other, hovering over the daily newspaper's crossword puzzle. She cuts her eyes at me over the rim of her mug as I grab a banana from the wire bowl on the counter.

"Is that what you kids call a bathing suit nowadays? The bottoms look normal, but the top does nothing for your figure, honey."

I should've known Memaw would have questions, but then again, when doesn't she? She stares at me, expressionless, as I spit out the usual explanation about how the rash guard keeps the board from chaffing my skin. For a minute, I'm sure she buys it.

Almost.

"So, where's this boogie board you speak of?" She scans the room, even walking over to the windows to search the ground below. The woman should've been on Broadway for her dramatic prowess.

I blow out a breath. "I don't have one."

"I see," she mumbles, chewing on the end of the pen still clutched in her fingers. I wait for another lecture, but nothing comes. She sits back down and leans over the table, doodling again on the spread-out newspaper.

Let it go, CJ. Now's your chance to escape.

Somehow, my brain decides to forego its own advice.

"I thought I should take advantage of living at the beach this summer."

She narrows her eyes, never glancing up from her work. "You should take advantage of a lot of opportunities here."

No explanation needed. Before I can haul ass out the door, she tells me to be back by 11:30. We have a lunch date.

Something's Fishy is nothing more than a roadside fry-house with a massive screened porch dining area attached to it, but Memaw swears it's the best food on the island. From the five-gallon bucket of used, partially solidified cooking oil beside the employee's entrance to the kitchen, I'm skeptical of her raves.

The chalkboard hanging on the handle of the screen door says "Please Seat Yourself", and Memaw beelines to a small table at the porch's far edge, which she declares is the best seat in the house because it provides a view of the ocean and of everyone coming and going. In other words, a Southern busybody's dream. She hangs her purse on the ladder-back chair and scoots herself in little spurts until positioned just so, then plucks a laminated menu from the metal holder and hands it to me.

"I don't even have to look. I always get the fried shrimp."

I glance at the main selection of entrees. Grease, grease and more grease. Not a salad or green vegetable in sight. Fried shrimp, it is.

"Now where is that waiter?" she huffs, craning her neck around me, scanning the room. A man, probably in his early sixties, pushes through the kitchen's swinging door with a tray on his shoulder and waves at us.

Memaw's frown reverses, the corners of her lips inching up her cheeks. Her eyes follow the waiter's every step. "You know, I've been thinking." She pauses, her eyes still glued to the man as she runs her tongue across her bottom lip, then pulls it in between her teeth. "You flirting with Jett. I think you're doing it wrong. Obviously the boy's interested in getting to know you, but you're not putting forth enough effort."

Our definitions of "effort" probably span night and day. This is the woman who happily bestowed upon me the right to drink and have sex under her roof should the situation arise. Not that it ever will. And besides, how does she know what has or hasn't happened between me and Jett?

She taps her finger against her temple, glancing at me briefly with a smile, before diverting her attention back to the waiter. "Watch and learn from a master."

As soon as the words exit her lips, the man walks to our table, notepad open and pen poised for our orders. His wavy salt-and-pepper hair is a bit shaggy, but his face is clean-shaven. He looks like the type of guy who probably smokes pot around the fire pit in his backyard. Suburban hippie.

"How are you two lovely ladies doing today?"

I give him a thumbs-up, but Memaw leans forward across the table, her humongous boobs piling on top like one fleshy mountain. "It's hard to have a bad day when the weather's this beautiful," she coos, her voice airy and laced with Southern honey. "I don't recall seeing you around here before. Are you new?" She reaches up to finger his name tag pinned on his T-shirt. "James?"

"Yes ma'am. Started first of the week, but I actually moved here last month. My wife died a couple years ago, and I finally decided it was time to get back in the ol' saddle. So, here I am."

"Yes. Here you are." She pulls her fingers back and trails the tips down her neck. "I'm local, too, so if you ever need anyone to show you around, let me know."

A grin spreads across his face. "That's mighty nice of you. I sure would love that..."

"Bessandra."

I roll my eyes, but she ignores me. Everyone calls her Bessie or Memaw, and here she is spouting off her full name in some breathy tone, making the middle "a" sound more like an "o." Guess that sounds more exotic while she's playing him like a fiddle.

He winks at her. "That's very friendly of you, Bessandra." He repeats it just the way she said it, except his eyes narrow at the "o" sound like a lion ready to jump its prey. Have they forgotten I'm even at the table? Surely that's the only reason they're comfortable with this senior citizen verbal foreplay in front of me.

"Well, that's me. Friendly." She throws both hands into the air in a coy shrug and giggles. "So, James, what are today's specials?"

Why does it even matter? Two seconds ago, she was fried shrimp all the way.

"Fried flounder basket or shrimp and grits."

"Shrimp and grits? Does that come with the usual bell peppers and...sausage?"

Oh. My. God. She did not just ask that. I gasp, sucking in a clot of briny air that makes me cough. They don't notice. The kinetic energy between them crackles, and while a part of me is disgusted, there's another part, albeit a much tinier one, secretly worshipping her confidence.

James swallows hard a few times, his Adam's apple bobbing and his chest moving faster. "Yes ma'am. I believe so."

"Mmmm. That's what I'll have. I do love some good sausage."

Fire rushes to his cheeks. "I bet you do," he mumbles, looking at his notepad. "Shrimp and grits then for the lady."

They stare at each other, so I clear my throat, hold up the menu and point. "I'll have the regular shrimp basket, please. With fries. Also, two sweet teas." I volunteer that part before Memaw can tell him how she'd like to drizzle it over her breasts or some other God-awful image that'll be burned into my head. He writes it down and dashes back into the kitchen.

Across the table, Memaw swipes her nails back and forth on her navy tank top, pleased with her performance.

"I so hate you. Know that now."

"There's nothing wrong with a little flirtation. Keeps you young."

"I *am* young."

"You're the oldest young person I know." She plunges her finger in my direction. "A little flirting—especially with a hunky racecar driver—might do you some good."

That was way more than flirtation. Flirting requires side-eyed glances and little giggles. Maybe a touch here and there. Not an X-rated discussion of sausage. And the thought crosses my mind that when he brings the food, I should excuse myself to the restroom before they sample the special together on top of the red-and-white plastic tablecloth.

She reaches across the table to grab my hand. "You like Jett, don't you?"

I stare at the napkin, a heat burning in the curve of my ears. "Like" is such a casual word. Meeting Jett has flipped a switch inside me, igniting a rainbow of emotions, good and bad, from distrust to jealousy to infatuation. But one thing undercuts them all: fear. He could hurt me, rip my heart into little pieces, and it's all because what I fear the most has already happened to me once. I did love, and I lost. And despite my best efforts, I care about him, even though I'd sworn to block myself off for good. Somehow, he's wiggled in the cracks of my armor.

"I don't really know him."

Memaw tugs at my fingers, and I glance over at her. "It's okay to take a chance. Happiness is worth the risk."

My phone vibrates, and I drop Memaw's hand to pick it up. A new text message from Jett "Jackass" stares back at me. No words, only a selfie of him in one of those zip-up suits standing by a camellia bush full of creamy blossoms. I can only smile.

"Jett?" Memaw grins at me from across the table.

I nod, just as James sweeps out of the kitchen with our food and drinks. He puts everything on the table, laying the bill face-down by Memaw with a wink. After he's gone, she flips it over. Underneath is a small sliver of paper with James's phone number. Memaw tucks it into her bra. "The bigger the risk, the bigger the reward."

After lunch, we rummage through beachy knick-knacks and racks of T-shirts in the souvenir shops off the boardwalk. In the back corner of one store, while rifling through a collection of framed art, Memaw squeals, hoisting a small rectangular sign in the air. A large rod and reel is painted on the front, and in white block letters, it says:

Reel Girls Like Big Rods.

As if her other suggestive signs littering the house aren't enough. This one might be the raunchiest yet.

"Do you even fish?"

"No...but maybe I should according to this."

I don't know how the idea starts. Maybe it's the way Memaw tugs at her collar as she daydreams about naughty fishermen with big rods. Maybe it's the lingering memories of the sausage from the restaurant. I grab the sign from her hands, ready to give her a dose of her own medicine.

"You're right, Memaw. It must be a sign. Jett rides around on a big ol' shrimping boat. I bet he has a real huge rod." I emphasize the last three words with a couple deep pelvic thrusts.

She clutches her hand over her mouth, stifling a laugh, but her eyes focus on something behind me. Or someone.

A dark-haired woman with shining hazel eyes walks up on my right. Her pale lavender blouse and slim-fit white capris make her look more like a movie star than a local. "This must be the Cami I've heard so much about!"

Please be a random townsperson. Please don't be Jett's mom. Please let it be a fluke she just called me Cami.

The fried shrimp threaten a resurrection on the tile floor.

"Jenniston! Yes, this is my granddaughter, here for the summer. She and Jett have already been…acquainted."

I stare at the woman in front of me. She can't be more than 35 unless Jett's dad is shelling out the big bucks for some really good plastic surgery. Or maybe she was a teenager when she had him. He's never mentioned her, so who knows. I search her face for signs of him but find none. There are no similarities in their looks, though they both share that charm-everyone-you-meet personality. I pluck my courage together, my stomach knotted. "So…you're Jett's mom?"

"Stepmom, actually, but mom for all intents and purposes. I've been in his life since he was six."

Jenniston fidgets with the strap on her purse while my mind kicks into hyper-drive. *For all intents and purposes.* I'm no PhD on family dynamics (Lord knows mine's a dysfunctional mess these days), but something about that statement strikes me. Lots of the kids back home have stepparents. Em's stepfather was about as close to her as any birth father would be, driving her to dance lessons and showing up at every school play. Still, she didn't refer to him as Dad, and neither did he. Her birth father remained a huge part of her life, too, so it wouldn't be right. *For all intents and purposes* makes it sound like Jett's birth mother is either a deadbeat or just…dead.

"When are the boys due back?" Memaw interjects, breaking the awkward silence.

"Couple days. Hopefully not longer. People talk about being a golf widow. Maybe I'm a racing widow?" Jenniston sighs, more from relief than exasperation. Like she's happy for the quick change in subject.

My phone buzzes in my hand, and everyone's eyes land on me as I swipe the screen.

<Jett "Jackass"> *you get my pic earlier? Couldn't spend the day with Camelia Jayne AKA Cami so I ate lunch with a camellia*

<Jett "Jackass"> *she didn't say much. Tough chick. Reminds me of you*

I snort-laugh then look up to two sets of wide eyes.

"Jett?" Memaw asks with a lilt.

Jenniston strokes my arm. "You must be pretty special. Jett doesn't take time away from his racing for just anyone." The blush returns back to my cheeks as she adds, "Nice to meet you, Cami…or CJ. Which do you prefer?"

"Either." My stomach somersaults at the lie. Cami is reserved for Jett's use only. It's his thing. "On second thought, CJ is best."

Jenniston nods, lips pushed into a sideways grin and a knowing glint in her eyes. "I look forward to getting to you know this summer. It'll be nice to have some estrogen in that sea of testosterone I call home."

As she walks away, Memaw turns to me, nodding toward the wooden sign still clutched in my fingers. "Let's get that one. You really sold me on it."

Chapter Eleven

"Pierce, she's fine. Got a job. Making friends."

Eavesdropping on Memaw's conversation wasn't my intention, but when she calls my dad's name, the curiosity claws within. I'd come to let her know I was going outside to read for a while when her exasperated responses caught my attention, so now I'm skulking in the hallway outside her bedroom.

"Why would I lie to you? CJ's happiness *is* my priority."

I ease to the cracked door. Memaw's sitting on her bed, back to me, holding the phone to her ear, head shaking back and forth. What's new? They're disagreeing on something. At least they're talking, I guess.

"You may *not* trust me—and for very stupid reasons I might add—but..."

She slams her fist onto the bed. It absorbs into the comforter. "I don't owe you any explanation. That was between your father and me. Maybe one day you'll finally understand."

She snorts into the phone. "Oh, so that's it. You felt cheated, so you cheated me? Out of my family? Time with my grandkids?"

Wondering what'd torn Dad and Memaw apart has always bothered me, but now, hearing their arguing, their using our family like a whipping stick to beat each other, turns my stomach. Funny how adults expect their kids to act with maturity while they run around kitty-scratching each other like a bunch of snot-nosed kids.

"Fine. I'll let you know if anything changes." She throws the phone onto the covers, mumbling under her breath. I tip-toe down the stairs, grab my magazine off the kitchen table, and disappear out the back door before she can catch me.

It's a hot one already, the late May afternoon sun's heat intensified by the ever-present coastal humidity. I slouch in the Adirondack chair and flip through ad after ad of designer clothing and perfumes in an attempt to keep my mind off Memaw's tiff with Dad or Jett's absence over the last four days. He hasn't said when he'll be home. In fact, I haven't heard much from him apart from a daily picture of him eating sandwiches with that stupid camellia bush. But at least the messages prove he's thinking of me during the day, and I thumb through them every night before bed like an obsessed fangirl. It usually ends when I either fall asleep, phone in hand, or threaten to kick my own ass. Whichever comes first.

I've also been stalking Facebook, and while Jett's page has been quiet, Rachel's continuous stream of pictures show her hugged between him and Trévon. In a few of them, a swish of blond hair and a sliver of tanned skin barely juts into the frame beside Jett. More than once, Rachel references catching up with Dani. Is that her?

I refocus on the page and a bikini-wearing model sprawled out on the sand underneath the headline "Summer of Love" when a high-pitched whirring breaks through the monotony of waves crashing in the distance. A small remote-control car—a Dodge Challenger no less—speeds up the sidewalk and onto the concrete pad. It stops in front of my toes, blaring its miniature horn twice. On top, secured by tape, is a lined notecard with simple block lettering.

FOLLOW ME.

I stand, glancing around the yard. Everything's quiet, the backyard empty. The car circles behind my feet and heads back up the sidewalk, pausing once again as the horn blows and lights blink. My pulse races faster as I run to catch up with the miniature bumper disappearing around the corner of the house.

He's invisible at first. My eyes are trained on the remote-controlled car whizzing through the grass when a pair of sneakers step into my path. I look up in time to crash face-first into his chest, the musky aroma of coconuts and gasoline wafting around me, a cross somewhere between a cabana and a gas tank.

Jett tosses the remote to the ground and grabs my arms, steadying me on my flip-flops. Sunlight glints across his emerald eyes, and my stomach kinks when he asks, "What's your hurry?"

It's the first time I've seen him in shorts, and his legs, though a tad bird-like from the knee down, sport well-toned and well-tanned thighs. The kind that ripple under the wiriness of his blond hair. The kind my fingers itch to touch. Maybe Memaw's right about it being time to put myself out there.

"Ironic coming from you, the guy who never slows down."

"I don't have time to slow down."

"Sure you do. You just don't want to."

He snorts and looks away. "Maybe you're right."

Of course I'm right, and not just because I'm always right about these sorts of things. Jett's running from something.

A couple days ago, Mrs. Baxter's new shipment of magazines needed to be filed in the display racks. On top was one of those glossy covered racing mags with cars and girls and testosterone, oh my. But it was the teaser for an article on page 43 that grabbed my attention. At first, I figured I'd skip it. It's not like you can trust a psychological breakdown of "the race mentality" when the headline shares the same cover as some half-naked model sprawled out across the hood of a racecar.

I read it anyway, and while it was no in-depth study worthy of a scientific journal, it did make a few key points about the 'need for speed' being akin to an addiction. Between the intense focus and the adrenaline rush, taking the wheel of a racecar was almost therapeutic, a way to compartmentalize all your shit and shove it in the background. Which makes me wonder—what's Jett trying to forget?

He cups my face in both hands and leans in, his lips within a few inches of mine. The proximity stirs something deep—a desire, a magnetic pull—I haven't experienced in over a year. If ever. "Who can slow down when the race is such a thrill?" he whispers, his breath hot against my earlobe.

He's so close his chest brushes against mine, and chill bumps scatter over my skin. My heart channels a hard rock drum solo that Jett can probably see pumping out in the vein on my neck. "You don't think going slow could be equally as thrilling?"

"Maybe. With the right person."

Am I the right person? Is he? And how do I even respond to that? A million butterfly wings beat against my chest, and I lick my lips, mentally searching for another topic.

"Have fun at your promo event?"

And what I really mean is did he have fun with Dani or the countless other fans there? Not that I have a right to know or be pissed if the answer is yes. But still.

He pulls back, nose scrunched, then bends to scoop the remote and car under his arm. "Same as always—smile for the camera, sign my name, meet people." He nods his head toward the driveway, and I follow along behind him, my mind spinning with questions I'll never have the courage to ask. Who's he meeting? Fans? Dani? A random hook-up?

Get a grip, CJ. This is insanity. You can't keep—

"What'd you do while I was gone?"

My mind zips back to the present and Jett, head cocked to the side as he waits for my answer.

"Worked. Hung out with Memaw," I offer and then snap my fingers at another remembrance. "Oh, and I met Jenniston."

"Great." He doesn't even look at me when he says it, just blurts it out in one flat syllable. Curt responses usually mean *drop the subject*. I know. I've perfected their use this past year, so I extend him the same courtesy, though my mind swirls with the possibilities of his silence. *Stop, CJ. He'll tell you when he's ready. If he's ready. If he wants to ever tell you at all. Good God.*

Jett fumbles in his pocket and produces a small silver key. "Here." He takes my hand, prying my fingers open, and drops it in my palm. In front of the house, a monstrous golf cart, complete with rugged tires and a custom orange and black paint job, waits on the shoulder.

I slam the key back into his hand, swallowing the electrical impulses slithering through my esophagus like a venomous snake, and dig in my toes, unwilling to budge. Surely he's joking. I don't care how much money he's sunk into that pimpmobile. No way am I taking that glorified tin can on wheels out on the road.

"You have to get behind the wheel for me to help you." Jett scratches his head and nods toward the cart. "How 'bout this? I'll drive us to the pier, and we'll practice in the empty parking lot. Just you and me."

The high-tide waves crash on shore, gurgling underneath most of the pier's wooden, crisscrossed support structure. The darkness of the shade and the wind tunnel effect send shivers over my arms as we walk to the beams beyond reach of the ocean's salty fingers. Jett yanks my hand, pulling me toward a post. "See this?"

High above Jett's head and all the way down to the sand, crude etchings, names, and dates cover the weathered wooden column. According to Jett, every teenager who calls the island home inscribes their name on the post. Why? No one knows, but it's tradition, and traditions rarely make sense anyway. In the center is the name Keith with 1952 carved underneath. Apparently, this Keith-whoever-he-is is the point of origin for this anthropological project.

"Here's Trévon's. Rachel's. Bo's. Gin's. And mine." His finger travels across the wood to each name and finally to a naked spot at the bottom corner of his. "Now time to add you."

"But I don't live here."

"Sure about that?" He nudges my shoulder with his, fumbling in his pocket to produce a small knife, which he uses to carve my name into the soft wood. CAMI. "Now you're officially a part of Edisto history."

"So I've been illegitimate until now?"

"Not to me."

I run my fingers over the carvings of our names, the fresh-cut letters splintering out from the otherwise smooth surface. At the end of summer, will this be all that remains—a tiny bit of history? A speck on the map of our lives? I know better than most that life isn't something you plan. You don't take it by the horns; it takes you. We're lying when we tell ourselves the key is to be proactive, because the truth is, we're all just reacting. The saying goes, "If life hands you lemons, make lemonade." Nobody's out there making lemonade for fun. They only do it because life hands them the lemons first.

Sour freaking lemons.

We can make plans with the illusion of control, but soon enough, life will find a way to shit all over it. I smile, imagining how my therapist's face would twist into a grimace from that deep-thought-by-CJ.

"What'cha thinking?" He stares at me, bottom lip tucked between his teeth, but I'm not stupid enough to rattle off that line of pessimism in all its tragic glory, so I shrug instead.

"You don't always have to keep your guard up, you know," he says. This from the consummate man-on-the-run, with his hunky-dory persona covering the quiet brooding that lurks in his eyes. Most people don't see it, but I can. "There's nothing wrong with being tough. Just don't be hard. There's a difference."

The corner of my lip twitches. "And you're the resident softie?"

The dimple in his chin deepens as he smiles. "I might surprise you."

That's the truest thing I've heard all day. "You usually do, Jett Ramsey."

"Then trust me on this." He dangles the little silver keys in my face.

"I...I don't know if I can."

It's not whether I can or can't, but if I will. Driving a car is a lot like riding a bike. Once you master it, it's pretty impossible to unlearn. It is possible, however, for the mere thought of sliding behind the wheel to morph into a paralyzing agent that literally sucks all energy from your body, replacing it with gut-twisting panic.

"That's where I come in." He reaches out and grabs my hand, twining his long fingers with mine, and pulls me toward the cart parked in the narrow side lot. It's deserted like he promised, and the lengthy strip of asphalt stretches out before us like a runway, with beach on one side and marsh on the other. A hedge of palmettos lines the far edge, creating a border between the main road and the Piggly Wiggly across the street.

At least there won't be a million people watching me make a complete ass of myself.

I get in and clutch the wheel. Jett slides into the passenger seat and eases his hand over my trembling fingers, his voice butter smooth. "You'll do fine. Circle to the end of the lot and back. Easy." If he's trying to calm me, it isn't working. His touch is like lighter fluid, and I'm incapable of calming down in the driver's seat or when he's near me.

I blow out a breath, turn the key, and push the accelerator. The motor putt-putts to life, purring as we pull forward at a snail's pace. My thighs and biceps scream under the tension settling in the rigid muscles. Jett nods in encouragement, leaning forward on his seat, elbows on knees. We parallel the Atlantic, driving across the painted yellow lines with all the ferocity of a hundred-year-old granny.

At the edge of the lot, I stomp the brake a little too hard, and we both lunge forward. "Now what?"

Jett points back over his shoulder. "Make a U-turn and drive back, then do it all over again."

His flat-lined lips say there's no point in discussion, so I ease off the brake, heading back toward the pier. Around lap three, my muscles finally relax. The sultry breeze tousles the unclasped wisps of hair around my face while Jett dances in his seat to the cart's radio, which blares full blast. Random whiffs of octane from the gas-powered engine dance in the air around us. I sniff harder, trying to capture the sweetness and commit it to memory. Freedom.

"Hey watch me!" Jett yells, hanging halfway out the side, arms swinging in the air as we approach the marshy end of the lot once again. His infectious laughter distracts me, and my gaze lingers on his bronzed skin flexing over the striations of lean muscles with each movement.

Damn, I'd love to touch him and explore each one of those peaks and valleys.

Without warning, the cart lurches to a stop. Jett smacks into the dash, and the steering wheel collides with my gut. My chest fills with bricks, lungs burning as a sudden lack of oxygen sears my cells. Panic radiates through me as I gasp for air and stomp the gas pedal, but each press only spins the front wheels, the quiet purr becoming a high-pitched wail, miring us further into the gray swamp mud.

I want to scream I'm sorry, that he should've never trusted me behind the wheel, but nothing comes out. Jett shuts off the radio and slides beside me on the bench seat, pulling my head to his chest. "Don't freak out," he says, stroking my back. "We're only stuck. No big deal."

Once my breathing steadies, he hops out the side, soft-stepping in the mucky goop to the front of the cart. "Put it in reverse, and I'll push. When I say so, give it some gas."

My muscles hug tight to my bones. I nod, shift to reverse and plant my hands in ready position.

"Okay, go!" He leans his weight into the front, arms bent for leverage.

My big toe taps the gas pedal, the engine giving a quiet rev without moving.

Jett continues to push, yelling above the motor. "Harder. Give it the gas!"

I slam my foot against the accelerator. A plume of muck sprays up along the sides as the cart barrels backwards onto the asphalt.

One minute, Jett's there. The next, he's gone.

The low rumble halts when I cut the engine and raise up, peering over the edge. Jett lays stomach-down in the mud, propped on his elbows as he wipes clumps of ick from his face.

I scramble out the side, tip-toeing through the muck to squat beside him. His green eyes and white teeth peek out in slivers from behind the gray mask. The mud clings to his T-shirt and shorts in big gooey patches, the champion racer morphed into a lowly swamp creature. I clamp my fingers over my mouth, giggles erupting between them.

He swipes across his forehead, large globs dissipating into horizontal smears, and a wicked grin curls his top lip. "Funny, huh?" He lunges for my leg as I jump to my feet, backpedaling out of his reach and directly into the ditch. My flip-flop disappears into the muck, which squishes between my toes, gluing my foot in place. Unfortunately, the rest of my body continues moving backwards, and in a dizzying tumble, I end up on my back, the soft ground cradling me like a baby.

Jett springs to his knees, crawling toward me on all fours. "Shit! Are you okay?" His hands slap through the muck, sending gray splatters pinwheeling in the air. With one hand at my left shoulder and the other at my right one, Jett straddles me, hovering over my body, which involuntarily arches toward his despite my best efforts to sink further in the goop.

That's when I know. He must pay.

"You asshole." I grin, raising my hand in the air with a juicy glob of swamp mud I chuck at his head. It lands on top, the more liquid parts trickling down his forehead in runny clumps.

"I'm the asshole? You threw me in first!" He laughs and smears a handful across my cheeks and nose.

The goo tickles the edge of my nostril, the putrid smell gagworthy. "That was an accident!" A quick swipe across the surface flings more muddy droplets onto his face and shirt. One lands on his lip, clinging strong despite Jett's attempt to spit it away.

I scoot closer, gather the one clean edge of my T-shirt and wipe his lip while he stares at me. "What?"

"There she is."

"Who?" I look over my shoulder toward the parking lot.

Jett grasps my chin, pivoting my gaze back to him, his Adam's-apple bobbing in a hard swallow. "The real Cami."

The truth shines in his eyes. I want to *know* this boy, not because he's cute or charismatic or has a nice car or any of those other things people swoon over. Because he sees me. Not as a victim like everyone else. Not as a rehabilitation project. Not as a damaged shell of my former self. No. He sees *me*. The person. The one tucked away behind a mountain of heartbreak, guilt, and fear. The CJ of yesterday. The Cami of tomorrow.

I extend my hand, and his fingers intertwine mine. "Let's go back to Memaw's and get cleaned up."

The water from the outside shower stall is frigid, and my teeth chatter as it soaks through my clothes, molding them to me like a second skin. Jett pulls off his muscle shirt, rinses it under the water, and hangs it on the metal peg by the door. The lean muscles of his back stack into a V-shape, disappearing into the waistband of his shorts. I shift my eyes to my bare feet when he turns around, watching the clumps of mud break apart in the water gurgling down the drain.

He steps beside me under the waterfall shower head, eyes closed and head thrown back, as the water races down his face and chest. Oh, to be one of those droplets, skimming over his skin, him underneath me, riding over the peaks and valleys on my way to——

"Cami?"

My heart pounds in my throat and I jump, inadvertently biting into my lower lip, which had been tucked between my teeth. I grimace but suck back the urge to scream out. He stares at me, a question floating in his eyes.

"Did you hear me?"

I shake my head, my brain inept at finding the right words when I'm standing this close to his half-naked body. He twirls his finger in the air.

"Turn around. I'll clean off your back."

I nod, still mute, and turn so the water courses down the back of my shirt. Jett's hands run from my shoulders to my waist, wiping away the last evidence of our day. When he finishes, I turn around as he lowers his head in front of me. "Can you get that last little bit out of my hair?"

"Sure," I mumble, scouring through the strands, letting the water loosen any residue.

Suddenly Memaw's voice echoes underneath the house. "CJ, there's a golf cart parked out front. Do you know who——"

The door swings open as she barges in, her narrowed eyes snapping open wide when they land on us. Jett's face hangs near my boobs while I'm running my fingers through his hair, both of us soaking wet and him barely clothed.

She smiles, bigger than usual, as her eyebrow flexes into her forehead. "Never mind," she singsongs and backs out of the stall, letting the wooden door slam behind her.

Chapter Twelve

The usually quiet island is abuzz with the hum of cars speeding along the main drag, their tow-behind trailers filled with colorful luggage and bicycles signaling the official arrival of vacation season. Mrs. Baxter said everything would change come Memorial Day weekend, and the uptick in traffic and the cackle of voices floating in the air prove her right.

"Well, there goes the neighborhood," Memaw grumbles. She stands beside me on the front porch, leaning her elbows on the railing, as we watch the parade of newcomers. "Every restaurant will be packed from now 'til September."

"Then I guess we'll have to eat in." I pat her shoulder, stepping back to the front door to grab my purse off the foyer table.

The natives have a love/hate relationship with the visitors who pour into their island for four months out of the year. Tourism is a lucrative business around here, and the majority of the money to be made happens during this sunny and spectacular stretch from Memorial Day to Labor Day. Memaw says the place becomes "damn near unbearable," but the Ramsey and Johnson families don't seem to mind it. Of course, the market and the seafood shop are hot commodities for those coming in for a unique "taste" of Edisto. I've only been around Jett's dad, Mr. Ramsey, a handful of times at the bookstore when he came in for a soda, but when he's not going on and on about racing, he's talking about how many pounds of shrimp he expects to sell this summer and the best way of advertising the Shrimp Shack. He's that proverbial "man with a plan" for everything.

Me, I don't have an opinion on the whole tourist thing, but while I can totally see Memaw's point, I can also imagine how nice it might be to see something besides all the usual retirees and locals. To be the tourists with their rainbow-colored beach umbrellas and wagons full of sand toys and little kids, running and screaming in the waves. To be oblivious again and living the dream.

Must be nice.

A ruckus arises from the sidewalk below. A couple and their children—two young girls—shuffle toward the beach, a stash of gear in a cart and the two littles trailing behind, arguing over a beach ball. The smallest one screams and stomps her feet against the pavement until the older one gives in and hands her the ball.

I smile. A few years back, that could've been me and Noli-Belle, our biggest concern in life hinging on who got to carry the ball. I would've given in. I always did where my baby sister was concerned.

Memaw pushes herself into my side and leans in close to my ear. "Damn near unbearable."

After the family disappears behind a thick palm grove, she reminds me she has a date for the evening. She's been out with James three nights in the past week alone. On at least one of those nights, it was nearly 2 a.m. before she came home. I tried convincing myself they must've innocently fallen asleep on the couch watching movies, but the extra spring in her step the next day painted a different scenario. One I don't want to think about.

I remind her I'm spending the night at Gin's, and her smile oozes with wickedness. "So, I have the place to myself?"

We've switched places. I'm the grown-up, and she's the hormonal teenager.

"I'll be right next door. I could drop in at any time." I shrug, my palms up. The last thing I want roaming around in my brain is an image of Memaw entertaining her 'gentleman caller.' Ew. Memories of the lunch date and her relentless pursuit of sausage sour my stomach.

She nods toward my purse. "Where are you going?"

"Work. Mrs. Baxter had an extra shift to be covered today." More people on the island means more people in the store, which translates to extra hours. Might as well take advantage.

"You're pretty chipper about having to work."

"Just following your advice. Embracing my new home."

The words barely cross my lips before the golf cart pulls up out front. Jett slides over to the passenger side and motions toward the steering wheel.

Memaw steps closer to the stairs, and Jett's eyes dart in her direction. "Morning, Ms. Bessie!"

"Morning, Jett!" She side-eyes me while waving in his direction. "Embracing something, I see," she mumbles under her breath. "Which also reminds me. How did you two enjoy your shower the other day?"

I lean in and kiss her on the cheek, throwing my bag over my shoulder, and bounce down the front steps without another word.

"Pepperoni or sausage?" Gin hovers above where I'm lying on the couch in the Johnsons' rec room, waving a delivery menu in my face.

"Pepperoni. Definitely pepperoni."

"Cool." She plops on the farthest cushion, tapping away at her phone, then slides it in her pocket when she's done. "Pizza's ordered. Should be delivered in a half hour. Until then..." She retrieves a large canvas bag sitting on the recliner in the corner and brings it over. With a quick shake, the contents spill out onto the sofa. Avocados, strawberries, a pint of local honey, a small canister of old-fashioned oats, and a plastic sleeve of paintbrushes. "Let's do mini-facials."

Although she's nearly three years older than Noli-Belle would be, Gin reminds me of her sometimes. My sister loved "girl time," when we'd watch cheesy movies and do each other's make-up and hair. Gin has the same excited look plastered on her face that Noli-Belle always did, somewhere in the neighborhood of Christmas morning meets innocent puppy dog.

Masks aren't generally my thing, though. There's something odd about sticking food all over your face and expecting some sort of beauty miracle. But when Gin smiles at me again with those wide eyes, I can't bring myself to disappoint her, so I give in. Sucker.

I slice and pit the avocado, mashing it together with a drizzle of honey and a half-cup of oatmeal while Gin uses a fork to mash together a red juicy paste from the berries. We take turns smearing the green and red concoctions on our faces and teeth with the fancy paintbrushes.

While the lumpy mixture hardens on our skin, Gin and I slouch on the sofa, and she flips through the CD/DVD wallet I snagged from Memaw's house, commenting about her eclectic tastes in movies and music like she's some kind of idol. "My grandma bakes cookies. Yours watches rated-R action flicks and wears cool clothes and..."

"Picks up old geezers at restaurants."

Gin crinkles her nose and cuts her eyes at me. The mere mention of anything boy-related gets her extra sappy heart fluttering every time. A hopeless romantic—the one thing I've learned is her kryptonite. I fill her in on Memaw's budding relationship with James, leaving out, of course, the sausage part. I'm not sure Gin would be able to stomach it. Even giving her the G-rated version, Gin's face still lingers somewhere between fascination and horror. It's the same look everyone gets on their first day of sex ed in school.

"At least Hippie James is a cutie," she says, her smile dissolving into a loud sigh. "I wish guys would pay attention to me."

"Gin, you're sixteen and gorgeous. Don't rush it."

She beams, her eyelashes flickering a mile a minute. "How about you? Have you ever been in love?"

I hardly know how to answer the question. If you'd asked me this time last year, I would've sworn to it. But now that I've had some distance, learned a few hard life lessons, the term itself is clear as mud. The things I thought were so important turned out to be nothing more than vapor that dissipated in one tragic moment.

But all that's too hard—and too heavy—to explain, so I give her the Cliff's Notes version. I dated a guy for nearly two years. He was a nice guy, but I pushed him away and he got bitter. So, hindsight being 20/20 and all, the answer is no, I've never been in love.

She nods. "What about Jett?"

"What about him?" I look down, toying with the drawstring on my cotton shorts.

"I mean...I've seen you two together, and..."

"When?" I glance at her.

Gin's lip quivers as if she's accidentally ratted herself out. "When he was putting together the new patio set at your house, and when y'all left on the golf cart the other day. And then there were all those questions Rachel planted in your head. Jett was upset when he called me for your phone number that night." She grimaces and holds both hands up. "But I didn't tell him anything. Swear."

"I know you didn't. Thanks." I slip in a little laugh, trying to disguise the tremble in my voice that takes over at the mention of Jett's name. "We're just friends. He hasn't said anything to Bo, right?"

She vigorously shakes her head. "Nothing I've heard, and Bo—" Three loud knocks on the door interrupt her. Gin glances at her watch. "Mom must have the pizza."

While Gin runs to the adjoining bathroom for washcloths, I walk over and throw open the door with a wide, strawberry-stained smile. "Thanks for—" The words hitch in my throat, my smile fading. It isn't Mrs. Johnson.

Bo's mouth drops open as he cocks his head from side to side, staring at every angle of my face. "What the hell? You look like a deranged vampire version of Oscar the Grouch."

Behind Bo's shoulder, another set of eyes fix on me—emerald ones—and my body goes numb, like at any moment I'll completely dissolve into a gelatinous puddle at their feet. A heat rushes to my cheeks, so hot I'm afraid the avocado will cook right there on my skin.

"I...uh...we were..." I stammer, my brain unable to string together correct words. Jett rubs either side of his chin with his thumb and forefinger, a wicked grin curling his mouth.

Before I can make any progress in my explanations, Gin runs beside me, flinging a damp washcloth in my hands. She stomps

105

her foot on the carpet, eyes wide and furious. "What are y'all doing here? It's supposed to be girl's night."

"Hate to tell you, but girl's night got hijacked." Bo pushes past us into the room and tosses the pizza box on the credenza. "Didn't you see the weather report? Severe storms all night. We can't tent camp, and all the cabins were full over at the State Park. So, here we are, like it or not."

Gin threads her arms over her chest, looking between me and Bo while Jett waits in the hallway. I take another swipe with the white washcloth, collecting greenish chunks from my face, and flick my eyes toward Jett, who smiles at his sneakers. Gin's pissed about the change in plans, but I can't echo her rage. Something about the idea of spending the night here with Jett in the same house ties my stomach in knots.

When no one says anything, Gin flies into a tantrum, complete with stomping feet, before she hurls herself on the sofa. Bo walks over and sticks his tongue out at her as she kicks her leg in his direction, narrowly missing his boy parts.

"All right. Keep the fight clean, guys," Jett says as he walks in and pushes the door closed behind him. He stands no more than a foot away, and my every pore feels magnetized, like an invisible force field sucks us together. As if at any moment, the resistance will break and I'll go flying into him. He leans in close and whispers so low only I can hear. "That Oscar the Grouch look is hot, and you smell good enough to eat."

The empty pizza box and two obliterated bags of tortilla chips the boys nabbed from Mrs. Johnson's pantry lay on the floor by the door. The credits rolling on the third movie of the night and the frequent flashes of lightning are the only light in the dim room. The predicted storms rumble outside with a vengeance, the wind howling like a pack of wolves. Rain pelts the roof in a barrage of loud thumps.

Bo, however, isn't fazed. He stretches out across the entire sofa, a river of drool puddling on the pillow beneath his head as he softly snores in rhythm with the movie's soundtrack. Gin lays belly-down in front of the TV, her pillow folded under her head where a mop of blond locks cascade onto the floor.

I sit cross-legged behind Gin, my back resting on the sofa's leg, and Jett's beside me, so close his knee brushes mine from time to time, each occasion sending shivers racing up my spine. More than once, I sense him staring at me in my peripheral vision, but by the time I gather the courage to look, his eyes are back on the TV. Other than a random comment here or there, we don't talk, but the tension between us builds like a rubber band pulled to three times its length. It may snap at any minute.

"Looks like everyone else is out." He nods toward Gin's sprawled frame, which hasn't moved in the last five minutes.

"Gin?" I call out her name and wait. No response, so I try again. "Gin?" Still nothing.

"So, what'cha want to do?" Lightning illuminates his face in flashes, each burst of light reflecting in his eyes. That's a loaded question. We could do all kinds of things, most of which we probably shouldn't do. Most of which I shouldn't even be thinking about right now.

"Another movie?"

Jett nods and grabs the case, flipping through the first few panels. He stops, scrunching his eyes at a DVD he pulls from its sleeve. "What are the ones with only dates on them? Home movies? Bootlegged copies?"

"I have no idea." With Memaw, it's a crapshoot into the grab-bag of weirdness. Jett gets up and loads the DVD into the player as I pull a throw pillow over my face, my eyes barely able to make out anything through the cotton fringe. "Watch that at your own risk. Don't say I didn't warn you."

He sits beside me, rubbing his hands together in anticipation. I fully expect to see some God-awful image flash on the screen.

The movie begins with a little girl's laugh, shrill and joyful and oh-so-familiar. Noli-Belle. I push the pillow away and clutch it in my lap as a steel column slides down my spine. She skips across the frame, auburn curls flying out behind her like weathered flames, the sight of her robbing my breath. I open my mouth and suck in air with a loud gasp.

Jett spins around, eyes burning into me. "Cami, who is that?"

The words don't come out voluntarily. I have to push them out, like thrusting boulders up a hill. "Noli-Belle. My dead sister."

"Oh my God," he mumbles, getting to his feet. "I'll turn this off."

"No." I tug his leg, holding him back. "I want to see it." It doesn't make sense. I've spent so much time trying to forget the worst parts that now the good ones are hazy too. My sister was so beautiful, so full of life. Why has it been so much easier to remember her broken and bloody than as this? Happy and young and free.

Jett nods and sinks beside me on the carpet. With no words, he reaches out and twines his fingers with mine. I squeeze. He squeezes back.

My dad's voice chimes in from somewhere off-camera. "What do we say when CJ comes out?"

"Surprise, CJ! Duh, Daddy." Noli-Belle flashes her full-toothed grin and sits on our front porch bench. And suddenly, I know where Dad is. He's holding the camera, and I know that because Noli-Belle is sitting beside Mama.

Her hair's thicker than I remember, lips fuller, face younger and fresher. Could it be the details of their images are slowly washing away from the memories I have left? The realization pierces me like a stake to the heart. This was just last summer. I remember this day so well.

At least I thought I did.

"Here she comes," Dad whispers as the camera pans around the yard, stopping to focus on the front door. What walks through is an even bigger surprise. So much so, Jett can't contain his gasp as he double-takes between me and the screen.

Last year's CJ.

Warm, bubbly, teenaged and carefree CJ bounces down the front steps, auburn hair flying in the breeze, hardly touching the bare shoulders exposed by a purple strapless sundress. I'm smiling and laughing as Noli-Bell wraps her arms around my waist.

"Tell her," Dad goads.

"Surprise, CJ!" Noli-Belle screams, jumping up and down. Mama steps beside her and stretches her arms around the both of us, hugging us into her sides.

"There's my girls!" Dad announces, the pride in his voice a faint glimmer of what used to be. "CJ, we have a surprise for you. It's in the driveway. Go look!"

The camera follows behind the three of us, across the lawn, around the side of our house to a four-door navy blue sedan parked in front of the garage. The same sedan that would end up a mangled heap of metal on the side of a country road a few months later.

I grab the remote and hit *stop*. Jett's hand clings to my other one.

"Cami—"

I shake my head. "I don't want to talk about it. I'm fine." But I'm not fine, and he knows it. His fingertips press into my hand even tighter. His body leans toward mine, as if he's a support beam ready to hold me up when I collapse.

And in this moment, the one thing I know without a doubt is if I'm going to fall apart, there's no one else I want by my side. That fact terrifies me. And excites me. And royally screws me up.

Jett's phone buzzes in the quiet, and he picks it up, thumbing over the screen to open a new text. "Shit," he mumbles. "My dad needs help at the dock. One of the boats came loose in the storm." His eyes connect with mine, moving back and forth between them.

"Go. I'm okay. Promise."

Jett slides his phone in his pocket and reaches to brush away a wisp of hair hanging from my loose braid. "I'll be right back."

He jumps up and slaps Bo on the arm. Bo rouses, glancing around the room in a daze before Jett grabs him under the armpit, hoisting him off the sofa. They disappear out the door, their footsteps thumping against the stairs. I walk over to the double windows and watch the rain come down in buckets, the wind blowing the palm fronds against the glass. The roar of Jett's engine cuts through the pounding rain, and his taillights disappear into the stormy night.

"Don't worry. He'll be back before you know it." Her voice startles me, and I jump, banging my head into the windowpane. When I turn around, Gin's sitting cross-legged, hugging her pillow to her chest.

"I thought you were asleep. How long have you been awake?" She doesn't respond, just drops her eyes with a sheepish grin on her face. "You were never asleep, were you?" I ask.

She glances up, eyes wide like a child expecting a scolding. "No. It's just—there were some heavy vibes going on between you and Jett. Bo was over there snoring like a bear, and I was a major third wheel. So, I pretended. Please don't be mad."

"I'm not mad."

"Are you okay...you know, because of the video?"

"I'm fine."

Gin purses her lips and nods, then suggests we play cards for a while. She doesn't push, and for that, I'm grateful. She slips a deck of cards from their box, shuffles them in her hands, and then deals us in. For the most part, we play conversation-free, but by the fourth round, I can't help noticing how she keeps nervously clearing her throat.

"What is it?" I ask.

"The guy you dated before, who is he?"

"His name is Trent. Trent Casey."

Gin flexes her eyebrows. "Is he hot?"

In short, yes. Trent is hot with his black hair, icy blue eyes, and a tall, athletic body. And he's genuinely a good guy, too, even if we did have a bad ending. We started dating my sophomore year, always together until the accident last year. After that, the silence became distance and the distance became a mortal wound that finished us off.

Gin balks when she hears the actual break-up happened right before I came to Edisto. "That recently? I'm sorry. I shouldn't have brought it up."

"We'd been over for a while. Just made it official." I smile and throw my cards, perfectly matched in suits, on the table. "Gin rummy."

She sticks her tongue out at me as she scoops them up and begins shuffling again. "That's the third hand you've won."

I glance at the digital clock on the TV. Nearly forty minutes have passed since the boys left, and the storm outside hasn't let up one iota. The usual anxiety rears its head, circulating grotesque images of car wrecks and bloodied bodies in my head. I wring my hands, my stomach suddenly heavy as if a dump truck just unloaded concrete into my gut.

Gin reaches over and taps my knee. "Bo and Jett are big boys. Don't worry."

I nod, knowing full well her words won't quell the bile rising in my throat. Telling me not to worry is like telling the Earth not to rotate. There's no way to turn it on or off. It's always there, sometimes a sliver but sometimes an F5 tornado. What *if* the worst happens? What *if* they're hurt, lying in a ditch, the rain pelting their bodies? What *if*—?

My phone buzzes.

<Jett "Jackass"> *Boat's fixed. On our way back*

A smile breaks across my lips, and a deep breath escapes. "They're on their way."

Jett's safe, and at any minute, he'll walk back in the door.

Chapter Thirteen

To say the video hadn't changed things between me and Jett would be a lie. It did. And in all the right ways.

In the weeks since, he'd attacked my "learning to drive again" with a renewed vigor, swinging by the house each day on the golf cart and waiting outside Beachin' Books every evening when my shift ended. He became a natural part of my day—a part I look forward to from the moment my eyes snap open on my pillow each morning to the last thought in my head as I snuggle beneath the covers at night.

Now, he stares at me more too. As we head down the trail, me behind the golf cart wheel, muscles tense and eyes peeled for anything and everything in our path capable of imparting certain disaster, he's there in the outer perimeters of my view, sitting catty-cornered in his seat with an ever-so-slight lean in my direction. He refines me with a laser-sharp gaze, like he's mentally cutting away my ever-crumbling barriers, shining and spit-polishing the girl inside. The one he saw in that video.

I'd worried it would warp his image of me, turning me into a victim to be pitied. It didn't. Rather, it seemed to validate what he knew all along—Cami's alive and well. Now I need to prove to him I'm willing to do the work and meet him halfway. Live life as much as I ever could.

I turn on the lamp. A ribbon of light cuts through the darkness of my room. This has become a ritual, but tonight, something's different. My heart doesn't throw itself into wild palpitations. There's no sweaty brow. Just calm.

The time is right.

I click open *Drafts* and pull up my email to Em, the words memorized from a million-and-a-half read-overs. I take a deep breath, in for four and out for seven, then hit Send. When the confirmation message pops up, I grab my phone and shoot off a quick text.

<Me> *I sent you an email. Text me when you read it*

A response registers almost immediately.

<Bestie<3Em> *K*

Silence. No news is good news, right? No. Not when it comes to begging your best friend for forgiveness. The phone is dead silent, so I shoot off a flurry of psycho-texts, my heart swirling into the pit of my stomach.

<Me> *OMG it's been like 20 minutes. Please respond*

<Me> *I know I have no right to ask but...please...*

<Me> *I miss my best friend*

<Me> *???????????*

My phone buzzes in my palm.

<Bestie<3Em> *took you long enough to admit it*

<Bestie<3Em> *emailed you back*

<Bestie<3Em> *read and think about it. Text me tomorrow*

<Bestie<3Em> *night CJ*

<Me> *K night Em*

This has to be bad. Very bad. Not sure exactly what I expected, but a return email isn't it. We haven't talked—not really—in months. I'm prepared for an *I hate you and die* or *I love you and am calling you right now* text, but whatever the response, I assumed it'd be immediate. Why would she send an email telling me to take time and think about it? Thinking about it means there's way more to this than simple forgiveness.

Ding. I look at the screen. *You have one new message.*

Double click. Deep breath.

To: <CJ Ainsworth>
From: <Emmalyn Henderson>
Date: June 7
Subject: RE: Long Time, No Talk

I should be pissed at you. I should tell you to screw off. But I won't. You're my best friend—always have been and hopefully always will be. Even if one of us is acting like an ass. (That would be you in this scenario)

So, I forgive you. The question is, after you hear what I have to say, will you forgive me?

There's a new guy in my life. He's someone I'm really interested in, but I can't be with him. At least not without causing a lot of problems. I've been wanting to talk to you forever about it, but, well, you weren't talking. And that's actually how this whole thing got started.

It's Trent. He texted me a few months after the accident to see if you'd talked to me. I didn't hear from him again until a few weeks before you left for Edisto. He was feeling pretty lost about what to do, how to reach out to you, and I could relate to what he was going through. I guess one thing led to another (God, I hate that cliché statement). We never meant to develop any feelings beyond friendship, but it's happened. Is happening. We haven't cheated. Right now, it's a bunch of tip-toeing around the subject because we both care about you too much to hurt you. It's hard to even write that because you're my bestie (no matter what), and I never want to ruin that.

Trent says y'all haven't been communicating, so I have to ask. Are y'all still together? I think he's weirded out discussing it, so it sort of slides under the radar. But I can't go on with this unless I know if you still have feelings for him. If you do, I'll forget it. Everything. Right now. But if you don't, I'd like to have your approval if and when Trent does bring up the subject.

I wrote this whole thing in like five minutes and have spent the rest of the time staring at the send button. Push it or not? Once things are said, they can't be unsaid. And more than anything, I never want to lose our friendship—we've come too close before.

And there you go, texting me again. Chill, CJ. You only made me wait almost nine months to hear from you! Read this. Think it over. Text me tomorrow.

I love you. Em

I walk over to my bed and lay on top of the covers, staring at my ceiling and gnawing on a fingernail. Em and Trent? So that explains the pictures of her at the baseball field I saw online. Obviously, Trent hasn't told Em we've broken up. Probably because he's too embarrassed to admit he did it with an impersonal email. That was a total jackass move, but in all honesty, I hadn't been so great to him myself. I won't tell her the details of our break up, I'll just say we're over. What happened between me and Trent is a moot point now, anyway. And they deserve a chance without all the baggage and drama. They have a lot in common. Why didn't I ever see that before?

My heart teeters on the edge of a happy explosion. Through it all, Em's still my bestie, and the aching need to fill her in on my first month here is like a vicious cat clawing at my nerves.

There'll be no waiting until tomorrow.

I dial her number. It rings twice before she answers in her melodic, soft-spoken tone.

"CJ? Is it really you?"

"It's me, Em. We have so much to talk about."

Riding in the backseat of Bo's Bronco shouldn't freak me out. It's not like we're not bigger than most every other vehicle on the road. And taller. His gargantuan tires and lift teeter on the verge of monster truck status. Still, my knuckles whiten in a death grip on the seatbelt strap. Maybe it's not so much the ride as it is the destination.

For the past three years, Jett's thrown a blow-out party at his house the second weekend of June. According to Gin, it coincides with some big shrimping conference Jett's parents attend, so when they pull out of town in their fifth-wheel camper, the preparations commence.

He invited me last week on our daily golf cart driving lesson. I hem-hawed a bit but finally gave in when Gin got wind of it and promised to stay by my side the entire night. Jett promised the same thing, but the guest list included tons of his racing acquaintances, and I'm not delusional. Trévon and Rachel will damn sure manipulate his face time in front of his adoring fans and colleagues.

Back at home, pre-accident, parties were no big deal. Every weekend there was somewhere to go or someone to go with. Of course, like the new measuring stick of my life, that was before. In the world of "this is your new life, CJ," parties don't blip the radar screen. Like, ever. It's hard to be invisible in the middle of a crowd staring at the girl who'd "been through so much" while they guzzle beers. Artificial pity at its finest. No thanks.

"Here we are!" Bo announces from the driver's seat, pulling into a grassy patch by the front drive. He reaches out to grab his date's hand. Laurel—the mysterious internet fling turned actual girlfriend for one week per year. Despite Gin's private claims that the whole relationship's "shady," Laurel's a sweet girl with turquoise eyes and long, chocolate hair, perfectly untidy when piled in her messy bun. Her easygoing personality syncs perfectly with Bo's.

"Same place as last year?" she asks from the passenger seat.

Her question catches me off guard, and I slide forward in my seat, elbows on the console. "Wait. You've been here before?"

"Last year's party."

Crap. I'm even newer than the newbie. Gin reaches out and grabs the small part of my arm exposed beyond the three-quarter length sleeves of my sapphire blue blouse. "Don't worry, CJ. I'll stay with you tonight. Remember?" Then she pauses, smiling, and points her finger out my window. "And I won't be the only one."

Jett bounces over the sidewalk in a half-walk, half-run toward the Bronco. He stops short as we throw open the heavy doors. "It's about time. Almost everyone else is already here."

Bo shoves his keys in his pocket, jumps out, and jogs around the front of the vehicle in time to offer Laurel his hand in jumping out onto the ground.

"I'm sorry. That's probably my fault," she giggles.

Jett nods and waves in her direction. "Hi Laurel. Just get in?" He doesn't wait for a response, but turns toward me, offering his hand to help me jump down. I slip mine in his and he threads his other arm around my waist, lifting me out onto the grass.

Gin jumps down on my heels, unassisted, and trails behind Bo and Laurel as they head inside, arms entangled. I alternate my gaze between Jett and the monstrous home in front of me. "So…wow. This is your house?"

"My dad doesn't do understated. Welcome to the Ramsey Family Compound." Compound is the perfect descriptor for a house like this—three stories on top of twelve-foot pillars, walls made mostly of glass windows, double-decker porches, sundecks all around, and a brick-and-iron gate surrounding the perimeter.

He grips my hand tighter as we walk in the front door, and the way his fingers fit in mine quiets my nerves, even in the presence of so many people I don't know. Though Gin has promised to never leave my side, my primary objective is to spend time with Jett to see what, if anything, is really going on between us. Everyone knows parties are the best way to overcome stubborn insecurities and find the (liquid) courage to get real. Could tonight be the night Jett and I make any sort of solid moves? I don't know, but I didn't spend two hours in the bathroom doing my make-up and hair for nothing.

We enjoy a good amount of time together before the inevitable happens. A handful of people, some our age and some looking to be in college, walk in with their T-shirts and jackets emblazoned with racing emblems. Different logos from the ones Jett wears, which I assume means they belong to a different team. Still, everyone seems friendly, slapping high-fives and shaking hands like long-lost buddies.

It starts with Rachel bending low to reach Trévon's ear while he sits at the kitchen table. She looks at us as she whispers, finally jutting her finger in our direction with a forceful ultimatum. Trévon nods, gets up, and heads our way.

"Shit," Jett mumbles. "You'd think they'd give all this a rest. At least for one night."

"It's okay. I've got Gin." He nods, squeezes my hand, and gets up to meet Trévon. I turn to Gin, but she's otherwise engaged, casting some serious flirty vibes toward the red-headed boy in a striped polo leaning against the staircase railing. He's talking to a small group of guys, but gives her The Eyes more than once.

When she doesn't make a move, I wrap my arm around her, accidentally sloshing a little of my drink on my leg. She laughs and points to my red Solo cup filled with PJ and fruit. "Go easy on those. Bo said Trévon made it, and he's heavy-handed with the grain alcohol. It sneaks up on you."

"Contrary to popular belief, I used to have a life, which *did* include a few parties in my day. This is only my second. Trust me, I'm good."

"Don't say I didn't warn you." Gin clicks her tongue and glances back over at the guy, who's now obviously staring in our direction. I dart my eyes between them, watching their mirrored reactions. He smiles. She smiles. He ticks his head up in a silent hello. She flutters her eyelashes. He strokes the collar of his shirt. She fiddles with her pinky ring.

I lean close in her ear. "So just go talk to him already."

She whirls around with wide eyes and a loud, "Shhh!" then mouths silently, "He. Will. Hear. You."

It's moments like these when the two years between us seem to span a decade.

"Unless he has some sort of hearing superpower, I'm pretty sure he has no clue I'm talking about him." I laugh and down another big gulp of my drink.

"You are talking louder than you think, CJ." Her voice morphs into some sort of reprimanding mother mode, all sweet and measured on the surface but seething with venom below. Sort of like when I was a kid and misbehaved at the store and Mom turned to me with that "We'll deal with this at home young lady" warning of impending doom. She pries the cup from my hand against my protest. "I think you need to slow down a bit."

I stick my tongue out at her. "Fine, but only if you go talk to him."

Gin stands up, both of our cups in her hand, and glances down at me. "I'll be right back."

As she saunters to the garbage can, the guy breaks away from his group and trails behind her. I readjust on the couch for a better view of the hallway where he stops her and begins talking. She giggles and bites her lower lip as he leans against the wall, hands in his pocket. While they chat, he angles his body toward her. Such a good sign.

As I spy on Gin, two brown-haired girls sit down on the loveseat opposite the sofa. When Jett's name comes up, I turn my head ever so slightly in their direction, mentally trying to block out the background noise.

"What's Tyler doing here?" Brunette One asks, flipping her hair over her shoulder. "You know how much he and Jett hate each other. I'm surprised Jett hasn't blown a gasket."

Brunette Two snorts and takes a swig of her beer. "Why should he? Jett's a better racer than him. Tyler's just jealous."

Tyler, huh? That must be the big competition Rachel keeps bringing up. I scan the room, but there are several guys with the other team's racing logo on their shirt. It could be any one of them. In the far corner, Jett leans against the kitchen island, still chatting with Trévon and Rachel and a few others I don't know, and he's perfectly calm. Smiling, even. If Tyler is anywhere around, Jett either hasn't noticed or doesn't care as much as everyone else thinks he does.

"Don't underestimate Tyler. He's Jett's biggest competition." Brunette One flounces back on the sofa, crossing her arms as if her declaration somehow seals the deal on the argument. The way she bats her eyelashes a million miles a minute when she enunciates Tyler's name screams that her interest in the matter is deeper than she's letting on.

Brunette Two rolls her eyes. "You only think that because you're all gah-gah for Tyler, but the truth's the truth. Jett's gonna cream him in the championship because he's a better driver and, just saying, he's better looking, too."

They burst into giggles when one's manicure catches the other's eye, and they ramble on into some stupid conversation about the subtle nuances of blue-pink versus red-pink nail polish.

I ease off the couch, careful to not draw their attention, and dart toward the drink table, far away from the gossip and just out of sight of Gin's infrequent well-check glances.

I grab a new cup of PJ and gulp some down, the fruity fire burning a trail down my throat. A chunk of pineapple peeks above the surface, and I grapple it with my fingers and pop it in my mouth. A gush of pure alcohol courses over my tongue when I chomp down.

"Easy. That's some high-octane shit." His voice is deep with a non-southern accent. I glance over my shoulder, mid-chew, at his hazel eyes, a little too close-set for my taste but handsome nonetheless, and spikey brown hair. A red racing emblem stares at me from the pocket of his polo.

"Good. Then I'm in the right place." I swallow the rest from my cup, ladle in another full round, and turn to face him, my back pressed into the wall. The stability helps. The entire room fuzzes in and out of my vision.

"A girl who knows what she wants and isn't afraid to say it. I like it." He props one arm on the wall beside me, leaning in and tilting his beer toward me.

There were a million guys like him at the parties back home. Smooth talkers with so-so looks who somehow thought they were God's gift to the female species. I stare at the bottle he's holding, choosing to ignore the gesture, and instead bring my cup back to my own lips for another swig. He really thinks I'm going to "cheers" him? On what—just being his perceived wonderful self? No, thanks.

He withdraws the bottle back to his chest and tilts his head, eyes narrowed. "You here alone?"

I glance over at Jett, who's talking to his group with a bunch of animated hand gestures. "No, I'm here with a...a friend. And you are..." I wave my free hand, prompting him to reveal his name.

"Tyler."

So, this is Tyler? Jett's racing competition. His nemesis.

"So, you're Tyler." My words slur, tongue turning to lead, as I poke my finger into his chest. "I've heard about you."

He smirks. "All good?"

The lights in the room turn from individual points of light into long gleaming trails. I blink a few times to stop the effect. It doesn't work.

I step forward, leaning in so close the pungent sweetness of the beer on his breath lingers between us. "Hardly," I whisper. "I'm here with Jett, and he...he doesn't like you. Like, at all."

At least that's what I've heard.

Tyler doesn't look stunned or angry. He laughs, and the throaty sound of it stirs a fire in my belly that shoots straight to my chest, drumming its way into my heart.

"Losers think about winners. But winners..." He pauses and thumbs back toward himself. "Winners think about winning."

Tyler laughs again and gives my shoulder a playful nudge, but the jarring movement sets off a tilt-a-whirl in my brain. The room spins, the lights blurring together in rainbowed arcs. The bass of the music pounds its rhythm in my temples. Too many cups of PJ and now a mammoth wave of swimmy-headed nausea bubbles in my gut.

"I don't feel so good."

Tyler gestures toward the door. "Fresh air?"

I nod with a quick glance back into the kitchen, but Jett's disappeared from sight. A lump knits together in my throat, the only thing holding back the vomit at this point. The bile, mixed with a near-lethal dose of booze, sloshes in my belly, burning upwards into my esophagus.

Tyler helps me out the door, directing my stumbling feet, and sits me on the front steps. The spinning increases, the steps blurring together into a single piece, and I prop my head against the bannister, searching for stability.

"Cami!" Jett's voice cuts through the darkness as he stomps down the stairs and squats by my side. "What are you doing out here?"

"She's with me." Tyler stands up, waving Jett off, then walks over and grabs my arm, his touch shooting chills over me. I wrench mine away.

Jett jumps to his feet, squaring off nose-to-nose with Tyler. "Like hell she is. She's with me."

My heart quadruples its pace. I'm with him. I want to latch onto his leg the way a little kid would, hugging it close to my body. Except that's probably not a good idea since it appears he has several sets of legs, and I can't tell which ones are real.

Damn alcohol.

"I'm warning you, Tyler." Jett balls his fists against his thighs, lowering his voice to a near-growl. "Get the hell outta here. No one invited you to begin with."

Tyler shrugs, holding his hands in the air. "Whatever. No big loss." He backpedals down the steps, jumps in his car, and disappears down the road.

Before the gravel dust on the road settles, Jett stoops by my side. "Are you trying to give me a heart attack? I turned around, and you were gone."

"I didn't think you'd notice." My stomach lurches, and I wrap my arms around my middle to absorb the pain.

"I noticed, okay? Tyler's not a good guy. He'd do anything to hurt me."

"He wasn't doing anything to *you*. He was talking to *me*."

"Exactly."

"How does that affect you?"

Jett deadpans, his nostrils flaring out. "This is a conversation for a different time. Not when you're drunk. Now grab hold. I'm taking you upstairs."

Jett wraps one arm around my back, one under my knees, and lifts me up. He carries me back inside and heads upstairs while I rest my head against his chest and let my fingers trace the outlines of his muscles through his shirt. I shouldn't be touching him, but I can't stop. The overwhelming desire and alcohol-fueled lack of inhibitions creates the perfect storm.

He sighs as his green eyes melt into mine. "Just so you know, it does affect me. *You* affect me, Cami."

I wiggle backwards in his arms, pointing my finger in his face. "Why do you call me Cami?"

"Because CJ doesn't fit you. It's too hard, too abrupt. It doesn't take into account all the things you keep hidden." He smiles. "That, and I like the fact I'm the only one who calls you Cami. Would it be as special if everyone called you that?"

"No." I grin, shaking my head, and press my cheek into his shirt. "You smell good. You usually smell like car exhaust and coconuts. Tonight, it's different."

"You've been smelling me?"

"Yeah."

"What else have you noticed?"

"Lots of things."

"Like?"

"Your chin dimple flattens out when you get mad. Out on the porch just now? Totally flat." I pause, trying hard to keep my words from slurring together. "And your eyes get so green in the sun. Like deep jade nuggets. Oh, and I like it when you wear your jeans with the rip in the thigh 'cause they make your butt look hot."

Oh my God, why did I say that?

Jett laughs. "I'll have to remember that."

We come to a landing on the second floor, and Jett starts up another flight of steps. I glance around at the hallway's blue walls to the door at the top of the stairs. "Where are we going?"

"To my room. You need to rest. You're hammered."

"Noooooo! I'm good." I wave my hands erratically but have to stop when my head once again turns into a tilt-a-whirl. "Hey Jett…" I mumble.

"Yeah?"

"Do you like me?"

"Of course."

"No, no, no. I mean do you *like me* like me?"

Jett frowns as he shifts his weight underneath me in order to grab the knob and swing open the door. "Cami, why don't you—"

"Are you ever gonna kiss me?"

Dear God, why did I ask that? Damn that stupid PJ to hell!

"What?" His eyes widen.

"Are…you…gonna…kiss…me?" I enunciate each word slowly, stabbing my finger at my mouth with each syllable. Please God, say this is a dream. That I'm not making a fool of myself. Still, the words pour out despite the crazy warning bells shrieking in my skull.

He pinches his lips tight and shakes his head. "Not tonight."

Not tonight? *Not tonight!* The rejection washes over me like a red-hot flame. I wrestle myself from his arms, my jelly legs bending and flexing below me as my feet hit the carpet.

"Screw you, Jett Ramsey. Who needs you anyway? I should've listened…Rachel was right…you're playing me like—" I stop and grab hold of the wall because the floor's shaking. Everything's shaking. The bile responds, burning in my throat, and I lurch toward the adjoined bathroom's open door. "Oh God, I'm gonna throw up."

I hug the porcelain and lose my supper and the reddish-colored hell juice. When I finish, I realize Jett is there, one hand on my back, the other holding my braid. He grabs a washcloth from the drawer, wets it, and holds it to my forehead, pulling me backward toward him. He rubs my arm, the silk from my blouse tickling my skin under his touch.

"I'll take care of you."

The anger leaves my body just as the alcohol did.

"I know you will, Jett."

And then everything goes quiet.

Where the hell am I? And what's that incessant buzzing noise? I pry open my eyes, the slivers of sunlight cutting through my pupils like knives, plunging straight into my brain.

The throbbing. Oh, the throbbing.

I fumble my hands beside me and find my phone buried in the soft folds of the cotton sheets. It buzzes against my skin, so I slide my finger over the screen and pull it to my ear, all without reopening my eyes to the blinding torture of day.

"Hello?" My parched mouth is dry and oddly sticky. Smacking my tongue against the roof of my mouth only exacerbates the effect.

"CJ. Thank God."

"Gin?"

"You sound like day-old crap."

"Ya think? What the hell happened last night? The last thing I remember..."

"Alcohol happened last night. A crap-ton of alcohol. You honestly don't remember?"

"Most of it. The last thing was Jett carrying me upstairs and I asked him...Oh my God."

"You asked him what?"

"Nothing." I stumble from the bed, using my hands to brace myself against the wall. Jett's bed in Jett's room in Jett's house.

What in the hell am I doing here? And why do I remember asking him if he was going to kiss me?

Now I remember why getting drunk sucks. It's all fun and games until you can't walk straight or control your own actions. Like being shackled inside your own head and forced to watch yourself do and say stupid stuff at will. Not to mention the morning-after headache and embarrassment.

Note to self: Never drink again.

In the bathroom mirror, my reflection stares back at me—disheveled hair, smeared make-up, and puffy under-eye bags.

"You passed out on Jett's bathroom floor. Both of y'all disappeared from the party, so Bo and I went upstairs to find you. Jett had your head in his lap. It was sweet."

I'm so stupid.

Gin babbles on. After my throw-up session ended, Jett shut the party down and threw everyone out. Apparently, someone called Memaw, who, unlike most normal grandmothers, was thrilled I'd finally "cut loose." Because I was sleeping (okay, passed out) in the safety of Jett's house, Memaw had said she'd be by in the morning to pick me up.

I walk to the large triple windows in the bedroom overlooking the dunes and beyond that, the Atlantic. The packed driveway and roadside from last night is empty, no evidence in the daylight of the craptastic party that went down here a few hours ago.

"I don't want to hear any more. I made an ass of myself."

"I wish you could've seen Jett's face when he was taking care of you, wiping your forehead with that cloth, holding your hair back. So, so sweet."

That's when it dawns on me. I'm in Jett's bedroom, but where is he? There's no note or anything. Maybe he had to go help at the docks since his dad's out of town, or maybe he wants to avoid me this morning, afraid I'll ask again for a kiss he so obviously doesn't want to give.

CJ Ainsworth, the walking train wreck.

My face presses against the window as a Cabriolet pulls up to the front gate, heralded by three quick bleeps. "Memaw's here. We'll talk later."

I grab my purse from the nightstand and dart down both staircases to the glass front door. The knob turns in my grasp and swings inward.

"What's your hurry? Want some coffee?"

My heart plummets to my feet. Crap, he caught me. All I can think about is my reflection in the mirror this morning. Scary.

"I...I can't. Memaw's here." The walk of shame would be much easier without him watching me, clumsy under the influence of a hurricane-sized hangover. His footsteps approach from behind, but I don't turn around. Instead, my shoulders swallow my neck as I stare at the hardwood floors. "Thanks for helping me last night. See ya later," I mumble, sprinting out the door and down the steps, never looking back and not allowing him a word about last night.

Memaw stares at me as I slide into the passenger seat, a smirk inching up her lips. "Must've been one hell of a night."

"Can we get out of here, please?" I slam the door, shrinking against the seat and shielding my eyes from the murderous sun trying to hard-boil my brains. As Memaw pulls away, he's there, standing on the porch, watching me leave.

Chapter Fifteen

Tink...Tink...Tink.

I sit up in my bed, the covers pulled tight around me. What's that noise? Am I dreaming?

Tink...Tink. No, definitely real. Easing out from under the sheets, I tiptoe to my door and press my ear to the woodgrain when it happens again. Nope.

It's coming from the window.

Tink...Tink...Tink.

I make it from door to window in three big leaps, unlatch the two brass locks, and slide the window open as another piece of pea gravel from the flowerbed pelts the siding.

The screen presses into my face as I squish closer to peer out below. Jett smiles up at me with a single white flower fisted in one hand and a palm-full of pebbles in the other. The moonlight gilds the messy spikes of his hair, lurching my heart into overdrive.

Nearly a dozen missed calls and texts sit unanswered on my phone because I couldn't bring myself to face him and the embarrassing way I threw myself at him in a drunken rant. I'd asked him to kiss me. I sniffed his shirt and talked about how he smelled. A blaze ignites under my skin just remembering my slurred words and the way I'd clung to him after violently throwing up in the toilet.

And now he's here, standing in the yard, forcing me to swallow the last crumbs of my pride as something inside melts like a marshmallow over an open fire.

"What are you doing?" My voice hovers barely above a whisper-yell so as not to wake Memaw, who's sleeping upstairs in the bedroom above mine.

He drops the pebbles into the flowerbed, holds up one finger, then disappears from view. I squeeze the bottom tabs on the screen and slide it open, stretching out the open hole, my abdomen flattened against the sill. He's nowhere to be seen, but the motion light in the parking slip under the house shines out through the privacy lattice, freckling the lawn in hexagonal patterns.

I dart to my bathroom mirror and flip on the light. Bed head's an understatement. My braid isn't so much a braid as it is a tangled mass of hair secured with an elastic band. More hair out than in. And then there's the volcanic zit sprouted on the side of my nose. I clasp my palm across my mouth, breathe into it, and sniff. Ugh, stale breath.

A hairbrush, concealer, and mouthwash lay on the marble countertop. All three are needed, but I only have time for one, so I loosen the mouthwash's cap, take a swig, swish, spit, and then dash back to my window.

The curtains ripple in on themselves. The humid air assaults my face, the dampness clinging to my cheeks as I peer over the edge. A ladder is pushed against the house, and Jett's halfway up.

"What are you doing here?"

A few rungs from the top, he pauses and smiles, genuine and familiar. "You wouldn't pick up the phone or answer a text, and I needed to see you. To ask you something."

"You could have just waited until tomorrow at work. Or maybe I would've answered…eventually…and you wouldn't have to do crazy stuff, like sneak in houses with ladders."

Jett snorts. "This from the girl who told me—and I quote—'actions, not words.'"

I lean out on my elbows. "This from the boy who told me he didn't have time to slow down?"

He climbs a few more rungs and leans in, his nose a mere fraction of an inch from mine, breath tickling my skin. "What can I say? You inspire me."

His words race through my veins like fire, the tingly sensation swirling to my toes, which curl against the cold hardwood floor. He is *so* NOT what I wanted this summer, but he is everything I need. My embarrassment from earlier tears away like leaves in the wind, revealing an ache for something new.

For him.

I'm ready for him and anything he has to offer.

He darts one hand in the window and nods his head toward the ground. "Come on."

Except that. I'm not ready for that.

Every muscle clenches. Me, go out the window with nothing between me and the ground but some tiny metal rungs? He's insane. I gulp back the knot lodged in my throat and look at his hand, palm up and open. My eyes travel up his arm to his face.

I sigh and slip my hand in his. He squeezes it.

"I'm afraid I'll fall."

"Don't be. I got you."

The air thickens between us, like we're caught in the midst of a heavy fog, the roar of the waves in the background louder now as we stare at each other. My heart accelerates and pounds against my ribs so hard, I have to open my mouth to breathe deep, panting as if I'd just finished a marathon. I'm pretty sure we're talking about more than sneaking out on ladders right now, and the very thought of it dances under my skin like a shook-up snow globe. The space between us is magnetized, every molecule in our bodies pulling us closer, preparing for the collision.

I step into my Chucks then slide my legs over the sill, letting go of his hand to death-grip the window frame on each side as I plant my feet on the top rung and pivot to face the house.

Jett's left fingers grip my hip. "I'm right here. We'll do this together."

He steps. I step. He steps. I step. We continue the majority of the way, my palms wrapped around the cold steel so hard it grooves my skin.

Jett's feet hit the packed sand with a thud, but before I can unclamp my eyes and find him, his arms circle my mid-back and knees, pulling me off into a cradle position against his chest. The metal frame slips from my fingers, and I grab hold of the closest safety net available—Jett's head.

His hair's barely visible in the tangle of my arms, clamped tight around his forehead as he's pressed face-first into my boobs.

Oh my God.

I drop my arms to his shoulders, and he lowers me to the sand beside him. The naked bulb burning under the house bathes us in a golden glow. His cheeks are red-splotched, eyes focused somewhere below mine. I follow them down. My braless form stretches the white cotton of my long-sleeve tee tight across my chest, my runaway heartbeat pumping blood through me so fast.

I wrench my arms across my chest, and Jett's eyes flick to mine. "Uh...I, uh..." he stammers. Rosy flourishes swirl over his neck and disappear beneath the V-neckline of his shirt.

My brain lurches into overdrive, desperately searching for a topic of conversation to break the awkwardness. Wait, didn't he say he'd come here to ask me something?

"You never did ask me that question," I remind him.

"What quest...oh...yeah." He plucks the white flower from his T-shirt pocket and holds it out. "I was an idiot last night at the party, leaving you alone to go talk racing. Not just that, but an idiot about so many things. What I want is a second chance, a do-over of last night."

I pull the blossom to my nose, its heavy sweetness a fond memory of Mama's gardenia bush beside the back porch steps. This smell blowing in our screens marked the official arrival of summer. Her favorite flower, she'd kept a constant supply of new buds in water bowls on the kitchen windowsill. "I was the idiot, drinking way too much, running my mouth. A do-over sounds perfect, but...isn't it too late?"

He shakes his head and taps his watch. "It's never too late for us, Cami. We're right on time."

I glance at the digital numbers on his watch. "4 a.m. is right on time? For what?"

"You'll see."

"We can't go in someone else's house."

An expansive one-story home on twelve-foot stilts towers above us from the front steps. The roof's low pitch is crowned by an elevated screened porch and above that, an open sun deck, which sits slightly higher than the surrounding palmettos. I size up the place, from window to window, waiting for lights to turn on once the homeowner hears us and figures out we're trespassing.

"Relax. It's my dad's." Jett pulls me up to the front porch. I almost have to run to keep pace with his long strides. "It's a rental property. No one's coming in until the afternoon, so this morning—it's ours." He motions toward the access stairs to the porch and the deck, which lay around the corner.

I follow him. At the top, the square deck spreads out before us like a private beach, open except for a couple teak loungers and an extra-large floral-printed papasan chair. During the day, this has to be one of the island's prime locations for ocean views, but at night, the landscape stretches out in pitch blackness beyond the deck's perimeter, despite the moon's best efforts.

My fingers fumble along the railing, clutching tighter when I peer over the edge at the top of a palmetto. *Dear God, we're higher than the trees.* My breathing quickens, the deck's spindles pressing into my skin as my head spins.

Then Jett's arms circle my waist, pulling me to him. His warm breath licks across my earlobe. "Hold on to me."

He directs me toward the deck's center, and I close my eyes, shuffling my feet in rhythm with his, absorbing the moment. The rustle of the breeze through the fan-shaped fronds. The chirping crickets playing soprano to the bass notes of the ocean's in-and-out roars. That slight rotten egg scent of the marsh I used to find so offensive, now completely ordinary. My eyes flutter open to Jett standing as my mirror image, staring back at me.

"Better?"

I nod and blow out a breath. "Much."

He leans forward, his lips brushing my cheek. "Now look up."

Above us, a million shimmering pin-dots freckle the inky night. The brightest ones blaze through the dark, the fainter ones dissolving in my focus then reigniting when I shift my eyes. The sensation of floating among the milky rashes of stars grips me, propelling my stomach to my toes. I grab hold of Jett's chest, my fingers slipping under the neckline of his shirt and sliding over his clammy skin.

He grasps my hips and tugs me closer, the roughness of his jeans rubbing against the fronts of my thighs. "You okay?"

"It's just...wow...there's so many..."

"This is the best time to see them." Jett glances at his watch. "Sunrise is 6:19, so we've got a good two hours."

I thump the watch's face. "You and that watch. You got somewhere else to be?"

With a grin, Jett steps back, flips his wrist over, unfastens it, and then shoves it deep in his pocket. He grabs my elbows, hints of coconut and spicy vanilla with an undercurrent of gasoline wafting over me.

His smell.

"No. I'm just here. With you."

"That's such a line." I roll my eyes and pull out of his embrace, trudging to the papasan chair. The disc seat tilts so far back in its frame, it swallows me, my body facing skyward, feet swinging over the edge a few inches off the wooden floor.

"It's not a line." He sits beside me, and the large rounded sides fold in, sandwiching us together in the middle, the contact points between our bodies like smoldering embers. "I've spent so much time running from everything. You're the first person to make me want to slow down."

The intensity in his eyes threatens to explode the embers into a full-fledged inferno.

"So you say."

"So I know." He crosses his arms behind his head, pushing himself back into the cushion. The motion makes me slide closer to him; obviously, this chair wasn't made for two. My arm overlaps his chest, my fingers nudge the top of his thigh. "I know something else, too."

134

I glance up at him, but he's not looking back, only biting his lip and staring into oblivion. "What's that?"

"You need to quit hiding." His words slap me across the face. He rolls his head towards mine, our foreheads a whisper apart. "If you ever want to talk ..." He slides his right hand down, reaching over his body to stroke my arm.

My throat tightens. Emotional one-on-ones are beasts I'd rather not confront. I once shared those with Mama and Noli-Belle, but since they've been gone, the words have piled inside, heaped in the murkiest corners of my brain. But here with Jett, a dam inside breaks, a flood of emotions roaring in my ears as I slide my palm against his, our fingers twining together.

Overhead, the stars pirouette in place as I contemplate the voids between them, as if searching for some hidden entrance to another dimension. Noli-Belle would've loved this view, would've stayed out here all night, and I would've loved to have shared it with her. Instead, I'm compelled to share a piece of her with Jett.

"My sister loved science, especially astronomy. She had this huge telescope in her room and one of those constellation charts."

She loved. She had.

Speaking out loud about my sister in past tense cuts to the bone every time. I sigh and add, "She would've been thirteen by now."

Jett squeezes my fingers and shifts on his hip, his body curving toward mine. My arm smooshes into his abs, our touch unhampered by the two thin layers of cotton lying between. "I have a brother. He's just turned fifteen."

It's the first time Jett's ever opened up about his personal life, and something tells me this gesture is significant. Like it's the reason he's been hesitant, and he's ready to fully trust me.

"Buck. My mom's son. He lives somewhere near Beaufort."

I scoot closer, facing him directly as we lay side by side in the papasan. "Somewhere? You don't know?"

Jett's Adam's-apple bobs up and down, pressing his lips into a flat line with each swallow. "It's been years since I've seen him."

The distance and heartbreak ring familiar. Missing my family and my old life consumes me every day, but it's never occurred to me Jett's missing someone too. I stroke his cheek with my free hand, the slight stubble from his last shave poking me like little thumbtacks. Tears lurk close behind his lashes.

"Buck's the product of my mom's affair. She left, married the guy, and started a whole new family without me. It doesn't make much sense when you're young, but then you get older and realize how everything went down. That's when I got heavy into racing...and it made my mom hate me."

"Hate you?" I grab his hand again, squeezing it in mine. I can't imagine a mom just up and leaving. Except when death creeps in and steals her away. My mother didn't get a choice; she never would've left under any other circumstances.

But voluntary separation? I can't help thinking about Memaw and Dad's non-existent relationship for the past decade. Dad refuses to discuss it and Memaw labels it a "misunderstanding."

All of it's stupid.

"Racing's the reason she cheated on Dad. He was never there, and she always worried something bad would happen." He takes a deep breath and continues. "When I started racing, she distanced herself, and told me if I kept on, she'd have no choice but to 'remove herself' from my life." He bites his lip. "She finally did. About five years ago."

The pain rolls off him in waves.

"I'm sorry. I had no idea."

Turns out no one does. Jett says it's not something he shares with people, and his dad flat-out refuses to discuss his mother. So, for the last five years, Jett's dealt with losing her, and consequently a brother, alone. Not even Bo knows the whole story.

Jett fidgets with the racing championship ring he wears on his pinky, twisting it in circles. "Trust doesn't come easily for me, Cami, but I...I trust you."

His words forge a steel connection between the two of us, and suddenly everything bottled up inside me spills out in a heap. "I'm so sorry I was drunk and stupid last night. I put you on the spot and..." I stammer. "And...I just want you to know that I'm here for you, especially for the hard stuff. If I could—"

He reaches over and presses a finger to my lips, his way of telling me he gets it. Because he's been there too. In actuality, though, he doesn't understand I have my own secret. A truth I've concealed from everyone around me wells inside, rising like steam off my guilty conscience. He's confided in me, and now it's my turn to trust him with what I can't bear admitting to anyone else. Only him.

"Can I tell you something no one else knows except my dad?"

Jett leans in closer, nodding his head, his cheek sliding against the floral fabric.

I lick my lips, mustering my courage. "I didn't tell you everything about the accident because...I didn't want you to judge me."

His eyebrows scrunch together above his nose. "Judge you? Why would I—?"

"Because the wreck was my fault. I was the one driving when my mom and sister died. It was me who overcorrected when that guy ran us off the road, when our car flipped and hit that tree." I look away, my breathing labored. The knowledge is bad enough. Saying it out loud is worse. "It's the reason why my dad wants nothing to do with me. Because I killed them."

Jett tips my chin up, forcing me to look him in the eyes. "Cami, their deaths are not your fault."

"And the distance between you and your mom is not yours."

We sigh in unison and recline against the floral cushion. The mood lightens, like a heavy blanket's been pulled off and tossed away. Maybe all we needed was someone who "got it" to listen, to hear the hard things. Ironic. A couple of messed-up kids with family issues comforting each other better than the highest priced therapist money can buy.

And then Gin and Bo with their perfect family life skip through my mind. Hating them for what they have, envying their happiness, would be easy, but I don't. Not even a little. They took me in and made me feel like family from the moment I rolled into town, a real-life example of what could be.

"I'm jealous of Bo and Gin. They'll always have somebody to lean on."

Jett swivels his head toward mine, and I stare back, our noses nearly touching. His voice is faint, a slight sound against the nighttime symphony of bugs and waves and wind through the palms. "Lean on me, Cami."

I turn back to facing skyward, the stars burning brighter than ever and giving life to the darkness. But now—now everything is brighter than before, the flame stronger, the need deeper. Even if our connection might only last for a season.

"At least until summer's over," I say.

He props on his elbow, hovering over me. "Even after."

"What comes after?"

"I don't know? Everything?" He shrugs. "Maybe we should focus on what comes now." He runs his fingertips along my hair, pinching at wisps frizzed out along the crown, and then tugs on the end of my braid. "Am I ever going to see you without this?"

I reach up and untwist the elastic from the end, sliding it onto my wrist before raking my fingers through the gnarled locks. They fan out around my shoulders, several chunky pieces swirling in the breezy night air.

"Happy now?"

He nods with a grin.

"So, what comes next?" I ask.

Jett smiles and leans forward, nose to nose. My heart pummels my ribcage when his arms circle my shoulders. I lick my lips, waiting.

"This," he whispers and crushes his lips to mine.

Chapter Sixteen

Jett's lips. Unbelievably soft and smooth when they pressed into mine. Everything I imagined, but so much more. The gentle pressure as he repeated the part-press-pucker rhythm a gazillion times. The way he slid his hand down my back, tugging me in closer. How my fingertips snuck under his cotton shirt and skimmed along his firm muscles.

He kisses with his eyes closed. I know because I looked, too afraid to close mine only to re-open them and find out it was all a dream. Jett's hands moved in rhythm with his lips, probing all the right places. My skin crackled under each sweep of his fingers.

We got back to the house around 6:30, and I spent another hour, after curling up in my sheets, reliving the moments over and over, finally succumbing to sleep well after the sun was streaming in my windows.

"Rise and shine!" Memaw bursts through the door, metal tray in hand brimming with a breakfast assortment of muffins, fruit, and a steaming cup of coffee in the middle. "I had a hunch you'd be sleeping in this morning."

"You did?" I scoot to sitting, my back pressed against the pillows at the headboard. She sits the tray in front of me, and I snatch a muffin, peeling the paper liner.

"After that party fiasco the night before last..." She pauses, her head tilted and eyes narrowed in my direction. "You were pretty mopey there for a while, avoiding the boy's texts." She crosses her arms and studies me as I heap in mouthfuls of muffin. "But something's changed this morning. You two kiss and make up or something?"

Kiss? There's no way she could know about this morning. A fire circulates into my cheeks and burns below the surface. How on Earth did she even piece it all together?

The CIA. Memaw's a freaking undercover CIA agent. There's no other explanation.

"Just a misunderstanding." The food in my mouth garbles my voice. "Fine now."

She nods, a glint in her eye and knowing smile across her lips, then sits on the bed's edge. "No use hiding from me, CJ. I know you and Jett have feelings for each other. That was evident from the moment you got here. It's time y'all finally did something about it." She gnaws the inside of her cheek as I sip my coffee, staring at the creamy brown liquid. "Talk to me. No subject's off-limits."

Since she brought it up...

I swallow hard, dredging up the courage to ask her something I've been dying to know. Something my "true confessions" episode with Jett last night rekindled.

"Memaw, what happened between you and Dad?"

She sniffs her nose and clears her throat. The whole forthcoming attitude evaporates in a blink. "Why are you bringing this up now?" Her bottom lip twitches, but I don't give in, hardening my stare even more. Her smile fades, eyes dropping to my comforter. "Misunderstanding?" she offers.

Same old excuse, and I'm not buying it. "A ten-year absence isn't a simple misunderstanding."

"Actually, that's the shitty thing, CJ. Most arguments stem from misunderstandings brought on by people's own prejudices or fears or egos. I bet we could solve half the world's problems if all the concerned parties would shut the hell up and listen."

I reach out and grab her hand. "I'm listening, Memaw."

She groans and launches into her side of the story. Dad cut ties with Memaw after accusing her of mocking Grandpa's memory and destroying what was left of their family. I remember only bits of the funeral, but one thing vivid in my memory is that nothing about it seemed sad. Instead, it was like a party with tons of food and guests who milled around, talking and laughing and drinking champagne from glass flutes. According to Memaw, the whole affair was pre-planned by Grandpa, who'd said in his gruff Southern accent that he "didn't want no sad-sacks looking at his dead body." He wanted to go out with a bang. Have people remember him as being the life of the party, not the stiff in the coffin.

He'd also begged Memaw to sell their Charleston house—the one where my dad grew up—immediately after and pursue their dream of living on the island, volunteering the last years of their lives in every near and dear cause. He didn't make it to that part, but he implored her to "live the dream" for both of them.

So she did, and Dad flew off the handle in a rage, refusing to listen, accusing her of losing her mind, and then cut Memaw out of his—and consequently our—life.

"Your mother realized it was a bad situation, and I'm thankful every day she sent pictures and videos of you girls. I got to see you, even if I couldn't be there." Memaw's bottom lip quivers as she swipes away a stray tear from her cheek.

"Are you and Dad talking now?"

"Only about you." She reaches over and pats my hand. "I'm sure he thinks I'm doing a horrible job."

At least he's getting updates on me through Memaw. God knows he hasn't taken any initiative to contact me himself. But if he thinks Memaw's failing me, he's wrong. The weeks I've been here have changed me.

Are changing me still.

I scan my room, the place I've come to consider home. "Ignore him. I'm right where I need to be."

Memaw folds me into her arms, squeezing so tight her bracelet pinches into my skin. But this time, no shudder ripples through me. Memaw's touch no longer crawls over my skin like a thousand stinging insects. Somehow, they—Jett and Memaw and Gin and Bo and the magic of this place—have found a way to break my walls, and instead of being scared, I'm happy. Content for the first time in months.

She heads to the door, pausing to dart her head back in, a wicked smile spreading her lips. "Oh, and CJ? When you talk to

Jett today, please tell him it's perfectly acceptable to use the back stairs and come to your door if he wants to visit you. That whole Romeo and Juliet shit with the ladder is going to destroy my siding."

Take a shower. Jett. Clean my room. Jett. Read a book. (Okay, *try* to read a book.) Jett. Walk on the beach. Jett. My mind roars like one of Jett's racecars going 100 mph in a loop.

I trudge through the sand to the pier and the beam where our names are carved. Mine, though still newer than the others, has begun weathering on the wood. It's more natural now. Fits in like it was always meant to be there. I sit, my back against the post, and pull out my phone. There's someone I need to share this moment with.

<Me> *You there?*

<Bestie<3Em> *what's up?*

<Me> *Holy. Freaking. Crap.*

<Bestie<3Em> *K this sounds good*

<Me> *Remember that boy I told you about?*

<Bestie<3Em> *Jett the racer?*

<Me> *Him! He KISSED me*

<Bestie<3Em> *WHAT OMG*

<Me> *IKR*

<Bestie<3Em> *And...*

<Me> *And what?*

<Bestie<3Em> *How far did it go?*

<Me> *Em...*

<Bestie<3Em> *That far, huh? And did you like what you found?*

<Me> *OMG*

<Bestie<3Em> *!!!!!!!!! Please call me tonight with all the deets*

<Me> *You have time now?*

<Bestie<3Em> *Too loud now. Can't hear*

<Me> *Where are you?*

<Bestie<3Em> *Baseball field. Is it weird I told you that?*

<Me> *What did I tell you? I'm fine with you and Trent. He made a move yet?*

<Bestie<3Em> *He's hinted. Think I should tell him we've talked?*

142

<Me> *No. Let it happen between y'all. He and I have been over.*
No need bringing me up
   <Bestie<3Em> *K. I'll keep waiting…patiently*
   <Me> *Fingers crossed. Call me later*

Jett finally contacts me a little after 8 p.m. I reread his text for the millionth time with a long face. He's leaving for a week. Unexpected racing promo event. Again. And right when we're finally making headway. Ugh.

Between my disappointment and Memaw's volunteering on the night shift at the nursing home, the night's a bust. I crawl under my covers. Might as well capitalize on extra sleep, but even closed eyes and a comfy pillow can't shut off my wandering thoughts.

A week away from me. A week surrounded by all those fangirls Rachel mentioned. And Dani. Let's not forget Dani.

I'm not insecure. Jett's more than proven he's interested. It's just, this lifestyle was engrained in him long before I was in the picture. And even though we kissed—a lot—it's not like we're an "official" couple, so I don't have any right to demand any sort of behavior. Still, I hope our connection proves stronger than any temptation he faces on the road. That he'll be thinking of me instead. Our kissing. Our touching. Our—

Thump. Thump. Thump.

The hard rapping on the French door startles me. I jump to my knees on the mattress, yanking the comforter to my chin, when I spot him through the glass panes, his freshly-showered, still-wet hair spiked up in the front. He adjusts the backpack thrown over his shoulder then motions for me to hurry and let him in. I dart to the door, swinging it open wide.

"I thought y'all left already?"

"Fifteen minutes, but I couldn't leave without doing this." He steps across the threshold, dropping the bag to the floor, and presses his lips into mine, hoisting me into his arms. I tangle my hands in his hair and wrap my legs around his waist.

The sweet, gentle kisses from before fade into tonight's hard and hungry ones, crackling over my nerve endings like a swarm from a kicked-over hornet's nest. Every part of me screams out to touch him.

He lays me on top of the covers, pulling back and hovering above as we pant for air like two fish out of water, eyes fixated on the other, mouths hanging open. His gaze reflects the same whirlwind raging inside me, yelling for me to pull him back down, take control of this opportunity. But time's running out. He has to go.

"Guess that'll have to last me for a few days," I whine, the mere thought of even one day without touching or kissing him hitting me like a bucket of ice water.

"That and this." He grabs the bag, loosens the strap, and pulls out a glossy headshot of himself. "The proofs came back for the promo tour, so I nabbed one. Even autographed it for my best girl." The orange and black jumpsuit skims his torso, the Ramsey Racing logo running lengthwise up the side of the arm. His jade eyes pierce the paper, still mesmerizing, but harder and edgier than they are with me. In the corner in black Sharpie, it says: *To Cami. You drive me _____. XO, Jett.*

"I drive you what?" I glance over the paper's edge, eyes narrowed.

"Depends on the day. Nuts. Crazy. Wild." He drags out the "i" in wild and leans in to nuzzle my neck. That's when his words finally register, and I yank backwards. He blinks rapidly. "What?"

"*Best* girl?" It was almost a verbal nod to my deepest fear.

"*Only* girl." He kisses me, but my lips stall. He sits on the side of my bed and grabs my hands, his palm hot against my skin. "Don't start that whole Rachel-blowing-smoke-up-your-ass stuff again."

I drop my eyes to his picture, now lying on the covers in front of me. My gut tells me to trust him, but every time I make that commitment, Rachel's nagging voice pops into the background. Like that annoying angel/devil thing. Except without the angel.

"You know my story now. How important trust is to me." He tips up my chin with his finger. "Rachel's right about my disappearing at these events, but I'm not hooking up with anyone."

He huffs out a long, hard breath. "It's overwhelming sometimes. Too many people. Too many expectations. So, I escape…and draw."

Huh? That's unexpected. My nose crinkles as I consider his revelation. "Draw? Like portraits?"

"Buildings. Houses. House plans, more specifically." He nods, eyes wide, but I can't seem to unfreeze my face from its *What the hell?* expression. Jett snort-laughs. "Why are you looking at me like that? Yes, I have other interests outside of racing."

Of course he has other interests. But architecture? "No…it's cool. Just surprising."

"Everyone assumes I'll follow my dad's footsteps. No one knows I want to go to college, get a degree in architecture with a specialty in sustainable design. Someone's got to figure out a way to keep growth from destroying all this." He pans his hand toward the window and all the natural beauty of Edisto.

Every time I'm positive there's nothing else to learn about him, he surprises me again. "There's so much I don't know about you, Jett. So much I *want* to know."

"We're just getting started." He takes my cheeks in his hands and plants a kiss on my forehead. "My Cami."

This time, he doesn't have to make the first move. I grab his shirt and wrench him to me, smothering his lips, face, and neck with a gazillion kisses, never letting up until the alarm on his watch beeps. Our fifteen minutes are over, and he has to go. But not without one last kiss and a promise to be back as quickly as he can. He disappears into the night, and I'm alone, not only with my memories but also with the hope that when Jett gets back, we'll finally be a true couple.

"You better put on sunscreen. Your legs are looking lobsterish." Gin snaps the lid closed on the tube of sunscreen with one hand and tosses it in my lap while smearing thick white cream across her chest.

"I'm pale with freckles. When do I not look like a lobster?" I laugh, stretching out on the blue beach towel for a better look. When I press my fingertip into my leg, the skin turns white then

145

quickly fills back in with a rosy hue. Obviously, the SPF 30 from earlier didn't do its job.

It's the first time in days I've been to the beach only because it's been the first opportunity. Five days without Jett meant five days with too much time on my hands, obsessing over every tiny detail of those last moments between us and agonizing over the prospect of what's to come. Sitting around like some loser-stalker-freak and wallowing in self-pity wasn't happening, so I begged Mrs. Baxter for extra shifts. And because the crowds are piling in due to the upcoming Fourth of July holiday, she obliged. Win-win.

As I recoat my legs, Gin pops up from her chair and bounces toward the foamy edge of the water, boogie board in tow. The incoming tide's waves are much bigger than the puny ones from earlier, and she convinces Bo to go out with her and catch a few. I snap the sunscreen lid closed and push the tube back into her pink polka-dot bag, using my slick, newly-lotioned legs as an excuse to sit this one out. Convincing at any rate, but not quite the truth. I bite my lower lip, peeping over my shoulder at the beach access and the deserted road beyond it.

No one.

"CJ?" Bo calls my name, and I jerk my head back in his direction. He's standing in front of me, arms crossed, one eyebrow jacked in a wicked triangle. "Quit stressin'. He said he'll be back today, and he will."

I didn't figure on being so transparent, and the words fumble off my lips. "I…uh, I…wasn't waiting…looking for…Jett…uh, I was just…"

"Uh-huh." Bo's smart-ass tone is echoed by the knowing glint in his eyes, which mocks my feeble attempt to cover up the obsessive waiting game. Bo laughs and runs out into the surf, trailing behind Gin to a calm area beyond the breakers where they kneel, boards in hand, waiting on the big one.

Em's the only one I've told about my make-out sessions with Jett. Not a word to Gin and Bo. Sure, they've asked—especially after the party debacle—but I've smiled and held them at bay with that same old *we're good friends and everything's a-okay* routine.

I want to tell them. Hell, I want to shout it from the rooftops. But the water's still muddy around the particulars of our relationship status, and like hell will I be the one to go around speculating without Jett first spelling it out. Besides, these are his life-long buddies. If he wants them to know, it figures he'll be the one to spill the beans.

Five minutes and fifty-million over-the-shoulder-peeks later, the only person coming from the beach access is some old geezer in a Hawaiian-print shirt over black Speedos with a Pekingese on a leash.

I get up, dusting the sand from my suit, and walk to the water's edge where the cool surf gurgles around my toes. What if he doesn't show? I burrow my big toe under the sand then kick my foot, sending a clump of sand flying just as I'm pulled off my feet and spun around in a dizzying spiral.

My squeals draw every eye on the beach. On the third or fourth revolution, the sand and ocean blur together and my stomach gnaws. "I'm gonna throw up!"

Suddenly, the bottoms of my feet hit sand, and I brace myself, my upper body still swaying with the momentum. As the motion eases, so does the nausea. He leans into me, coming so close his chest hugs into my back, his breathy words tickling my ear. "I'll hold your hair back if you do."

I glance backwards over my shoulder and meet his green eyes, sparkling in the overhead sun. "Wait, you've already done that."

"I'll do it again. And again. And again. And again." With each "again" he kisses my temple, ear, cheek and slope of my neck while his hands grip my hips, creating a firestorm in all the places beneath my suit.

"Everyone's watching," I whisper, pressing into him and inhaling his coconuts-and-gasoline scent. The lean muscles in his chest squeeze into my shoulder blades, bringing to life the secret fantasy that's played in my head for weeks now.

"Let 'em." Jett presses even closer, his lips hovering so close to my face they brush across my temple as he speaks. I tilt my head, and he plunges his lips into mine, erasing everything and everyone around us until...

"Get a room!" Bo yells as he stomps out of the water.

Jett and I pull apart, words flying from my head, and the excuses for why I haven't told them come out in a jumbled mess. "Oh...I uh...we were just...I mean, I didn't..."

"Save it. We've known all week." Gin walks behind Bo, giggling, and jumps up and down. "And you thought you were smooth."

Jett snickers and tugs me to his side, my shoulder lodging underneath his armpit. His grip's protective yet gentle, and the way he trails his fingertips over the dry-weave fabric of my long-sleeved suit scatters chills over my body, prickling every hair straight to my toes. "What did you tell them?"

"I told them we kissed...a lot." Gin and Bo laugh out loud, but Jett leans to my ear and whispers, "Nothing personal we discussed."

Bo nudges my shoulder. "Come on, CJ. Jett's my best friend. You know he had to tell me."

I slap his arm, then wag my finger at Gin. "Then why did y'all keep asking me all those stupid questions?"

"It's funny watching you squirm." Gin giggles as she and Bo nod in unison. "Just like y'all both have since CJ got here. Trying to be all secretive about your *obvious* feelings for each other."

Jett squishes his mouth, nose, and brow together, mocking them. Then he gets serious and says, "That's all over. Cami and I have no secrets anymore. We know everything there is to know." Jett smiles at me, a shimmering hint of his gold tooth making his smile look like one of those hokey toothpaste commercials.

The double meanings in his words aren't lost on me. We share more than feelings. We share personal truths, secrets no one else knows, hesitations no one else appreciates. But it's through our fears we understand each other. Maybe that's all we ever really needed.

Chapter Seventeen

Jett's lips are a drug whose side effects include the euphoria of floating on a surreal wave, rising and falling, opening and closing, each one new and adventurous but also homey and familiar. I love that the first thing we do now when seeing each other is move steadily together, as if magnetized, meeting in the middle, moving in perfect rhythm.

An addiction.

A necessity.

I pull back, his mint Chapstick burning into the creases of my skin, and wipe my thumb across his swollen bottom lip, rubbing away the remnants of my glittery pink lip gloss. The ride from Memaw's house to Jett's made two miles feel like an eternity as I sat in the passenger seat, secured tight in my seatbelt, gazing non-stop at his lips. The ones I'd devoured in Memaw's driveway. The ones I attacked as soon as we pulled up in front of the brick-and-iron gate of the Ramsey Compound.

He captures my hand in his, bringing my palm to his lips, and then slides it down, holding it open against his chest, his heart thumping beneath the muscle shirt. "What took us so long to start doing that?" he whispers.

I lean across the console and bury my face in his neck. "I don't know, but I never want to stop."

"Then don't." He cups my chin and pulls me into another kiss. His eyes are closed as his lips move over mine, his tongue jutting out to part my lips slightly.

I swoon, my insides like melted wax running down and pooling in my toes. I could stay here all day in his car, nuzzled into the curve of his body, except for the fact that we're parked in front of his parents' house and his dad's truck sits just inside the gate. I tear my lips from his and glance over my shoulder.

There's no one in the yard or standing by the windows, but it doesn't take a genius to figure out what's going on when we're parked here, not getting out.

"Maybe this isn't the best place," I hint, ticking my head toward the house, and Jett opens his eyes, following my direction.

"Eh, they don't care. But if it's privacy you want," he says, a mischievous grin lighting his face, "I've got the perfect place."

He pop-kisses my forehead and hops out, running around the front of the car to hold my door open. I slide out across the leather seat. "About that. You said to dress for a day on the beach. Why are we here?"

"I didn't say *this* beach. I said *a* beach." He grabs my hand and pulls me toward the five-car garage connected on the side of the house. "We have to drive to the marina and then use…alternate transportation…to get to my beach."

"Alternate transportation?" My belly flip-flops. When Jett starts using vague terms, it usually means he's cooking up some scheme. Something that's going to test the limits of my comfort level. "If we have to leave from the marina, why'd you come here first? You're already in your swim trunks," I say, pointing toward his orange and teal plaid shorts.

He shoots me a sly smile as we walk into the first bay where the golf cart is parked by the wall. "Figured we might as well get in a little practice on the way."

Of course. His commitment to have me driving again before the end of summer. "You're never going to let this go, are you?"

"A bet is a bet, Cami, and I always follow through."

A bet is a bet. And here I was hoping our newfound penchant for lip-locking would somehow scrub that score from the board. I sigh and climb inside the golf cart, settling back against the orange vinyl seat.

Jett laughs—a short, almost sinister sneer—and leans in, draping his arm over my shoulder. "Not on that. We're taking Jenniston's car."

Slowly, the realization of his words filters in like ten pounds of concrete on my head. "Jenniston's car?" I repeat, the blood drumming in my temples. I swallow hard and shake my head.

"No. No, I can't." I stand up beside the cart, my knees wobbling and threatening to go kaput. "This, okay, but not a real car."

He loops his arm through mine and pulls me toward the neighboring bay, my feet struggling to actually come unglued from the floor and participate. "Perfect then, because I'd hardly call this thing a *real* car."

I peer around the edge of the partition, not immediately seeing any sort of vehicle in the slot. Jett pulls me forward until my focus lands on a tiny blue car that looks swallowed whole in the enormous space, like a little blue fish in the cavernous belly of the whale. "It's a Smart car."

"Yep. Compact, eco-friendly, half the size of a standard parking space, and..."

"What?"

"Slow as hell." He rolls his eyes. "Sea turtles move faster than this thing."

Okay, so it's slow. That doesn't mean it won't flatten into a pancake in an accident. The fact that it's about the same size as the golf cart doesn't give me the warm fuzzies, either. All it means is there's a lot less room between us and the outside world with speeders and texters and general idiots.

I grapple in the recesses of my brain for an excuse. "I don't know. Jenniston may not want me taking out her car. Maybe, instead, we—"

"Oh, it's perfectly all right with me." Her melodic voice breaks in from behind, shattering my argument to a million pieces as her floral perfume swirls around us. The smell perfectly embodies her personality—sweet, happy, peaceful. A calming force. She steps between us wearing a white sleeveless blouse and black straight skirt, her only jewelry a simple, very Southern strand of pearls. Mr. Ramsey is in tow, standing behind her, hands shoved in the pockets of his khaki trousers. It's the nicest and most put-together I've ever seen him. No team logos or The Shrimp Shack T-shirts in sight. "Jeff and I are going to Beaufort tonight to meet with a potential new restaurant coming on board as a client. And then, he's taking me out." She lifts her shoulder to her chin, glancing back at him. His stone face softens around the lips. "Right, hon?"

He nods, almost imperceptibly, and reaches for her hand.

Jett folds his arms over his chest, rocking back on his heels. "No harm in mixing a little business with pleasure."

Jenniston beams, but Mr. Ramsey's eyes steel as he turns in Jett's direction. "None at all, just as long as I get the business part done first. And speaking of which, I've got the paved track over at Gilmore's reserved tomorrow for team practice. You're expected there at 7:30 sharp. No excuses this time. The championship is in just a few weeks, and every bit of track time helps."

The hard edge in his voice is undeniable, like he's issuing a warning for Jett to read between the lines. I figure he'd be much more candid if I weren't standing here, and my mind begins to dwell on the subtext to his words. Is he indirectly accusing me of sucking up Jett's time and energy, or have I just become paranoid?

Jett tilts his head from one side to the next, stretching out his neck. His chin dimple disappears into a flat line. "I'll be there."

Mr. Ramsey's gaze zeroes in on him harder, with laser precision, and Jett huffs out a loud breath. "I said I'll be there."

The tension in the air is fully-loaded, like a rubber band stretched to the hilt and ready to snap. Jenniston steps toward Mr. Ramsey and pinches his chin between her fingers. "Isn't he cute when he's playing the grumpy race manager?" she says in a sing-song voice. His stiff jaw releases and he grabs her hand, bringing her knuckles to his lips. "Jeff, seriously. Let the kids go have fun. You have Jett all tomorrow morning, but tonight..." She steps back and twirls in front of him, her long hair and blouse billowing out. "Tonight, you have me."

Like that breath of fresh air, Jenniston diffuses the tension with ease, and a big smile spreads across Mr. Ramsey's face. He glances over between us and gives me a wink. "She's right. I'm just stressed. It was really nice seeing you again, CJ." He steps toward Jett and pats him on the shoulder. "Have fun tonight, son, because tomorrow, we work."

They wave good-bye and head out the garage door, and within a minute or two, his truck fires to life and the engine's rumble dies away, taking along with it the sour expression on Jett's face. He turns to me, dimple restored, and dangles the key in the air. "Are you ready?"

Am I? There's no way to tell, no accurate measuring stick of what's going to go well and what's not. All I know is that with Jett by my side, I'm willing to try.

"You've got to be kidding me."

I stand on the dock, looking down at a black and orange jet ski bobbing up and down in the slip.

"You got this," Jett says, tossing two life jackets onto the wooden floor. "You just drove a car all the way here with no problem."

Correction. I drove a Smart car—a glorified golf cart, in Jett's description—for one mile down a two-lane road going twenty miles per hour. I got passed by four cars and flipped off by one in that short stretch. I somehow managed to not break down in a panic attack, though the muscles in my arms still ache from the death grip I had on the teeny-tiny steering wheel.

"I thought you were the one who said it wasn't a real car."

"It's real enough. You passed that test, and this is the next logical step. A harmless jet ski on the ocean."

Anything capable of going seventy-five miles per hour, skimming the waves with nothing between me and the water's surface but air, is definitely *not* harmless.

"I know how fast these things go. It's like a motorcycle...on water...which is as unforgiving as splatting into the asphalt." Images of us floating face-down in the ocean, broken, bloody, encircled by hungry sharks, swim into my brain, and I take a few steps backwards.

Jett steps forward, life jacket in hand, and swings it around my shoulders, physically manipulating my unwilling arms into the proper holes. With a *click, click, click,* I'm suited up and ready to go. He slides his on too, fiddling with the straps until they're tightened and secured. I walk beside the jet ski and sit on the

155

edge of the dock, per Jett's instructions, as he lowers himself onto it.

He extends his hand, and I stare at it a moment, not moving.

"Trust me. I'll take care of you."

I gather my courage, slipping my hand into his, and step one foot onto the flat footrest. He scoots back on the seat, pulling me down in front of him. His legs and arms surround me, wrapping me into a safe cocoon. Our thick life jackets create a barrier between his body and mine, but I lean my head back and he leans forward, pressing his lips into mine.

"We're headed to that island over there." He lifts his arm and points toward a small patch of palms and golden sand in the near distance. "All we have to do is cross the Sound. That's it. And you're going to help me drive over there."

He takes both of my hands and lays them on the handles, covering mine with his. Small beads of sweat form between us, giving each movement a sort of burning friction that rockets through me and turns to longing. He plugs in the safety shut-off and turns the key. "We're going to do this nice and easy," he says, fingers squeezing into mine as he twists his wrist on the throttle. The engine fires to life and I gasp as we begin to move forward, clamping my eyes shut and sinking backwards into him.

The wind whistles in my ears, tousling strands of hair in every direction, and the seat bounces hard under my butt a handful of times. Leftover wake from a passing boat, Jett says, but I don't open my eyes, only grip the handles tighter, trying to focus on his legs rubbing against mine and the warm comfort of his body wrapped close behind me, instead of the fact that we're whizzing across the ocean with nothing to save us but a flimsy life jacket.

"You're doing great," he yells in my ear, his voice barely discernible over the roar of the engine and the hiss of the water as we cut through it. "I know you're afraid but open your eyes. You don't want to miss this."

I take a deep breath and slit open one eye, watching the blue water disappear under us like silk, and the yellow rays of the sun sparkling over the top like a thousand diamonds.

"Look to the right!" he yells again, and I glance over just as a gray mass appears, the hump of a back breaking the water's surface before dipping back below in a trail of bubbles. A dolphin, so free and happy. Not worrying about our intentions or mistrusting us, only content to enjoy its journey. It swims along beside us, playing peek-a-boo in the wake until we approach the shoreline and then divert toward the inlet. I watch the dolphin until it becomes a small dot on the horizon.

Jett lets off the throttle and we begin to slow as we approach the shoreline. A dense stand of palms and sea oats congregate in the center of the small island, but the outer rim is clear, golden sand, dotted only by a few deadwood tree skeletons and some large washed-up shells.

He maneuvers the jet ski into the sand, stabilizing it so it won't float away, and then helps me off the side. Up ahead, half-buried, a blue and gray conch shell pokes out of the sand. I yank it out, my fingers barely able to grasp it fully.

"This place is amazing," I say, gripping the shell to my chest as I turn in circles, taking it all in. Jett steps in front of me and grabs my hands, sliding the conch's open slit to my ear. A loud whirring emanates from deep inside.

"Conchs hold all the ocean's secret wishes." The sun glints off his green eyes and they glimmer like polished emeralds. "That's where the whirring comes from. The conch is remembering and repeating them. Breathing them into life."

I snort and hold it out. "A hollowed-out shell can do all that? Isn't this just some sea creature's abandoned home?"

"I guess it used to be a home of some sort, but just because circumstances have changed doesn't mean it's no good." He takes the shell in his hands, turning it over and over, inspecting every inch. "The conch changes, sure, but it's still beautiful. Think about it. It's been through all that," he says and points toward the waves in the distance, "and it didn't break. It didn't give up. It just waited here on this sand for the right person to come along and realize what a treasure it is."

157

He steps forward and brushes his hand over my cheek, fiery swirls springing to the surface under his touch. "Sounds just like someone I know."

My heart somersaults in my chest. I step forward, coming up on my tip-toes, and pull him down until my lips find their home base.

He pulls away and brings the conch to his mouth.

"What are you doing?" I laugh.

"Legend says that whatever you whisper into the conch comes to fruition." He offers it to me, and I take it with both hands.

"So, what did you wish for? A racing championship? Fame and fortune in NASCAR?"

"Can't tell. It negates the magic."

"Magic, huh?" The conch turns to lead in my fingers. If only this little conch could really make dreams and wishes come true. I wouldn't be a half-orphan with no sister. I look up and meet his eyes. And I'd have him beside me to kiss forever.

I pinch my eyes closed, pulling the conch to my lips, and whisper into the depths. "Him. I wish for him. For always."

Chapter Eighteen

The sun blazes overhead in a cloudless sky, and the mid-summer humidity thick and heavy, making the beach feel more like an oven stuck on broil than a refreshing reprieve.

Gin and Bo, complaining about the strangling heat and the assault of pesky gnats in the sand, declare it's time to call it a day, but Jett and I barely notice. We can't keep our hands off each other, our bodies like magnets sucking us back together every time we're separated by more than a couple of inches. Holding onto him keeps my head above water, especially when for so long, I refused to let go and focus on enjoying life instead of regretting it.

Tonight, we'll all attend the annual Fourth of July bonfire on the beach, but for now, we plow through the burning sand, heading toward Memaw's to relax before we have to get ready. Jett clutches me to his side, gently massaging my left shoulder as we walk, and I circle my arm around his waist. His leg rubs against mine, the wiry hairs tickling my fresh-shaved skin. They're all part of a string of subtle touches and gestures kindling the heat between us. The July sun can't even compare.

It continues all the way back to Memaw's house where we shower off the excess sand and sit around on her new patio set, the oscillating fan on high, drying off and relaxing in the shade.

In the middle of Bo's story about an epic, record-winning cantaloupe on display at the market, a car creeps down the road and turns into the driveway. The conversation stops as we stare at the stranger in the driver's seat, who's straightening his hair in the rearview mirror.

My stomach drops, my brain unable to make sense of why he would be here. Especially now.

Oh God, is that really who I think it is?

Jett visors his eyes with his hand and squints at the silver Honda Accord purring in the midst of a swirly sand cloud kicked up in the driveway. "Who's that?"

I plant both feet in front of me and slide off the swing's edge, still clinging to Jett's hand. My heart slams into my ribs as the car door squeaks open and the sun's rays illuminate the baseball-sized dent below the driver's window. I put that dent there nearly a year ago on one of the last truly fun days I remember having pre-accident. We'd been goofing off and I told him to think fast, and, well...he didn't. I swallow hard and push down my shoulders, standing arrow-straight.

"Trent."

Gin gasps and slips forward on the edge of her chair, craning her neck toward the tall boy now sauntering toward us. She turns her head in my direction, clicking her fingers. I glance over at her wide eyes and gaping mouth, the perfect mirror to my internal state. "*The* Trent?" she whispers.

Bo frowns and throws his hands in the air, palm-up. "Who's Trent?"

The sand on the concrete pad crunches beneath his sneakers, and everyone freezes except for four sets of eyeballs following his movement. He stands there smiling, hands shoved deep in his pockets, rocking back and forth on his heels. "I'm Trent. CJ's...um...boyfriend?"

"What the hell are you talking about? I can't believe you're showing up here unannounced calling me your girlfriend." I glare at him, coming up on my tiptoes as if my vertically-challenged 5'4" self could stare down someone a foot taller than me.

He shrugs, his eyes nearly black from the expanded pupils. "You are!"

"No, I'm not!" I glance over my shoulder, my words rebutting Trent as much as they are meant to reassure Jett. But his flat-lined lips and steely glare don't look reassured in the least. "We hadn't been together in months before I came down here, but that break-up email pretty much sealed the deal."

160

"I didn't send you a break-up email. God, give me a little more credit than that!"

Is he really standing here offended? That's laughable, considering he's shown up here out of nowhere claiming we're still an item after I clearly saw The Email.

A river of fire courses through me, starting at my toes and racing upward until the pressure throbs beneath my skin. The sweltering coastal humidity is a feeble contender with the inferno raging in my gut. Exactly when did I enter the Twilight Zone where my ex-boyfriend who *dumped me* crashes in on a perfect day with the new guy in my life? Never mind the fact I already know Trent's crushing on my best friend back home. Does crazy stuff like this happen to other people in the world, or has fate decided to kick me in the teeth once again?

Better go back. A dead mother and sister aren't enough. Let's nix the only person who she's made any connection within the last year. That'll teach her.

"You did."

"Did not."

"Yes, you did!"

"No, I didn't!"

"Oh my God, so you're saying I imagined it? I'm so not having this stupid conversation with you right now!"

"Then pull up this so-called email, CJ. Read it out loud."

"Fine." I glower at him over the rim of my phone. Beside me, Jett blows out a loud breath and crushes my fingers in his palm. A lopsided grin is plastered on his face, but I'm not stupid enough to trust it. When Jett smiles—really smiles—it lights up his whole face. It pulls everything toward the corners of his hairline. His eyes, eyebrows, even the bridge of his nose crinkles when he's happy, and then those creases across his forehead appear. Right now, everything's smooth and hard, except the flimsy twist of his lips. Nope, so not trusting that.

With my free hand, I tap my browser icon and sweep down the list of messages, all the way back to the first of May and his name. "Here it is, and I quote: 'CJ, things have changed so much this last year I think....'"

161

Trent steps up beside me and grabs the phone from my hand, holding it close to his eyes, then flips the screen out in front of me. "God CJ, you didn't even open the email! You just read the first few words of the preview."

I peer at the screen. His name's still highlighted in bold with the word *unread* in tiny, slanted font on the right-hand side. I'd never actually read the email in its entirety. I'd just assumed. I yank the phone from his hand and press my thumb to the link. My breath catches in my throat when the words appear, and I can hardly read it out loud without pausing to swallow the air that keeps expanding against my chest.

To: <CJ Ainsworth>
From: <Trent Casey>
Date: May 6
Subject: Decisions

CJ, things have changed so much this last year I think that time away will do you good. Do us both good. Sorry if I acted like an ass the other night when you told me. You need to clear your head. I get that. So do I. We used to be good together. There's still something there, right? Let's use this summer as a reset. I'll give you your space, but I'll be here when you get home in August.

Trent

Oh my God. How could I have been so stupid?

But even that's not the worst part.

My other hand's empty. When I read the email, the part about there "still being something there," Jett's fingers, which had been interlaced with mine, went limp and slipped to his lap. Now they're balled into fists so tight I can't see his nails, only the blue veins that spider across his wrist pulsating in quick rhythm. He springs to his feet and the swing arches backward, then slams into the backs of his knees with a thud as he stands at arm's-length from Trent. They stare at each other; the spot in front of Jett's ear throbs with each jaw clench. Without a sound, Gin sneaks her hand out and grabs Bo's arm. He leans forward as if waiting to break up anything Jett's thinking of dishing out.

But Jett doesn't draw a fist, only shakes his head. "So nice to meet Cami's...boyfriend." His rigid jaw nearly flattens out his chin dimple, and before I can ease in a word edgewise, he waves his hand toward me, offering me up like a Price is Right show-case. "By all means, dude...come get your girlfriend. I'm all done here." He turns and stomps across the property line to the Johnsons' driveway, the metallic jingle of the keys in his pocket following behind him.

I run to the edge of the yard and yell, "Jett!" He won't look back at me. He doesn't even flinch when I scream out his name again and again. Bo steps behind me and grips my shoulder, his fingertips pressing to the bone. I angle my head to catch his gaze, his eyes dark and intense.

"Bo," I whisper in his ear. "Please make him understand this is all a colossal mix-up. He'll listen to you."

He nods and takes off across the lawn, sliding into the pas-senger side as the Jett's Dodge roars to life. After three thunderous revs, the Challenger flies backward into the street, back wheels spinning as it jerks into gear and speeds away. My stomach crawls to my throat as the rumble fades into the distant hum of the waves breaking on shore. All that's left in the John-sons' driveway are two long smears of black and the stench of burnt rubber.

Gin paces back and forth along the underside of the house, hands on her hips, flip-flops slapping against her heels in the yard's one patch of green grass, saturated from the hose run-off where we washed the sand from our feet earlier. *Slap, squish, slap, squish, slap, squish, slap squish.* Pause and repeat.

I toss my phone into Trent's hands. "Take this and wait for me upstairs on the front porch. I'll be there in a minute." He stares at me, flipping my phone over and over in his fingers, not moving. There's no time for this crap. "Move!"

He and Gin both jump when I scream. Trent darts to the front of the house, and once his clomping on the wooden steps silences, I turn to Gin. "I have to handle this." I point above me then grab her hand in mine, the ragged nails she's chewed away poking into my skin. "Text Bo. I need to talk to Jett. This is not

163

what he's thinking." I squeeze her hand harder, and she grimaces like I'm crushing her knuckles under the pressure.

She nods and jogs toward her house, stopping midway to look back over her shoulder. "CJ? What are you gonna do with two boys who care about you?"

I force a smile and shake my head. "Trent's confused, and Jett..." I swallow hard and motion toward the empty street. "I thought he cared, but then he just...left. Now I don't know."

Gin snorts. A smile stretches across her face as the sun glints off the row of metal on her top teeth. "Funny. That's how I know he does." She winks, then turns and runs to her house.

"You want to be with him." Trent leans back in the wooden rocker and props his feet on the porch railing. He massages the stubble on either side of his chin.

I prop myself against the porch column, pretending the wooden beam is my second spine, and stare back at him. My gaze is locked on his icy-blue eyes; the same ones that used to send shivers coursing through me. Now it's more like reconnecting with an old friend. "So what? You're into Emmalyn."

He jerks his feet to the porch floor, sliding to the chair's edge as cherry-swirls tint his cheeks then crawl across his neck. "I...I mean, we..."

I cock my head to the side and bite my lower lip, watching him fidget with his class ring. "She's my best friend, Trent." I pause, take a deep breath, and look out over the front lawn. "Yeah, I know...I've pushed everyone away this past year, but she never gave up on me. I'm trying to be a better friend."

His eyes widen and the muscles in his neck flex as he swallows over and over.

"She felt awkward about the two of you, but I told her to go for it."

He sighs and drops his shoulders, looking at his shoes. "Are you mad?"

I push off the post and sit beside him in the matching rocker. "No. Y'all make more sense than we ever did. If there's one thing I've learned in this past year..." My mind spirals backwards in time, spinning like an out-of-control merry-go-round. Everything's blurry, the memories mixing with the dreams in an abstract mishmash of sirens and screaming and crying and sulking alone in my room. I sink my head in my hands. "Okay, I don't know what I've learned..."

"CJ?" Trent tugs my hands from my face, forcing me to look in his eyes. "I see a difference. This guy Jett must be good for you. It's like the old CJ's finally coming back."

A warmth covers my shoulders like a sweater and filters down from there. "That might be the best compliment I've had in a long time."

He nods and then frowns, forehead wrinkled. "From the way he glared at me when I called you my girlfriend, it's obvious the guy is falling for you."

The words spawn a tornado in me, fueled by the thought of Jett somewhere out there thinking I lied to him. Why didn't he wait five minutes so I could explain? Why did he leave me? Fiery flames lick my stomach, and I wrap my arms around my middle, pressing into the twisted guts. "I thought maybe he was starting to, but now...I'm not really sure."

It's a little after six when Bo stomps in the Johnsons' front door. It slams behind him so hard, Mrs. Johnson's display of collectible bells tinkle on their glass shelves. Trent slouches on the couch, perusing the movie channels, while Gin and I sit in the open foyer in front of the full-length mirror. She smears a boatload of make-up on my face, dabbing the sponges in little circles over my cheeks and eyelids, obviously trying to keep my mind off the Jett situation.

Bo squats beside us, sweat rolling off his forehead, T-shirt soaked underneath the armpits and chest heaving in and out with each pant.

I grab Gin's hand, stalling the eyeliner pencil in mid-air. "How is he? Why didn't he come back with you?"

"He wouldn't listen. He kept..." Bo pauses and looks at the floor.

"Kept what?" When Bo hesitates, I shove his shoulder, and he topples backward, catching himself on one arm.

He huffs out a loud breath. "Kept saying he wished he'd never met you. That he should've known better."

The words are bullets, ripping through my heart. Shredding it. Obliterating it. Being mad is one thing. Regretting me—us— is another. Jett's hurt. He believes the worst because he's been conditioned that way. Still, it's me. He should know I'd never lie to him.

I pick up my phone and check again. Nothing. "He won't answer my texts. I've sent like a million and he won't..."

"He turned his phone off. Then his racing team showed up and started drowning him in beer." He shakes his head, teeth gritted. "I tried to reason with him, but it's useless."

My heart crumbles. I've got to find him. Make him listen. Make him remember I'm still the one he can lean on.

Trent's footsteps sound behind us. He stands there, hands shoved in his pockets. "Should I talk to him?"

"No." Bo's jaw stiffens as he hurtles to his feet. "If Jett won't listen to me, he sure won't listen to you."

The one thing I'm absolutely confident in right now is Trent should NOT be the one to talk to Jett. And if he refuses to listen to Bo, then it has to be me.

It can *only* be me.

I just hope it's not too late.

The half-sun piggybacks the water, painting the salty ripples in smears of orange and gold. The party's only been going for about an hour when we get there, but the bonfire flames lick the darkening sky and the sweetly-sour stench of beer floats on the breeze. The beach is thick with scantily-dressed bodies running, dancing, and falling into each other. We push through them, rocking back and forth with the flow of people shoving beside us in all directions. Bo grabs me and pulls me back to standing when I nearly trip on the legs of a couple making out on a beach towel at the far edge of the crowd.

I'm not paying attention to them. I scan the mob for Jett, the only face I want to focus on in this sea of craziness. I lift up on my tiptoes as we walk, searching the nameless heads for his face, when I spot a pink ponytail bobbing across the uppermost edge of the crowd. Rachel steps into a clearing, hand-in-hand with Trévon, and I wave my arms in the air to nab their attention.

"Rachel! Trévon!"

She stops, glancing around. When her eyes land on me, she nudges him with her elbow and points in my direction. I jog toward them with Bo, Gin, and Trent in tow. "Have y'all seen Jett?"

Trévon nods his head down the beach. "He's by the water on the other side of the jetty."

The four of us collectively turn in that direction when Rachel grabs my arm, her grip tight and uncomfortable. "Let him be, CJ. Can't you see this is for the best?"

"No one cares what you think." The tension oozes through my gritted teeth. Bo steps forward, wrenching her hand from my arm, and pulls me in the direction of the monstrous rock-and-cement jetty.

Bo and Trent scale the rocks first and then pull up both me and Gin. The top affords us an expansive view of the beach, and it only takes a minute to locate Jett.

Frayed jeans and a black T-shirt, Jett sits alone in the sand, out of reach of the water lapping the shore. His fingers grip the longneck of a bottle.

He stares out across the horizon where slivers of waning light dance on the water as they're swallowed by the purple haze of night. Today got so screwed. We should've come to this party together the way we planned. It should be us down there. Not him there and me here.

Gin nudges my arm and nods her head toward Jett, but no sooner do I step forward on the rocks than a shrill giggle cuts through the dusk. That's when I see her, running along the water's edge in the shadows of the jetty. I freeze, my breath trapped in my throat as a pain shoots through my chest. Weird pinpricks of fire scatter throughout my limbs.

She skips along the water's edge, kicking up fans of ocean foam that rain down on her cut-off jean shorts and cropped, sleeveless blouse, tied up under her breasts, exposing her impossibly perfect body.

"Who's that?" Gin leans in, glancing back and forth between Bo and me. Her voice is barely audible over the waves crashing just a few feet away.

Bo rolls his eyes. "Dani…somebody. I can't remember her last name."

Dani. The famous Dani. The one Rachel claims is Jett's perfect match. The Dani who shares his passion for racing. The one who's been in his life way longer than me and will still be here after summer's come and gone.

Another giggle rings through the silence. I squint my eyes, straining to see her against the shadows. As much as my insides are twisting on themselves, I need to know how this will end. So, I stand motionless, quiet.

Watching.

Dani drops to the sand beside Jett, their bodies only inches apart, and leans her head onto his shoulder. Every muscle in my body turns to steel, immobile and paralyzed. I can't breathe. I can't rip my eyes away, and on the inside, my silent screams bubble up but find no voice.

What are you doing? Did I mean nothing?

Not so many weeks ago, I was numb. Nothing affected me. But now, the pain snakes in, constricting itself around my heart, squeezing it to the point I'm sure it'll burst. Tears sting my eyelids, puddling to the point they run over and trickle down my cheeks. It's been months since I've cried. The last time was before the memorial service.

I swore I'd never cry again.

I force my eyes open. She reaches up to ruffle his hair, the same way I had earlier on the beach, and then trails her fingers over his neck. Jett doesn't move. At all.

My friends' hands grip me, pressing into my muscles, consoling me, holding me back from murder, or possibly keeping me standing on two wobbly legs now threatening to collapse.

"I can't do this." I spin on my heels and face plant into Rachel.

Nose to nose, she purses her lips with fake concern. "Sorry, CJ, but I tried warning you." As I elbow my way past her, she grabs my shoulder and spins me back to facing her. "Jett needs to focus on all things racing. That's what he's doing. I get that you're hurt, but this is for the best. For everyone."

"For everyone"—I shake her hands loose and thrust my finger in her face—"or for *you?*" When she tries to swat my hand away, I grab her wrist and shove. She trips over her own feet and lands butt-first in the sand.

Trévon steps between us, holding out both of his hands like stop signs, but there's no need. She and her games can lie there in the sand like the slug she is. Gin and Trent stare at me—obviously waiting on me to scream, cry, explode, something—but the shock glues me in place. Gin's fingers wrap around Trent's forearm.

"Ouch," he groans. "Let go."

It's enough to break my trance.

No. I will not cry. I will not fall apart. Not in front of all these people.

The lump in my throat gets bigger and rises, pressing on my palate, making my nose and throat burn. I grit my teeth, sending subliminal messages to my tear ducts. *Don't cave to the pressure. Be strong.*

But the tears betray me. They sting until they stream down my cheeks, faster with each passing moment.

I backpedal out of the group, the only thought in my head being how quickly I can get off this beach.

"CJ, wait!" Gin yells, her voice so loud it echoes above the blaring music, but Bo grabs her arm, holding her in place with a head shake.

The ruckus, however, draws a crowd, including the pair down the beach. Dani jumps to her feet, giggling, and clamps her hands over her mouth, and Jett jerks back, looking over his shoulder. His hand slips in the sand, throwing him sideways onto both elbows. He lifts his head, eyes zeroed in on me. The soft glow of the bonfire is the only light dancing through the darkness at this point, and it faintly illuminates his face. His mouth twitches, then his lips enunciate one word.

Cami.

Chapter Nineteen

A row of houses peek over a cluster of palmetto trees, faintly illuminated in the yellow glow from the streetlight. No cars or people crowd the main highway that parallels the beach, which is perfect because I just want to be alone.

Except I'm not.

"CJ, stop! Wait a minute!" His voice booms over the waves and I pick up speed, the sand grains spraying up on my legs like a thousand tiny razors as I slog through the dunes. He has nothing to say to me. Let him go check on his girlfriend.

Up ahead, the pier breaks the horizon, its underneath dark and quiet. If I could just get there I could disappear into the shadows, away from the drama and the excuses and the pain.

"CJ, dammit, I know you hear me!" Closer this time. He keeps gaining on me, his heavy breathing in sync with the crashing waves. I dig in with all my strength, but instead of going faster, my feet sink lower into the drifts and slow me down. A heavy hand grabs my shoulder. "Listen to me, chick."

Chick. I hate being called chick. The memory of the first day I met Jett in the market floods my brain. My first instinct was to push him away. Why didn't I listen?

I stop and whirl around as we come face to face. "Who are you calling chick?"

"Ha!" He laughs and juts his finger at me. "Jett mentioned...one time...how much you hated that. I knew it'd get you...to turn around." He pushes out the words through heavy pants and presses two fingers to his neck, so dramatic-like. "Dang. Are you...trying to kill me with that marathon sprint?"

I deadpan. "What do you want, Trévon?"

He takes a deep breath and plants his hands on his hips. "I know you're pissed…and hurt…but don't give up on Jett. You're good for him."

My jaw about hits the sand. No way would he say something like that if his girlfriend was in earshot. I snort and jab my finger at some indiscriminate spot down the beach where I know she's standing. Probably laughing. "That's not what Rachel thinks."

Trévon glances over his shoulder as if following the invisible line emanating from my finger. He turns back and waves me off. "What Rachel said back there…she—"

Oh no. I'm in no mood to listen to some lame excuse. "Why defend her?"

"She *is* my girlfriend."

"That's your bad decision-making. Not mine." I pivot on my heel and trudge toward the pier. *Just shut up and leave me alone already.*

"Hey!" He claps his hands together hard, three deep echoes in the dark. It's the same thing I've seen him do when pissed off at the impromptu race meetings outside The Shrimp Shack, when Jett's dad is chewing him out for something. "I know you think she's just some mean girl with an agenda, but—"

"You're telling me she doesn't have an agenda?" I yell into the night air, refusing to spend any more face time with Trévon and his laundry list of Rachel-isn't-that-bad propaganda.

"She does, but it's not what you think." Trévon runs past me and steps into my path. He grabs my shoulder, forcing my attention. Nothing he says is going to change a thing, so he might as well save his breath. I roll my eyes as he continues. "No, really. Hear me out. Rachel's dream is to race with the pros, but she can't get there…not on her own." He licks his lips and bites down on the lower one for a quick beat. "She needs Jett to carry her. She needs him to win this race to get her—our team—to the next level. You're a threat to that."

Go figure, she's hopped on board the blame train to guilt me for her shortcomings instead of pointing the finger back at herself. "That's such bull! I've never tried to take him away from—"

"He's missed practices lately to see you. He's texted you continuously throughout strategy meetings. The track is dangerous if your head isn't in the game. Rachel thinks you're distracting him, and she wants you gone. Plain and simple."

My stomach drops. Jett *had* been calling me more, texting when I knew he was at the track, but the thought of him sacrificing his racing for me never crossed my mind. My stomach drops to my toes. *The track is dangerous if your head isn't in the game.* A terrible image of flipped race cars and smoke filter into my brain, my knees wobbling. "What do you think?"

Trévon lifts his eyes to the expanse of beach behind me, a small grin creeping onto his face. "I think Jett's happier than ever, and if he can focus and harness that for his racing, he'll be unstoppable."

I snort and shake my head. "Don't let Rachel hear you say that. You'll be minus a girlfriend. Besides, why would Jett want me when he has Dani the racing model fawning all over him?" My eyes focus once again on the pier, and it pulls me like a magnet. My feet fumble forward in response. "Rachel said Dani was better for him. Maybe she'll make him happy."

"I don't want Dani. I never did."

The words rocket icicles through my veins, icy hotness sprinting down my spine and turning the muscles to stone. Everything seizes: my breath stagnates in my lungs, my gaze homes in on a lone crab scuttling in and out of the long beams of light radiating from the pier. When he steps beside me, I shift my eyes diagonally to his sneakers and let them run up the length of his body. Trévon pats Jett on the shoulder, ducks his head, and jogs back up the beach.

Jett moves closer, so close the sourness of old beer assaults my nose. He trails his fingers down my arm; the wake of his touch leaves tingling phantom paths on my skin.

"We need to talk."

I shrug my arm away. He says he doesn't want her, but the images of him and Dani together on the beach gut me like the fish his dad puts on display in the refrigerator case. My insides are hollowed out.

173

"Please, don't shut me out. I have to tell you…" He grabs my shoulders and spins me toward him but pulls back when we come face to face. "You've been crying?"

Looking in his eyes is torture, so I shift my stare to his T-shirt. "Consider it another win, Jett. First place for being the person who finally got CJ to cry." I slap both hands against his chest and push him away. He stumbles backwards in the sand, then steadies himself and charges toward me again.

"I don't want that prize. You think I want to hurt you?" He grabs my hands, holding them tight in his. "I did *not* hook-up with Dani tonight. I never have. I don't want to."

"Not according to Rachel."

"Screw Rachel. She makes up shit because she's trying to ride our team to the big time."

"Whatever."

"Why don't you believe me?"

"Why don't *I* believe *you*?" His questions kick the hornet's nest in my gut. My entire body begins to sting. "I came out here to find you and explain about Trent because you didn't stick around long enough to give me a chance. You took off."

Jett exhales and rubs his hands over his face and through his hair, then threads his fingers behind his neck. "He showed up saying y'all are together. I freaked. Forgive me if I'm a little jaded."

"I'm *not* your mom, Jett." I plunge my finger into the V-neck of his T-shirt. "And I've never lied to you. How could you think—?"

"I have trouble trusting people because of her. I told you this. That kind of rejection scars people."

"Scars?" A guttural laugh seeps out of me like one of those horror movie moments. "You want to talk to *me* about scars?" I grab his arm and pull him with me into one of the broad bands of light shooting across the sand. In one fluid motion, I criss-cross my arms, grab the hem of my T-shirt, and yank it over my head. Anyone might think I'd be self-conscious standing in front of Jett in my bra, but there's no point. He's looking at something else. Something that, besides me, only Daddy and Memaw have seen.

"Oh my God." He steps forward and traces his fingers along the silvery-pink chasm "From the accident?"

"Where else? I don't just feel my scars on the inside. I see mine every day. It's a reminder; I'm here when they're not." More tears streak my cheek as the secret words I've pondered a million times push their way across my tongue. "Why didn't I die, too?"

Jett circles his arms around me, pressing my head to his chest. I don't push him away this time. Instead, I inhale his familiar coconut scent that reminds me more and more of home.

"The world needs you, Cami. I need you. After tonight, I know that more than ever."

I wrap my arms around his waist and squeeze, holding him in place until I finally get to tell him the entire truth. "Jett, I'm not with Trent. He—"

"Bo and Trent told me what happened. I get it now. I mean, I told the guy it probably would've been better to call, but…"

"But what?"

"But he said breaking up needed to happen in person. Not some random phone call." Jett laughs. "Ironic since you were the one who thought he broke up with you in an—"

"Yeah, yeah, yeah."

"Anyway, he said to tell you good-bye. Seemed pretty eager to get back home."

A smile inches up the corners of my mouth just thinking about *that* reunion, when Trent finally puts Emmalyn out of her misery. Good for them.

Jett's lips press into my temple and stay there for a minute; curlicues of warmth circulate from the spot. "I should've trusted you. I should've listened earlier and saved us all this drama. I'm sorry."

"Me too," I whisper, and then pull back just far enough to look him in the eyes. "So, does this mean we're okay?"

A smile breaks across his face, the corners of his lips and eyes stretching upward. "We," he whispers, "are so much better than okay." He lunges forward, scooping me into his arms, and crushes his lips into mine with so much force we lose footing and tumble to the sand in a tangled mess.

Chapter Twenty

The gold racing championship ring won't fit any of my fingers, so now it's threaded on a delicate chain around my neck. We were lying side-by-side in the sand beneath the pier when Jett propped on one arm and slid it from his pinky, offering it to me. His most prized possession for me to wear as an outward symbol of our togetherness. "So you—or anyone else—can never say we're not official." He smiled as he slid it on my middle finger, but the band swallowed that one and even my thumb, so when we got back to Memaw's, I dug a simple gold chain out of my jewelry box, and it became the ring's new home.

I fiddle with it, leaned across the Beachin' Books counter, and stare into space, reliving those moments under the pier from this past weekend. Cuddling on the sand. Jett kissing away all my tears. His hands—

Snap! Snap! Someone's fingers pop in my face and deflate my daydreams like a punctured balloon. "Earth to CJ." She barely gets the words out before spotting the ring dangling from my chain, which she grabs and yanks to her eyes. "Shut up! No freaking way!"

I straighten, and the ring slips from her fingers. It bounces back onto my chest. "Yep."

Gin slaps her hand over her mouth, but the edge of her broad grin peeks out from her fingers. "Bo said you and Jett made up, but"—she giggles—"this is huge."

The door chimes interrupt us as Rachel and Trévon step inside. They walk to the freezer case. Rachel wags her head childishly but stops when Trévon jabs her in the ribs with his elbow. After they grab two drinks, he approaches the counter. Rachel follows behind, using him like a shield. Though she stays quiet behind Trévon's blockade, her very presence spews venom into the atmosphere.

I hand Trévon his change with the usual, "Thanks and come again."

He offers a quick smile, grabbing the drinks with one hand, and ushers Rachel out with the other. But her focus lands on Jett's ring.

"What the—?" She pushes past Trévon and plunges an accusatory finger in my direction. "Why do you have that?"

I twirl the ring between my fingers, holding it out. "Jett and I are together. You're just going to have to get used to it."

Rachel balks, jerking backwards. "Get used to it?" She huffs out a loud breath and shakes her head, as if the mere thought of "getting used to it" is preposterous. She jabs Trévon's arm. "Now it makes perfect sense why he blew off practice yesterday. A total no-show. He was with you, wasn't he?"

I pretend to shrug off her accusations, but a rush of dread bubbles inside. He was with me—all day—with his phone turned off.

When I don't respond, her eyes bug out a bit. She clenches both fists in the air, looking ready to explode. "He's crazy. He's gone loopy! He's throwing everything away, and for what? Her?"

"Let's not do this," Trévon mumbles, trying to corral her.

"No, no, no, wait." She slams both her hands on the counter. "I want to hear what you have to say about it, CJ. Are you really okay with Jett blowing off practice, not putting in time at the track, and then going out there unprepared? Because I can tell you, this is *not* going to end well. Tyler is already talking crap and threatening Jett. You think it's fine for him not to be on his A game? You're willing to risk his career, his life, for your 'relationship?'" She accentuates her verbal jab with air quotes. Her laser-intense gaze stares holes through me.

The words trip over my tongue. "I...I didn't know about yesterday's practice...He never mentioned it. How was I to know?"

"You couldn't have," Trévon reassures me and then grabs Rachel around the waist, pulling her to the door.

Her mouth drops open, and she jerks away from his grip. She takes a few steps backwards, shaking her head. "Yes, let's all protect poor, fragile CJ from the truth. You'll ruin him. He needs to focus on his racing...on his team! You're a distraction that's gonna cost him his career...or his life!" Trévon reclaims her hand and with a final yank, shuffles her out the door. It slams behind them, leaving Gin and I in stunned silence.

"What a witch," Gin mumbles, reaching across the counter to grab my hand. "Don't listen to her."

I swallow hard and force a grin. "Already forgotten." But it's not. Not completely. If Jett spends so much of his time thinking about us, then how can he be putting his full attention into racing? How can he be preparing for his race when he's not even bothering to show up for practice? *Could* I cost him his career, or worse yet, his life?

No. I won't let that happen, and neither will Jett. Our relationship will bring strength, not division. It's just another one of Rachel's attempts to derail us, and she's not getting her way.

Never again.

"Come with me to the race this weekend? I want you to see what I do." Jett's eyes sparkle in the dim lamplight as he shuffles across my room and stretches out on the bed. He drops his backpack to the floor and kicks his sneakers off beside it.

"You know, you're gonna have to quit showing up to my room in the dark of night. People are gonna start talking." I laugh as I walk across the room to lock the door to the hallway. Memaw wouldn't give two craps he's here, but still...privacy.

"A little after ten is not exactly the 'dark of night,'" he laughs, looking up from his watch as I slide onto the covers beside him, propping myself on my elbow. He immediately stretches his arm around my shoulder and draws me in, capturing my lips in an easy, smooth kiss.

"You're an idiot, Jett Ramsey."

"Maybe, but you're a question-dodging subject-changer." He laughs and falls back against my pillow.

It's not that I don't want to go to his race. Of course, nothing would be better than watching Jett zip himself into that cute orange and black jumpsuit. Part of being with him is supporting him, and I want to, but Rachel's prophecies parade through my head non-stop. They won't shut up.

I questioned him about the skipped practices, and he shrugged it off with a dicey explanation that his Dad knew about it, so Rachel's opinion didn't matter. No big deal, he's got this, and all the usual deflections. But what if it's just a sugar coating to what's actually going on? What if Rachel's right, and I *am* a distraction that pries his thoughts away from the track, causing him to wreck? It's scary enough he's chosen a path that requires being behind the wheel at break-neck speeds, but if something happens to him because of me...I can't even.

"I'm not dodging your question." I sit up, criss-crossing my legs in front of me, my knees grazing his hip. "I just...I don't know...if I should go...I mean, racing's your thing...and I don't want to be in the way."

He turns onto his side and props himself up on his elbow. With his free hand, he cups my cheek; his skin burns like embers against mine. It's all I can do to focus on what he's saying and not lunge toward him, especially when he launches into a speech about how I'll be his motivation above anything else, then sweetens the pot with the promise of some quality one-on-one time afterwards. His dad and Jenniston are camping overnight, and we're invited. Of course, that could also be an excellent cover story should we want to spend some alone time elsewhere.

"You need to get used to the track, because you're definitely coming to the big race in August, right?" His gaze is hopeful, like an expectant puppy.

"When is it exactly?"

"The second Saturday."

My stomach clenches. "Oh."

"Is that a problem?"

No, the second Saturday is open. It's the day before—the second Friday in August—that's already slated to be one of the hardest days of my life. Testifying in court against the man who ran us off the road won't be a cake walk. Only the day of the accident could ever compare in my book, and I've tried so hard to block it out, just to have all this court stuff throw a stick of dynamite into the memories. "I have court that week. The day before actually. Back home."

My own words deliver the one-two punch. Court. Back home. Bam-bam.

The words sit like hundred-pound dumbbells on my tongue. Home doesn't feel like home anymore. Edisto's home now, the only place I can channel some version of the new CJ—the one who survived the worst and is somehow still standing. With Jett and Memaw and Gin and Bo by my side. As the truth sinks in my gut, the huge implications of what I have to do in court loom before me. And once it's over, I have to move on. Away from Edisto. Back with Dad. The summer I'd initially wanted to fly by has done just that, except now I need a pause button to freeze-frame things the way they are.

To pause us here in this moment.

Jett pulls at a loose thread on my comforter. "I didn't realize you'd be gone by then." His voice cracks over each word.

"That's when I have to testify."

He swallows hard, his eyes searching mine. "Are you prepared for that?"

I clasp my hands behind my head and lie back, looking at the ceiling. How do you prepare for something like that? In truth, how can I prepare for anything I have to do by summer's end? All the good-byes to be said, the chapters to close. It seems inevitable and impossible all at once. But right now, I only want to focus on what's in front of me. "Let's not talk about it. Tonight, only happy thoughts...about me and you." I lean forward, our faces a whisper apart, and nibble his earlobe.

"You're good at changing the subject," Jett says through a throaty moan, reaching for the lamp switch, which is just out of

181

reach. He swings his legs off the side of the bed and accidentally kicks his backpack, which falls over with a thud.

"What's in the bag? You bring me another headshot?" I crawl behind him as he sits near the edge of the bed and circle my arms around him, kissing his neck until I reach the stubble on his jaw.

"Something better." He opens the zipper and hands me a thick, black spiral-bound book.

"What's this?" The book's supple leather cover is smooth under my fingertips. I settle against the pillow, my back to the wall.

"My portfolio. My drawings. Thought you might wanna see them." The weight of the book increases three-fold. These are Jett's secret talents and dreams, ready to be shared with me. I open the front cover and peruse the first plastic-protected pages as if they're sacred relics that might crumble in my hands. But nothing about the designs are fragile. Massive coastal homes with expansive windows and open living spaces spring to life from the dark precision-perfect strokes. Notes about green construction materials, renewable resources, and energy-efficient mechanics crowd the outer perimeters. He fidgets his feet and chews on a hangnail. It's the first time I've ever seen him unsure of himself, but examining his designs, I can't imagine why he'd ever doubt his abilities. My mouth can't formulate anything discernible from the whirlwind of thoughts swirling in my mind. "You're looking at me weird," he says.

There's only one thing to say. "These are amazing." I fasten the book's silver clasp and lay it beside me on the bed, then lean forward to cup his face in my hands. His green eyes, pulled back at the corners in a wide smile, connect with mine. "You are amazing," I whisper. Our lips meet in the middle, and we collapse backward onto the covers. Jett hovers above me at first before I yank him to my level, running my hands up and down his back, under his T-shirt and against the rippled landscape of skin stretched over lean muscle. It's impossible not to touch him when our lips lock. Some urgent need to pull every bit of him as close to me as possible hijacks my motor neurons and demands it. It's as if I'm trying to absorb him. His own hands explore my body too; his roaming fingertips fill my veins with fire. My skin might melt like hot wax. His lips brush over my scar, my hidden shame, but the old instincts evaporate. I don't pull away. I push closer.

After a few minutes, when we're both seriously in need of oxygen, Jett settles on his back and pulls me to his side, wrapping his arm around my shoulder. I rest my head on his chest; the steady *thump-thump-thump* of his heart drums against my cheek. Our legs tangle together. My niche, the place where my body magically seems to conform to his. He kisses the top of my head and whispers through the dimly lit room.

"Promise you'll come back to me."

"What?"

He inhales deeply, holds it a minute, then blows out a loud breath. My head, still on his chest, rides the wave of air to completion. "When you have to leave...in August...promise you'll come back."

I grab his hand, weaving my fingers around his, and pull it to my lips. "Promise. I'll always come back to you, Jett."

Chapter Twenty-One

My eardrums might be busted. Surely, the stabbing pressure means the flimsy little things have ruptured deep in the canals.

Okay, so that might be dramatic, but only a little.

Jett said it'd be loud, but nothing quite prepares me for the mind-numbing, decibel-cracking whine of revving engines and rubber meeting asphalt. Each thunderous lap rattles my bones, as though it's emanating from somewhere inside instead of the track in front of me. It's what I imagine it'd be like standing in the middle of the football locker room after a Superbowl win. Sweaty, gritty, and brimming with testosterone.

As of tonight, he's only two races away from The Big One. He has to be on point.

My nerves have teeth sharp enough to chew my own head off, and if I think too much about what he's doing out there, I'll likely face-plant in a jerking, heaving pile of panic. Instead, I focus on the things that make me happy, like the way Jett's butt looked in that jumpsuit or the way his body slid through the car's window.

And then there's Gin, sitting on the stool beside me, relentlessly tapping her foot against the metal rung. Since Bo's working on the pit crew, she came with him to keep me company while Jett's on the track.

The massive headphones fit snugly against my ears as I slide them back on, instantly blocking out the monotonous mechanical hum and reconnecting with the Jett/pit crew dialogue. The verbal back-and-forth is light speed. Some of it I don't understand: stuff about drafting and finding a low groove near the apron and dirty air. Some of it needs no explanation.

"That Tyler's a son-of-a-bitch. I 'bout burned my brakes up trying to get around this shithead."

In all fairness, I was also warned the unfiltered feed might be vulgar. It doesn't disappoint. And I don't know what I like better—Jett's commanding tone over the naughty expletives pouring from his mouth or the way Gin's cheeks shade crimson each time a new torrent unleashes.

"Two laps, son! Pace yourself. You got this little jerk." Mr. Ramsey's hard voice crackles over the radio. We're all in the Crew Chief's booth, which is nothing more than an uncovered rectangular platform raised about eight feet off the ground. Meager quarters to say the least, and with the five of us up here—Mr. Ramsey, Jenniston, the spotter (some guy named Darren), Gin, and me—it's more like a sardine can.

Mr. Ramsey's stool is pushed against the front railing, though he's not sitting. He just stands beside it with one leg propped on the bottom rung and a set of binoculars shoved to his face. His head makes circular rotations as he watches the cars loop around.

"Bumper! The five car is coming up on the bumper!" the spotter screams into the mic.

"Five ain't shit!" Jett's voice fires back. "It's this damn twelve car that needs to clear outta my way!"

Tyler's in the twelve car. The entire race has been a switcheroo: Jett first with Tyler second, then Tyler first and Jett second. Over and over and over again. Now, coming into the last lap, Jett's slightly behind. My nails are chewed to oblivion, and a queasiness rocks my stomach.

"White flag! Slingshot the little asshole!" Mr. Ramsey belts out. He's leaned so far over the railing I'm terrified he'll tip over and splat on the pavement below. Jenniston catches me staring and side-shuffles toward me, never taking her eyes off the track.

Below, the seventeen car looks almost attached to twelve's bumper. That can't be safe. I hold out one side of the headphones; the deafening growls from the engines filter back in.

"Jenniston?" I yell above the noise, and she darts her eyes in my direction. "What's he doing?"

186

"Drafting. Getting ready to make his move." She ticks her head toward the track and taps her own headphones, signaling me to listen in.

"Approaching the straightaway! Show this idiot who's boss!"

I ease off the edge of my stool, crushing Gin's hand in mine. My heart pounds against my ribs in a heady mix of anxiety and adrenaline. Whatever maneuver Jett's about to pull will definitely be risky, but as much as I want to cover my eyes, I can't look away.

"Watch this, Cami!" Jett hollers into my ear. Then in one quick, blurring moment, he fakes high, drops low, and in a sudden burst of speed shoots past Tyler, capturing the checkered flag.

The platform and pit crew erupt, jumping up and down, slapping hi-fives and yelling, and of all the people celebrating Jett's win, I'm the loudest. For once I don't care who's looking or listening. That's my man!

But my cheeks catch fire when, through all the hoopla, Jett's voice crackles over the headphones with a private message in front of a very public forum. "Let me finish with this winner's circle stuff, Cami, and then I'm coming to get my real victory prize."

His arms circle me from behind. The smell of exhaust is stronger than ever even though his hair is still wet from a shower in the track's facilities. The way his breath wafts over my skin, slinking down my neck into the hollow of my chest, bristles the hairs on both of my arms, and I pinch my shoulder to my ear reflexively.

"Someone's ticklish," he whispers. His lips move against my earlobe, sending a million more chills over my body. I cross my arms to hide the obvious reaction. My brain goes all stupid for a minute, unable to form any sort of a rational response.

Jett doesn't notice. He's too amped up on the speed and the adrenaline rush of victory. True, it's been hard to keep our hands off each other the last couple weeks, but this? This is a bolder, more affectionate side than usual.

"Can I tell you how hot it was to see you in the booth with those headphones on?"

I feel a flushing heat on my cheeks, and I'm melting. The stir-rings surge through me like never before. Like the cars on that track—frenzied, fiery, and fast.

"Yeah?" I turn around and toy with the zipper on his team shirt, tugging it down an inch or so. "Can I tell you how hot you were in that racing jumpsuit?"

Our bodies press together. Jett's lips hover millimeters in front of mine, so close, but not touching. He's teasing me, and it's working because right now, between the shallow panting and the aching in my lungs, the only thing I can think about is running my hands—

"Blech! Blech! Blech!" Gin and Bo are standing there fake puking. They're both doubled-over, fingers stuck in their mouths.

Bo straightens up and slaps Jett on the shoulder. He narrows his eyes and glares, but a slight smile betrays him. "And did I ever tell you how much I miss you winning races without being so disgusting afterwards?"

My cheeks burn. Jett, unfazed, moves back to me, hooking his fingers into the belt loops of my shorts and tugging me to-ward him. "I can't help it. Another win and this hot girl to cheer me on?" He leans forward and trails kisses down my neck. "You'd be feeling it too."

"On that note, we gotta get going." Gin wags her finger be-tween the two of us. "You two, please be good. Great race, Jett. See you tomorrow, CJ."

I grab her hand. She's stayed with me all night. The last thing I want her thinking is that I'm throwing her over once Jett shows up. "Don't go, guys. We'll behave I promise."

"No, you won't," Bo says. "But we really do have to leave. Early morning delivery at the market tomorrow."

As they walk away, Jett swirls his car keys on this finger. He has no intention of our spending the night in the camper with his dad and Jenniston, announcing instead we have our own plans back on the island. Apparently, it's a colossal secret, and he remains tight-lipped except for one hint. "I got my victory to-night, Cami. Now let's go get yours."

Within minutes, we're flying down the two-lane marshy highway toward Edisto, windows down, briny air whipping a few loose tendrils of hair around my face. I squeeze the arm rest, keeping my eyes closed for most of the ride. Sure, Jett's a highly-skilled racer, and he's been working with me all summer on overcoming my fear of driving, but that's only been baby steps. I slit one eye and lean over to get a good look at the speedometer, instantly wishing I hadn't.

As if reading my mind, he pulls my knuckles to his lips, kissing in a line up to my wrist. He says nothing, even when I pry my eyes open and gaze in his direction. No words are needed. The way his gaze locks on mine for the briefest of seconds tells me I'm safe.

Jett pulls into a short gravel drive and stops in front of a metal gate fastened with a chain and lock. Chain link fencing spans the perimeter, partially covered in what looks to be honeysuckle vines. Ahead of us, a set of headlight beams break through the inky darkness, illuminating a whole lot of open space and some sort of dirt drive. If I wasn't with Jett, I'd probably be running for my life; this place seems like a TV crime drama set, where a bunch of dumped bodies might be found.

"Where exactly are we?" I ask, scooting up in the seat and scanning the empty lot.

Jett flips open his console and removes a keyring with two keys. "One of my favorite places in the world." He leans over and kisses my cheek. "Be right back."

I watch him run to the gate and unlock it, pushing it forward to make enough space to drive through. He pockets the gate keys on the way back to the car and slides behind the wheel.

Chill bumps scatter over my skin and my teeth begin chattering, and I'm not sure whether it's from the night air or the eerie place. We pull forward slowly, the car bouncing up and down with the rough terrain until we reach the dirt road, which is broad and flat and curves to the left. At the far edge, a tall building with garage-style doors stands amid a group of palms.

"You're not bringing me out here to kill me or something, are you?"

He circles his hand in a halo over his head. "Purest intentions, I swear. Welcome to my escape, Cami. My personal practice track—the one I started out on—and hideaway," Jett says. He cuts the engine and gets out before sticking his head back in. "Give me a minute to turn on some lights."

He heads toward the building and disappears into the shadows, and for a moment an intense ache of loneliness creeps through me. The night sounds of the swamp grow ten times louder; the trill of tree frogs and cicadas rise and fall into oblivion.

I pull my feet underneath me and nibble on a hangnail when a sudden burst of light erupts, shining through the windshield. It's so bright I have to squint until my eyes adjust, and the mysterious place takes shape. Large posts with stadium-style lights dot the perimeter of the field, illuminating an oval dirt track. The building we're parked in front of looks to be some sort of utility space. One of the garage doors slides up, and inside, fluorescent lights reveal some large machines and a row of toolboxes along the back wall. Jett's silhouette darkens the doorway briefly before he saunters back to the car. He sticks his head in my rolled-down window.

"Are you ready?"

"For what?"

A broad grin spreads over his face. He winks and holds up the key to the Challenger. "I promised you your own victory tonight."

For a moment, his words don't register. My victory? Then like a thunderbolt, it all comes together. I scramble out of my seat and slam the door, running to catch up with him as he rounds the trunk.

"No, Jett. Absolutely not. I'm not ready." My arms shake, the tremble coursing down into my fingers. "I can't."

He stops, grabs both of my hands, and stoops down nose to nose. "Yes, you can, and you will. I'm going to help you."

"But this is a *car* car. Not just any car. A fast one. With gears."

He drops my hands and makes his way to the driver side door. He gets in and slides the seat as far back as possible, then pats his lap. "Well, come on."

"What?"

A little nod and a grin. That's all he gives me.

"Am I supposed to know what that means?" I ask.

"It means get over here." There is a lilt in his voice as he beckons me with his finger. "You sit here, steer, and press the gas. I'll control the clutch, and we'll shift together."

"What if something happens?"

"Nothing's gonna happen."

"I don't know..." The thought of getting behind the wheel makes me seize up like an engine with no oil, and I turn to stone. Still, there's a big part of me that doesn't want to let him down. I want him to see I can be brave. That he's helped me.

And I really—*really*—want to sit on his lap.

"Other than Bo, no one else has ever driven my car. Doesn't that tell you something?"

"Yeah, it tells me you're gonna be super pissed when I wreck it."

He deadpans and blows out a loud breath. "It should tell you that I trust you. Now the question is, do you trust me?"

One hundred percent. No question in my mind. I nod a few times as if summoning my courage and climb into the car, situating myself on his lap. A lump knits itself in my throat, so huge I have trouble swallowing, and it's not only because of the butterflies in my stomach. There's something about the way our bodies hug tight to each other sitting like this. How the rippled muscles in his thighs press against the bottom of mine. How I can feel exactly how much his excitement is growing by my being on top of him. When he cranks the engine, the deep hum of the motor vibrating only intensifies the aching.

He trails both hands down my arms to my waist, where he grips me above the hip before moving his hand to the gear shift.

He eases into first gear and slides his foot off the brake, and the car rolls slightly. I stomp on the brake, throwing us both forward. Jett's face is plastered into my shoulder.

Surely now he can see how stupid this is—how hopeless I am—but he says nothing, only runs his hand over my right arm, covering my palm with his and lifting it onto the gear shift. His voice is easy in my ear. "Calm. Steady. I got you."

Boy, does he ever.

I nod and lift my foot from the brake, then press on the accelerator. I apply super-soft pressure at first, then harder and harder until we gather enough speed to actually warrant changing gears. As Jett pumps the clutch, his leg rubs against mine. We shift gears, his hand over mine, moving in sync.

As we approach the first curve, my heart beats triple-time until his lips brush my earlobe. "Lean into it. Natural. Easy." Again, his leg slides along mine as he pumps the clutch, setting off a million little explosions all over my body, but I drag my thoughts back to the dirt course. "Great job," he reassures me and plants a kiss between my shoulder blades. "That's my girl."

With him so close to me and his reassuring voice in my ear, my confidence grows with each curve and straightaway. We zoom forward, picking up a little speed so that the cool night air slips through and around the building heat between our bodies.

After ten laps, Jett takes the steering wheel and pulls off the track in front of the garage. He cuts the engine and we sit in silence for a minute, absorbing the gravity of the situation. His hands once again wrap around my waist, and warmth radiates over my skin.

"You did it, Cami. I knew you could."

I did it. We did it.

"I drove!" I scream, pumping my fists. A rush of excitement careens through my body. The space between Jett and the steering wheel is tight, but with a few creative foot placements, I finagle myself around in the seat to straddle him. "And it's all because of you."

"No. This is your victory. You earned it," he says and wraps his arms around my back. But he stops short, concern knitting his brows together. "You're shaking. Was the driving too much for you?"

My breath is hard to control, coming out in short, fragmented puffs. "It's not the driving," I mutter and bridge the gap, smashing my lips into his. The full aggressor, I grab handfuls of his hair and pull him deeper into the kiss. He responds with roaming hands that scour every surface of my body and settle cupping the curves of my butt in his palms. I run one hand down the front of his stomach and grab hold of the waistband of his pants.

A low moan escapes between our lips, and he mumbles, "Remember those pure intentions?"

"Uh-huh," I whimper, my mouth still on his.

"Yeah, those are out the window."

"Good." I grab the hem of his T-shirt and pull it over his head, clenching it in my fist as if it's a trophy. His bare chest ripples under my fingertips as I trail kisses down the slope of his neck. His breathing comes faster, the warm air coursing over me in waves.

He throws open the door and maneuvers us both out of the seat, never releasing his grip, only hoisting me higher in his arms once he's standing. I wrap my legs around his waist as he shuts the car door. His coppery skin is slick against mine, and he carries me toward the garage.

"Where are we going?"

"There's a studio apartment upstairs," he whispers before pushing his lips back against mine. He sets me on my feet and unbuttons my blouse with one hand while his velvet lips wash up and down my neck and over the top of my breasts. We stumble up a flight of stairs, littering the steps with the clothes yanked off in our hands-on exploration. At the landing, Jett twists the knob and kicks the door open with his heel. He pulls me with him to a bed in the corner where we collapse on the comforter. I still grip his T-shirt in one hand, so I fling it onto a small chair in the corner.

He hovers above me on the bed, kissing and groping, starting at my belly button and ending at the ribbon trim lining the bottom of my bra. With a sly grin, his fingers slip under the elastic, trailing pinpricks of fire and ice over my skin as he makes his way to the back, and in one quick motion, sets me free. The black lace lands on his rug, joined shortly by its match.

Jett's wide eyes roam over every hill and valley as my aching for him swells inside like a wave rushing to shore. He leans over and fumbles in his wallet, then quickly slides off his boxers and tosses them into the pile.

A swell of butterflies beat against my ribs, an assurance I want Jett in every way possible. Right now.

His lips brush over mine, softer than before but enough to stir the craving even more. My body arches into his as he whispers, "Are you sure?"

His eyes search mine, waiting for my answer. I twine my fingers in his hair and wrench him to me. "Yes."

I lift my head off the pillow. The silence of the room is broken only by the distant song of the cicadas outside. The red digits on the alarm clock say 3:12 a.m., but the pillow beside me is vacant. A small sliver of golden light cuts through the dark, and in it, Jett's silhouette hunches over his desk. An art case filled with colored pencils and gum erasers sits beside him.

I ease from the tangle of sheets and sneak to the chair in the corner. Grabbing his T-shirt, I slip it over my head. Immediately, the blend of gasoline and coconuts envelops me.

"I like you better without it," he says without turning around.

"Jett! How did you know I was up?"

"The secret to racing? Gotta have eyes in the back of your head. Know your six at all times."

"Guess I can't get anything over on you." I walk behind him, lacing my arms around his shoulders, and nuzzle his neck. On the paper in front of him is a delicate vine with flowers. Camellias. "What's this?" I ask. The petals on each blossom are expertly shaded, so much so they seem to leap off the page like an optical illusion. But the vine—something about its snaky, winding path seems familiar.

"It's for you. A tattoo design."

"A tattoo?"

He stands up with the thin paper, lifts the T-shirt, and presses it over my scar. An exact match. I gasp. "I traced your scar after you fell asleep, and then designed this. Figured it might be good therapy to dress it up. Maybe realize good can come from the bad."

Tears slide down my cheeks as I clutch the paper—so fragile in form, so heavy in meaning. A simple thank you will never be enough. I cup his cheek in my hand, his stubble pricking my palm. "You're the good in my world, Jett."

Chapter Twenty-Two

"See you later, Mrs. Baxter!" I yell over my shoulder.

The day's been unusually slow with only three customers during my shift, probably because of the picture-perfect sunshine and the fact Saturday's a "turnover day" on most of the rentals. Everyone's either on the beach, packing, or unpacking. Right now, nothing sounds better than spending an afternoon with Jett, cuddled under the pier, possibly reliving some of those moments we shared after the race. But when I round the corner to The Shrimp Shack, he's not the one waiting for me.

Jenniston gazes at me over the rim of her sunglasses with a mega-watt smile, looking as model-esque as ever in a bright pink halter-style sundress. She waves from the porch and motions me over.

"Hey there! I came by looking for Jeff, but it looks like he and Jett had to make another shrimp run this afternoon. They should be back soon according to this." She holds up a half-sheet of lined paper with a few short lines scrawled on the front and shakes her head. "He could've saved me a trip. That man refuses to use his cell phone."

"In that respect, Jett is *not* his father's son," I say with a laugh. "He's never without his."

"Tell me about it. Even more so now that you're in his life." She threads her arm around mine and nods toward the dock. I amble along beside her, trying not to obsess over what she inadvertently revealed—a confirmation of what Rachel's been saying about Jett always being preoccupied with me.

"Maybe we should take my number out of his Contacts." I force another laugh to hide the gnawing in my gut. "Get his head back in the game."

The slatted boards of the dock creak under our weight, and Jenniston directs us to a long expanse with no railing. She tucks her dress underneath her and sits on the edge, dangling her legs over the side. I join her, and we sit for a moment. The soft lapping of the rising tides sloshes against the barnacled posts.

She leans toward me and nudges her shoulder into mine. "You know, Jett's never paid much attention to anyone outside of his racing team until you came along. It's still so funny to see him squirreled away in the house, texting you non-stop."

There it is again. I chew on the soft fleshiness of my inner cheek, debating whether or not to ask Jenniston the simple but loaded question that's been haunting me. One I might not want to hear the answer to.

I clear my throat, and she looks over at me. "Do you think I'm distracting him?"

Jenniston purses her lips and takes in a big breath, holding it for a beat before blowing it out. "Is that you or Rachel talking?"

My jaw drops open and a fluttering kicks up in my chest. I readjust on the dock and fidget with a rusty nail that sticks up from one of the boards. How does she know about Rachel's beef with me?

Jenniston reaches over and pats my leg. "Don't look so surprised, CJ. This is a small island and an even smaller racing community. I know all about Rachel's meltdowns where you two are concerned. She's complained more than once to Jeff about Jett's lack of focus on the track and how it's going to cost her. Her future. Her spot in the big time. Her, her, her." She nods her head back, punctuating each "her."

So, this has grown bigger than just bickering. Rachel really did go through with her threats and took the problem she has with our relationship to Jett's dad. Jett always dismisses Rachel's talk as the rantings of an opportunist, but would he casually ignore his own father's advice? A father who's been the only real parent to stick around and who also happens to be his manager? Probably not. The gnawing in my stomach clenches harder.

"What does Mr. Ramsey think?" My voice wavers as I say the words.

Jenniston stares out at the horizon toward the afternoon sun. The amber light dances around her like a halo. "Jeff's always focused on the race. Sometimes too much. He forgets Jett is a 17-year-old who, in some ways, just wants a normal life. But he also trusts his son and stands behind him. I personally think it's great that you break things up for him a bit. Get him off the track. Remind him there's more to life than asphalt and octane." She bites her lip and stares down at her lap. "Jett's a good kid. Always has been. I've been very lucky to be his stepmom."

From the way her eyes twinkle when she talks about him, I can't help thinking that maybe Jett's the lucky one to have someone come into his life, love him like he were her own, and choose not to leave. Choose to be there when other DNA-linked people didn't.

"Jett told me about his real mom," I blurt out without thinking and immediately wish I could suck the words back into the depths.

Jenniston stops cold, surprise seizing her face. "He did?" She raises her hand to her mouth, shaking her head. "I'm shocked. I mean...not that he told you...but he doesn't talk about it—about her—ever."

I shrug. "His feelings are all mixed up. He's confused, and he has a right to be. What I don't get is...how could she just—?"

"Walk away?" She glances at me, tears rimming her eyes. "This is a hard lifestyle. Janice isn't a bad person. She just couldn't handle it. She hated when Jeff and Jett were on the road, and the constant worrying and loneliness finally got to her." She blows out a loud breath. "That's obviously no excuse for her cheating or leaving her own child, but it's an intimidating task, to fit in when you've not been brought up in this world."

The thought of being caught in the middle like that—having to choose between love and self-preservation—wrecks me. But one thing Jenniston says twists my heart the most. I've not been brought up in this world. Everything about it is still so foreign to me.

A lump builds in my throat, and I whisper my one gut-wrenching fear. "Maybe Jett would be better off with someone else. Someone who understands what it takes to be a part of this. Someone who helps instead of hinders him."

Jenniston gasps and grabs my hand, gripping it between hers. "Oh no, honey. That's not what I meant. Growing up in this life isn't a pre-requisite to be happy with him. It just takes character and strength to deal with this type of lifestyle. You have so much of both."

"Sometimes I wonder about that." I pick up a broken shell from the dock and launch it into the water. Circular ripples surface and spread out, dissipating.

"Can I tell you something?" she asks, scooting closer so that her rose-petal perfume encircles us. "When Jett first met you at the market, he said he saw something familiar in you. Something that hit home with him." She reaches up and brushes away a few strands of loose hair from my face. "If you're not into racing, so what? The connection between you and Jett is stronger than that."

A breeze kicks up. I lean back on my elbows and close my eyes, letting the sun warm my face. "I hope so," I whisper, so low my voice melts into the whoosh of the moving tides.

"I think you and Jett deserve a nice night out." She rummages through her purse and pulls out a white envelope and hands it to me. "Here."

I open the flap and pull out two dinner vouchers to a restaurant in Beaufort. "What's this for?"

"Our new client couriered these over earlier. Five-star quality food, according to their ads, but I do know their seafood is divine, supplied fresh from some awesome local shrimpers you and I both know." Her eyebrows move up and down, and she points down the canal where a large shrimp boat teeters on the horizon.

"Jenniston, we can't—" I begin to protest, but she waves me off before I can manage another word.

"Take them. Jeff hates getting dressed up to eat out. He'd much rather go grab a bite from Something's Fishy. Besides, you and Jett deserve a real date instead of hanging out at the beach all the time."

A short distance from the dock, much closer than before, I can make out Jett's figure standing at the front of the shrimp boat, waving in our direction. A quiet night away from the island and the racing and Memaw's prying eyes sounds phenomenal. A moment to slow down and just be us without any expectations or interferences. I slide the vouchers back in the envelope and slip them into my purse as Jenniston beams, and I'm compelled to hug her.

I lean over and wrap my arms around her, squeezing tight. "Thanks. I really appreciate it."

The spinach salad is of the wilted variety with some sort of artisan, gingery-tasting dressing I can't pronounce. The fact we're sitting in one of these upscale, coat-and-tie dining establishments with the real china and the authentic crystal goblets verges on the hilarious. It's so not our style, but I guess when your dad's company is providing the fresh-caught seafood, and the restaurant owner gives you two vouchers for dinner on opening weekend, you dress up and go.

While picking the cucumbers from my salad, I notice a woman staring at our table with an odd expression, somewhere between confusion and surprise. Go figure. We've garnered more than a few wary glances since walking in, as if all of the dressed-up, professional couples and families naturally expect us to be obnoxious just because of our age. And maybe we do look a little conspicuous, two teenagers eating at what the local newspaper called "Beaufort's swankiest taste of the South."

Still, one glance is acceptable. Two, irritating. But this is some sort of relentless gawking that scatters chill bumps over my skin.

I try not to stare back. No use encouraging her. But when it continues into the shrimp scampi main course, the warning bells in my brain go off. Something's not right about her full-on ogling, fork paused mid-air between her plate and open mouth, or the way she never acknowledges the man and the teenaged boy sitting at her own table. While they load forkfuls of the night's special in their mouths, laughing and talking together, she remains rigid and cold until she turns her head and catches my eye. She issues me a small grin that pinches up the corners of her eyes. I can't place her, but the face is familiar. Maybe she'd been a customer at Beachin' Books. So many come in each week, it's impossible to remember every one.

I nudge Jett's elbow. "There's a woman at the far table who keeps staring at us, and…"

He leans back in his chair, craning his neck for a better look.

"Don't. Too obvious. Just gradually check it out in a minute. I swear she looks familiar."

Jett smirks, stretching his arms wide with a fake yawn while swiveling himself in the direction of the back table.

I roll my eyes at his obvious lack of smoothness and stab a bit of potato with my fork. "So, what's the verdict? Do we know her or not?"

Jett doesn't respond. He's frozen in place; his lips and chin dimple both flat-lined, and his eyes are wide, unblinking. The woman sits across the room, still staring, though her expression has changed. Her lips are downturned, and her hands knead the linen napkin in her lap. Tears streak her cheeks. Why?

"Jett?" My fork clangs against the china as I grab for his hand. His fist is clenched tight like a rock. "Who is she?"

I don't have to ask again. When I look at him, I know who she is. The coloring, the chin dimple, the smile—I have seen it before.

On Jett.

Oh my God.

"She's my mother," he spits out, jaw clenched tight. "If you can call her that."

Across the room, she sweeps her hand over her open mouth. Her dinner company, the man and the boy, glance in our direction. The boy's eyes shine a rich emerald green.

Jett's expression softens for a moment before he throws down his napkin, fumbles with his wallet, then tosses the dinner vouchers and a hefty tip on the table.

"I'm done here. Are you ready?" It's not really a question. He's on the run, and nothing I say is going to sway him from getting the hell out of dodge.

I manage a meager nod, all the right words sticking in my throat. Helping Jett find the strength to face it head-on would be best, but I'm in no position to be handing out family relationship advice. So I scramble from my seat, having to run-walk behind him to keep pace with his angry strides, which are twice their usual length.

Jett shoves open the double doors. Within seconds, the humid night air shrouds us like a heavy blanket. He walks straight to the large metal garbage receptacle at the building's corner.

Bam! Jett slams his palm against the bin's green metal top, and the sound echoes through the park. Passers-by stop and stare in our direction. I know from experience there are times when no words can help. This is one of those times. So, I step closer to him and run my fingers along the stony muscles lining his spine.

"I'm sorry. I can't..." He turns to me, anger subsided; the timidity of his expression catches me off guard. Suddenly he looks so much younger, so vulnerable, as he turns and folds himself into my arms. He clings to my waist, mashing his face into the braid draped over my left shoulder.

I want to tell him it's okay, that I'll help him through it, but before I can open my mouth, we're interrupted by a voice that echoes Jett's Low Country drawl in a higher pitch.

"Jett?"

Those green eyes look totally different on the boy, young and innocent, and I can't help noticing how they're rimmed with tears. Jett whips his head toward him, standing by the restaurant's entrance. He's slightly bent over with his hands on his knees, panting from his quick jaunt out the door.

"Buck? My God, you don't look anything like the last—"

"You know, just because you and Mom fell out doesn't mean you had to forget about me," Buck interrupts, his voice more pleading than accusatory. "I needed you. I wanted us—"

Before he can finish, Jett steps forward and wraps him into a bear hug. Buck hesitates at first, then slides his arms around Jett's back. His fingers clench in the folds of Jett's shirt as if he's afraid that at any minute, it'll all disappear.

I know the feeling. It's the same one I get when waking up from a dream about Noli-Belle.

When they finally part, Jett tugs me closer. "This is my girl-friend, Cami."

Red swirls blush Buck's cheeks as he gives me a slight wave, obviously still suffering in that awkward, just-now-talking-to-girls stage. "Hi. I'm Buck."

"I know who you are," I say, patting Jett on the shoulder. "Your brother's told me all about you."

Surprise flashes in his eyes, his mouth dropping open. "Really?"

"Of course I did," Jett insists. "How many brothers you think I got?"

Buck shrugs, fidgeting his fingers against his jeans. "I guess it's been so long..."

"Too long." Jett snorts and stubs the toe of his sneaker in the sand. "You get your license in what—a couple months? Then no one can stop us from getting together." Jett fishes in his wallet and produces one of his promotional business cards. "Here. This has my social media handles, my email, and my number. Call me. Text me. Anytime. I'll pick you up if I have to."

Buck slides the card in the front pocket of his jeans. "I'd like that."

Jett pulls him in for another hug. "I love you. Don't ever forget it."

The door swings open again, and the woman emerges with the man hot on her heels. "Buck! You can't go running out into—" She doesn't finish the thought. When her gaze lands on Jett, her entire body freezes mid-action. The tension on the sidewalk is more oppressive than the humidity. "Je...Jett? What are you...doing here?" She fumbles and wraps her hand around her throat as if easing out the choked words.

He steps back from Buck and grabs my hand. The hairs on his arm bristle. "Leaving. You should know all about it." Before she can respond, he yanks me toward his car parked at the far end of the street. Jett's feet pound the cement, but I sneak one quick glance over my shoulder. Buck stares back at me, lips flat-lined, but Jett's mom manages a feeble smile before collapsing into the man's waiting arms.

The salty ocean breeze tousles the ends of Jett's hair as he sits, sullen, on the small balcony outside his bedroom. He didn't say much on the drive back from Beaufort. I'd figured our date was over, but when we got back on the island, he never offered to drop me off at Memaw's. That gesture is enough to let me know he needs me, even if he can't find the words to express it. At least he isn't pushing me away.

"Want to talk about it?" I snuggle into his arm and lay my head on his shoulder. He shrugs, then turns and kisses my forehead.

"What's there to say?" Classic avoidance. I, of all people, know he has plenty to say, but he doesn't want to. Or know how to. He bites his bottom lip, and we sit, cuddled together in silence. Lightning bugs dance to the wild concert of cicadas and swamp frog croaks floating with the breeze.

"Any advice?" he finally whispers over the bugs' grating hum.

"Only you would trust me with dispensing psychological advice." My laugh bounces off the balcony's stone tile. "But I do have some...if you want to hear it."

He blows out a hard breath. "Bury the hatchet and talk to my mother?"

"Obviously, because that's worked so well for me." Jett smirks when I point toward myself and roll my eyes. "No, you should write out your feelings. Put it in an email."

"An email?"

"You don't have to send it. You can save it to drafts. At least for now."

Jett cocks his eyebrow. "So you *do* plan on me eventually sending it?"

"Only when you're ready. That might be now, in a couple months, or never. You'll know when the time's right." There's no better way to explain it. For me, there was no *aha* moment of enlightenment. I just knew. "It helps to put it in words."

"You know this from experience?"

"It's how I made up with Em."

A few lines crease the area above Jett's nose. "I had no idea."

"I know," I giggle, nuzzling into him. "I'm such a mystery."

"No, Cami. You're the one thing in my life that makes perfect sense." He leans in and crushes his lips to mine. His absolute faith in me is evident, but any idiot can see we're the proverbial two peas in a pod. Neither one of us is willing, nor properly equipped to face our demons. At least not until forced.

Chapter Twenty-Three

"Could you two be any more sickening?" Gin laughs and nudges my arm. We sit together on the short brick wall near the parking entrance of the Piggly Wiggly, letting our legs dangle over the side. Behind us, the Ramsey racing crew is finishing a last-minute promo event before tonight's race. "Y'all are so sweet, it makes my teeth hurt."

"I'm not sure I'd call us sweet."

"You kidding me? The way he looks at you? The way you look at him?" She stares at the broken bit of clam shell she picked up off the side of the road, twirling it in her fingers. "I don't think that's ever going to happen for me."

"Quit talking that way. I hate clichés, but this feels appropriate here, so work with me," I say, turning sideways to grab both her shoulders. "There's plenty of fish in the sea, Gin."

She rolls her eyes and swats my hands away. "That's the problem. I don't want some ol' fish. I want what y'all have. The real thing. The mahi-mahi, not the crappie."

"Is Jett aware you refer to him as a mahi-mahi?"

"Shut up. You know what I mean."

"Yeah, I do." Jett's not just one of the crowd. Both of us are far from perfect, but there's something about the way we are together. Like a jigsaw puzzle that clicks into place. All the crazy pieces fit.

"What y'all have is the real thing, right? Like forever?" she asks.

Forever. What does that mean anyway? Is forever until the end of all time or just your time on Earth? And if it ends there, what becomes of those left behind?

I still don't know.

"If I've learned anything in life, Gin, it's nothing is forever. Even when we desperately want it to be."

She frowns. "Well, that's a downer."

"I'm not being cynical. I don't know what's going to happen. I leave in a few weeks, and from there…" I don't finish the sentence, because deep down, I don't want to face the truth. The red X's on the calendar prove the greatest test of our relationship is lurking just around the corner. Sure, they say absence makes the heart grow fonder, but try telling that to the millions of people who've had their hearts broken in long-distance relationships.

"No way. You and Jett are tight. I mean, you're wearing his ring, and have you…" Gin trails off but searches me with narrowed eyes, a question dancing behind the sapphires.

"Have we?"

"Anything else?"

"What exactly are you asking me?"

She widens her eyes, tilting her head to one shoulder. Obviously, I'm supposed to know what she's hinting at—and I do—but teasing her is fun. She sighs. "Okay, you don't have to say it. Just nod if you have."

I purse my lips and sit perfectly still. Gin's not breathing, not blinking, while she waits for my signal. I nod my head three times, and she squeals so loud that a few seagulls take flight from the nearby seagrass, and even a few of the racing fans turn to check out the commotion.

"I knew it! Oh my God, y'all are so meant to be!"

Gin's romantic heart rushes headlong into its wild goose chase of forevers and meant-to-bes and all that other star-fated bliss. God love her.

Across the parking lot, Mr. Ramsey whistles. Once he's got our attention, he waves us over. Gin and Bo don't get to attend the race tonight. Their grandma is in town, and Mrs. Johnson insists they stay for a big family dinner. Gin's only told me fifty million times how sorry she is to leave me alone, but I'm not sweating it. Now that I've been to one race, at least I sort of know the drill.

Gin waves good-bye and heads down the sidewalk toward her house, and I'm left alone in the parking lot. Where is Jett? Everyone else is busy packing the trailers and trucks, but he's MIA. I navigate the maze of folding tables and leftover fans mulling around the promotional banners. As I step beside the ten-foot decal of Jett on the trailer, I hear them. He's talking to someone, a female, but I only recognize the hard tone when I slink a little closer and peer around the corner.

Rachel has Jett backed against the trailer doors, wagging her finger in his face while she lectures him. Her pink ponytail flits angrily with each punctuated word.

"Don't dismiss this, Jett. I'm telling you what I've heard."

"Whatever. I'm not worried." He looks at his nails, all Joe-Cool style, pretending to buff them against his shirt.

"Are you dense?" Rachel shouts and slaps his hand away. "Tyler's out for blood, and he's planning on getting it tonight."

"I got this." Jett's voice is monotone. No inflection. No emotion.

It only pisses Rachel off more.

"What's with you? I don't even know you anymore! This is the kind of shit-talk that used to get you all riled up." When Jett shrugs, she blasts him again. "You need to get your head in the game and out of your girlfriend's ass."

Jett pushes himself off the trailer and bucks up to her, the fire finally returning to his words. "Don't bring Cami into this!"

"So *now* you're pissed? Tyler's making threats—valid threats—and you blow it off, but God forbid I point out the fact you're totally distracted by your precious girlfriend."

Jett nudges her out of his way and walks toward the opposite side of the trailer. Rachel jogs behind him and grabs his shoulder, spinning him back around. "This isn't just about you, Jett! It's about all of us—the team. Your success is our success. You used to know that."

"I still know it. Nothing's changed."

"Seriously? Then remember what your dad preaches. Distraction equals death on the track. Every time your mind wanders from the asphalt in front of you and the cars around you

209

is one chance closer to losing it all." She grabs at her scalp in frustration then plunges her finger square in his chest. "Get your head on straight or you're gonna get hurt out there...or worse. And it's gonna be CJ's fault!"

Fifty laps to go, and Rachel's words still haunt me. Each time Jett throws in a *watch this, Cami* or *that's for my girl* over the radio, it reminds me his head's not where it's supposed to be. Of course I want him thinking of us. Just not now, on this track. Later.

One thing gives me a glimmer of peace. Despite Rachel's warnings about Tyler being out for blood, he's underperformed tonight, hanging back in fifth place and never even coming near Jett.

"Twenty-two car on right quarter," the spotter's voice crackles over the headphones. "Three approaching your six."

"10-4," Jett's voice answers. "These bitches ain't shit. Race's in the bag."

"Pace yourself, son," Mr. Ramsey's voice cuts in. "Last big one before the championship. Eyes on the prize. Need to finish strong here first."

"10-4."

For twenty more laps, Jett easily maintains the lead, and the spirit on the platform soars. Mr. Ramsey's actually sitting on his stool for once, his hand rubbing up and down Jenniston's back. Seeing that is better than any self-induced pep talk. He's the professional, and if he's not sweating it, neither should I.

For the first time since the green flag, my shoulders sink to a more natural position, allowing me finally to take the deep breath that's proven so elusive. I lean forward on my knees. Jett's ring, dangling from my necklace, sparkles in the track's glaring lights, and my earlier conversation with Gin rears its head.

Two weeks.

In two weeks, I'll go to court and relive the worst day of my life. In two weeks, he'll be out here again on a championship quest. But what happens after that?

"Son of a bitch! Twelve's on the move!" The spotter's angry words blast in my ear, sending my heart into overdrive. Mr. Ramsey lurches off his stool so quickly it topples over behind him.

"He's got his team behind him! Pushing from the rear!" His fingers curl around the railing so tight his knuckles seem to explode out from the skin. "Dammit! It's partin' like the Red Sea out there!"

"Little bitch wants some, huh? Been waitin' on this all night," Jett growls.

I jump to my feet and press myself into the railing, leaning over as far as possible to catch sight of his car. Jett's coming out of the curve, and Tyler's hot on his bumper. My chest caves in. This is exactly what Rachel predicted.

"Rear fender!"

That's when it happens. Suddenly, everything that's been so fast slows into some surreal frame-by-frame action sequence. At least, that's what it feels like. Like a movie. Not real.

But it is real.

Tyler nips Jett's back fender, spinning him out. The nose of Jett's car scrapes the asphalt, the tail end off the ground. Tyler darts high, blowing past him, but the twenty-two car comes underneath Jett's back bumper, hitting him again and sending him airborne. His car flips mid-air and slams into the fence. Debris flies in all directions before his car comes to a stop upside down.

"Jett! Jett! Oh God, please no!"

Someone's screaming.

It's me.

My knees buckle, and I hit the metal platform.

Oh my God. Not again.

Where's Jenniston? And why hasn't anyone come to tell me anything? Unless...

No. I won't consider it.

I move toward the nurse's station, but the hard stare from the heavyset, gray-haired one stops me in my tracks. She responded politely the first six or seven times I checked in. But the last time, she told me curtly I wasn't immediate family and there was nothing she could do until one of them came out to speak with me.

So instead, my shoes burn grooves in the tile floor just outside the big double doors. What's taking so long? I'm not a blood relative, but dammit, that boy means everything to me. We're as close as any two people can be. I need to know he's okay.

I grab a paper cup from the dispenser by the water cooler and fill it but can't choke any down. The moment the water hits my tongue, my throat gives a violent thrust, and I have to spit it back out into my cup. I chuck it in the trashcan so hard, droplets spray the wall and floor.

Dammit. This sort of thing was never supposed to happen to Jett. Two people I love have already been taken this way. Sure, I realize the inherent risks of his job, but everyone knows lightning doesn't strike twice. Unless I'm some sort of bad luck charm.

Or distraction.

Shrill screaming echoes in the ER's vestibule as Rachel and Trévon push their way past the security guards. Rachel charges toward me, double-fisting my shirt and throwing me into the wall. My head smacks into the painted concrete; the impact radiates pain down my neck.

"Are you happy? I knew you'd eventually kill him!"

Trévon waves off the nurses who, upon hearing the commotion, shoot evil glances our way. He threads one arm between us, pulling Rachel back into his hold, mumbling, "He's not dead."

"Do we know that? Do we know he—and all our dreams— are not gone?"

"Jett's tough. He's always—" Trévon reasons, before Rachel cuts her fiery eyes back at me. Whatever he's selling, she's not buying.

"He's always been focused until she got here." She lunges at me again but Trévon's tight grip holds her back, her arms and legs swinging erratically. "You won't be happy until you've ruined all his chances, right? Kill him or hurt him bad enough so he can't race? Is that your plan? His championship is in two weeks!"

"Come on, Rachel. This isn't helping." Trévon again tries dragging Rachel away, but she fights against him.

"This is your fault, CJ. Jett's in there because of you!"

The words drop in my stomach like a ton of bricks. Every-thing's my fault. She's right. Mama and Noli-Belle are dead because I overcorrected. Jett had to be rushed to the hospital because he was too focused on me instead of the race. Now he's paying the price somewhere in a cold hospital bed unless...I killed him, too.

Oh God, no.

I can't go through this again—watching the people I love die because of me. They deserve better, and I can't stand any more loss.

I feel behind me for the wall, using it as a crutch to make my way to the blue padded chair where I sink down and bury my face in my hands. My tears free flow, coming out so fast and heavy they squeeze into the cracks between my fingers. "I care about him," I mumble. "So much."

"If you care about him, then leave him alone before you kill him," Rachel growls in my ear. "If you haven't already."

"That's enough," Trévon says again, jerking her away. Their voices fade beyond the sliding glass doors, but her words still ricochet in my brain.

It's my fault. I'll ruin his future. I could kill him.

I can stop this. I have to.

Unless it's already too late.

The overhead lights smear across my vision and begin spin-ning like a pinwheel as a strange blackness creeps in from my periphery. I stagger to my feet, desperate to search for the near-est restroom. But everything's hazy, the sounds all muted, and I'm covered in sweat. Someone grabs me by the shoulders and puts me back in the chair. They push the back of my head until it ends up between my knees.

"Breathe, child. Just breathe." As my vision clears, a pair of white, chunky support shoes stare back at me. Someone helps me sit back up; it's the cranky, gray-haired nurse. Only this time, she wraps her arms around me and gently rocks back and forth.

A click-clack of heels stops behind the wooden door. It eases open, and Jenniston walks out. Her cheeks are streaked with mascara and a wad of tissues are clutched in her fingers.

"CJ?" Her voice cracks. "Come with me, please."

Chapter Twenty-Four

The door closes with a thud behind me. Suddenly, it's as if the sterile corridor is a vacuum, sucking the air from my lungs. My stomach plummets to my toes and I grab the handrail affixed to the wall. I imagine it's here for moments such as these—moments when you have no idea if the next words you hear will knock your legs out from underneath you. Mine are barely holding me up now, trembling with every step we take. Jenniston stops and turns to me, fresh tears streaming again as she gathers me into her arms and squeezes me tight.

Oh, God. No.

Everything about this is all too familiar, all too painful as the memories of another such hospital visit crash into my brain. Except then, I was the one in the hospital bed, covered in tubes, watching through the sidelight window as a doctor put his hand on my Dad's shoulder and held it there a while. Dad's eyes went blank, and he sank straight down like the floor swallowed him. Only his hand had remained visible, clutching onto the wooden rail much like the one holding me up now, as if it's a life preserver.

"Jenniston?" My voice is weak, barely more than a whisper.

She releases her grasp and holds me at arm's length. I try to swallow, but the lump is in the way; it's like a brick lodged in my throat, threatening to strangle me.

That's when she smiles, wide enough to reveal most of her teeth. "He's okay, CJ. Jett's fine. A few bruises and some stitches. A mild concussion. But the doctor says other than a little soreness, he'll still be able to race in two weeks. Isn't that terrific news?"

The relief floods through me, and for the first time since the accident, my lungs suck in a deep breath. She reaches down and squeezes my hand in hers.

Before I can speak, the door swings open wide. "Y'all coming in or what? The patient has lost his patience." Mr. Ramsey laughs and steps back, waving us into the room. Jett's in the bed, elevated to sitting with the generic gray-blue hospital gown untied and pulled away from his chest. A congregation of beeping monitors and machines crowd the head of his bed.

"Cami, check it out!" He smiles and traces a long line of puckered skin, neatly stitched together with small black knots. It snakes across his chest and out to his arm. Like mine.

I'm pretty sure he wants me to laugh about it, but I can't. Right now, I just want to put my hands on him. I need to touch his warm skin and feel his breath going in and out under my fingers. Make sure that this isn't all a dream. Authenticate his life.

I drop Jenniston's hand and charge headlong into the room, plowing by Mr. Ramsey so hard he fumbles backward a bit. The wires and machines are no obstacle for my hands, which slip around his ribs and clench into his shoulder blades. After a sharp exhale, his muscles tense under my arms, and the beeps from the heart monitor pick up speed as his lips brush over my earlobe. "Easy tiger, I'm out of commission."

I can't loosen my grip though, so I bury my face into his chest, sure I'll dissolve into him.

He whispers in my ear. "You're good, right?"

The words stick in my throat, so I nod and sit as close to him as the tangle of wires allow, pushing everything—the wreck, Rachel's accusations, and my own haunting memories—out of my mind. The important thing is he's alive. That's what I *have* to focus on. Nothing else.

The orange light for medium roast blinks as the machine whirs to life in front of me. I never expected our night to end with a hospital stay and a Styrofoam cup full of lackluster vending machine coffee. But at least it's ending with Jett still alive.

This is the first time since I saw him in that huge, impersonal bed, looking so small against the pillow, that I haven't had my hands on him. Even through the vitals assessment, the nurse let me sit on the foot of his covers and grasp his ankle. It's a defense mechanism because inside, a storm's brewing. A howling around my heart says he wouldn't even be here right now if it wasn't for me. I'm trying to ignore it.

They're keeping Jett overnight for observation. Just precautionary. At least that's what the doctor said when he encouraged everyone to go home, get some rest, and let the patient recuperate. But the thought of leaving him nearly knocked the air out of me. Thankfully, Mr. Ramsey—surely noticing my death-grip on Jett's hand—asked if I wanted to keep Jett company for the night.

The answer was unequivocally yes and for very selfish reasons. My fried nerves ache for his comfort and the reassurance that he is totally fine.

Afterward, as Jenniston left to pull the car around, she hinted it might be good for me to call Mcmaw and get something to eat or drink. A protest rose in my throat when Mr. Ramsey grabbed the reclining chair and slid it alongside the bed's rail. He needed some time alone for a little father-son talk, probably to reassure Jett and tell him how grateful he was to see him alive.

Three short beeps bring me back to present as the vending machine's clear plastic door automatically lifts and reveals my cup, brimming with fresh coffee. I slide it off the platform and blow away the ringlets of steam before sipping. The hot liquid singes my lips, but I drink it anyway. If I keep busy, the darkness lurking at the edge of my thoughts won't consume me.

I turn the corner and walk down the hallway when a loud voice—not angry-loud, just firm—spills out of room 212's partially ajar door. I shrink against the wall, nearly spilling hot coffee down the front of me as I lean in to listen.

"...it's been all summer, son. Not just tonight."

"You're sounding more and more like Rachel."

Mr. Ramsey snort-laughs. "I normally wouldn't take that as a compliment, but under these circumstances, I do."

"You've gotta be kidding me." There is a faint rustle of sheets, and Jett's groans bleed out into the hall.

"Rachel's attitude is shit, Jett—we both know that—and I don't like some of the underhanded stunts she pulls on the track, but…"

"But what?"

"She has a point. She's been warning you, me, everyone all summer that your focus is off. You're too…consumed…by other things."

"Oh, I see. So you're next in line to start in on me and Cami? First Rachel and now you? That whole line is a bunch of bull—"

"Give it a rest, Jett." Mr. Ramsey's voice is cool, hard. "This isn't some sort of witch hunt. I like CJ. She's a terrific girl. And I get it. But listen to me, what good are you going to be to her if you're dead?"

"I'm not dead." Two loud smacks, like skin on skin, ring out between his words. I imagine him slapping his chest the way I've seen him do when and he and Bo are smack-talking. "Still flesh and blood right here."

"You're damn lucky you aren't dead after tonight. But you could very well end up that way if you don't get your head in the game."

"My head's fine." His voice is flat without intonation. Almost robotic.

"Missing practices? Showing up late, then leaving early? Stopping every 10 minutes to text on that damn phone?" Mr. Ramsey pauses but Jett doesn't respond. Not even a discernible sigh. "Rachel says she warned you about Tyler's plans, but you blew her off. You should've seen that trick coming a mile away, but you didn't. You got too cocky out there, showboating for your girlfriend, and you got sloppy."

The beep-beep-beep of monitors increases again. "Sloppy? I won the last race, and I was well on my way to winning another before that jackass Tyler—"

"You're saying that with a straight face? You barely pulled out the last win, and tonight? Well, that's a whole different story."

"Oh yeah?"

"Tyler would've never had the guts to try that maneuver if he didn't think he could pull it off. He's good technically, but he's always lacked that fire, that determination that used to set you apart."

"So now I suck?" Jett laughs, sending a thousand ice cubes down my back.

The chair legs screech across the tile. "God, son, are you listening? Word's getting around, and the vultures are circling."

"What word?"

"Have you looked at the online forums? Even the fans see it, saying you're off your game, screwin' up left and right. Spending so little time at the track that your skills are suffering. I've been trying to ignore it all summer, but after tonight…I can't ignore it anymore."

"What exactly are you saying?"

"You're becoming a liability to the team and to yourself. Get your shit together or you're off the team. I'll pull the plug before you ruin your career or get yourself killed."

"An ultimatum? Really?"

"Learn from my mistakes, son. When you're with CJ…be with CJ. Focus on her, make her feel special, be involved, all that fun stuff. But when you're on the track, focus on the track. Only on the racing. It takes one mistake to end your career…or your life." The doorknob twists, and the crack in the door widens slightly. "Just think about it. I love you, Jett. I only want the best for you."

The wooden door squeaks the rest of the way open, and I step behind a large rolling cart of medical supplies so Mr. Ramsey won't see me. I peer out between the boxes of bandages and rolls of gauze. He steps out into the hall, pausing long enough to stare back in the room for a minute, then sighs and heads off toward the red exit sign.

It's only then I realize I'm holding my breath. My chest tightens from the lack of oxygen. My hand shakes so violently that ripples of coffee slosh against the sides of my cup. The thought of another drop on my tongue spikes a churning nausea. I drop it into the garbage can in the empty room across the hall and step back into the hard glare of the fluorescent lights as I dart toward the family lounge, where I can be alone to digest Mr. Ramsey's words.

By the time I return to Jett's room, the nurse is pushing her mobile instrument panel into the hall after having checked his vitals and given him a dose of pain medication to last the night. She whispers he might have a good five minutes before they take effect, so I slip through the door to his bedside. The hospital gown is crumpled in a pile around his waist, all but the pulse and blood pressure monitors disconnected and pushed to the background, and his chest is bare except for the snaking black strings suturing the gash.

Jett slits his eyes and grins, patting the bed on his right, uninjured side, and I ease onto the mattress, curling up in the small void beside him.

"Where've you been?"

"Getting coffee. Calling Memaw." I clear my throat of the lump rising deep within. "How are you feeling?"

"Much better, now that you're here."

"I doubt my presence is the cure-all for your pain. But rest is. Why don't you close your eyes and relax?"

"If I close my eyes, I can't see you."

"I'm right here. You need to focus on your healing, not me."

"I'm always focused on you. All the time, every day. 24/7."

His voice takes on a slight slur as the medicine infiltrates his blood. I swipe my hands over his eyes, closing his eyelids. The drowsiness keeps him from re-opening them. I scoot farther down and loop my arm over this waist.

Before he totally gives it up, he pushes out a few more words, garbled and breathy. "You...make me happy...Cami." He stops and smacks his lips a few times. "You're all...I could...think...about...tonight at the...track..." His voice trails off as he succumbs to sleep, but his words cut deep. His dad was right. Rachel was right. Jett just admitted it. He was thinking about me when the wreck happened. His dreams—his life even—are in jeopardy, and it's my fault.

I demanded too much of his time and focus—attention he should've been putting on his racing. Rachel's words ramble around my brain, but even more, the private discussion she had with Jett before the race is omnipresent. She hadn't known I was there, so there was no reason to showboat. No, that discussion had been pure honesty, but he'd brushed off her warnings. The only time he'd shown any fire at all was when he took the words as a slight to me.

I pull my phone from my pocket and click the link for Jett's racing social media page. His dad said people were talking. Maybe it's time to find out what they're saying. The discussion thread has five new comments in the last hour since Mr. Ramsey posted details about Jett's condition.

Ir8 Drvr *Rookie mistake. Didn't look like championship material tonight*

RamFan17 *Tyler coming on strong. Don't underestimate him.*

Axlr8 *Heard he has a new gf. Reckon she's been keeping him up late? LOL*

Jettster *@Axlr8 If so, he needs to drop her like a bad habit. Ruining a good thing*

Ir8 Drvr *Glad he isn't dead. Could've been much worse. Might not be so lucky next time.*

I click off my phone and shove it deep in my pocket, swallowing hard. There's the evidence in plain view. Next time? My stomach churns.

There can't be a next time.

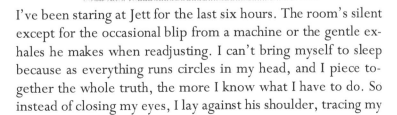

I've been staring at Jett for the last six hours. The room's silent except for the occasional blip from a machine or the gentle exhales he makes when readjusting. I can't bring myself to sleep because as everything runs circles in my head, and I piece together the whole truth, the more I know what I have to do. So instead of closing my eyes, I lay against his shoulder, tracing my fingertips over and over again across the curves of his arm and hand. Feeling him. Memorizing him. Because one day soon, this will be all I have left of us. Memories. And it makes me sick.

Sometime before dawn, I kiss Jett's lips, steady and slow, then slip from the bed to the reclining chair.

An hour later, he flutters his eyes and scans the room. When they land on me, he smiles and pats the bed beside him. "Morning. Come snuggle?"

Oh God. My heart is blowing up in my chest, but I have to stay calm. I bite my lip, shaking my head. The words stick in my throat like glue.

He squints and pushes himself up in the bed. "What's wrong?"

"Do you trust me?"

"With my life."

"Good. It's your life I'm concerned about."

"Here it comes." He tosses his hands in the air with a small snort. "You're still freaked about the wreck. I saw it in your face last night, but Cami...it's only one wreck."

His words slap me across the face. "Only? You could've died."

"Wrecks happen in racing all the time. It scared you and dredged up bad memories, but—"

"It dredged up a lot of truths, too." I jump to my feet, pacing beside his bed. "Things I've been trying to ignore. Things you've been denying."

The beeps on his pulse monitor accelerate as his voice hardens. "What do you mean?"

"I overheard you and your dad talking last night. He thinks your focus has been slipping all summer. Exactly like Rachel said. Your head's not in the race."

Jett slams his hand on the bed rail; the attached TV remote falls to the floor. "I don't give a damn what anyone thinks! They don't—"

"See? That's what I'm talking about." I grab Jett's hand, squeezing his fingers in mine. "Your dad didn't threaten to kick you off the team for nothing. You're not listening to their warnings. I wasn't either. At least, not until last night."

"Look, Tyler snuck up on me. He got the better of me this time. It won't happen again."

"No, it won't. Because I won't be there to distract you anymore."

He rips his hand from mine and crosses his arms. "What are you saying?"

"They're right. I've been taking up too much of your time. Time you should've been committing to the track, and—"

"That's not true!"

"Please. Let me finish while I still can." I sit on the edge of his bed near his feet, unable to get closer for fear of the look on his face when I tell him everything. "I want you to get that championship. I want you to get that architecture degree. I want you to be happy...and alive. What I *have* to do now is make sure that happens."

"Why are you talking like this?" Jett's face softens. His eyes are wide, almost pleading.

"Because two people are already dead because of me, and you mean too much for me to let you be the third."

He shakes his head. "No. You're not doing this to us. It's you and me, remember? If you walk away, we've lost each other already."

I want to give in. Nothing would taste better than his lips against mine. Nothing would feel better than wrapping my arms around him and nursing him through this. But how can I stay if his feelings for me might be the very thing that kills him?

"Jett, please understand..."

He drops his head for a minute, then lifts it again. He's glaring at me. Stone-faced. Hard. "Oh, I understand. You swore you wouldn't do this. You said you'd always come back. That you cared about me, but...you lied."

"That's not fair! I'm not leaving you because I don't care about you. I'm leaving because I do! I can't watch you..." Tears slip down my cheeks as I watch everything we had—could have had—circle the drain. Oh God, this is killing me. I bury my face in my hands as the door clicks open. From between my fingers, I see Mr. Ramsey walk into the room.

"Just leave then. The door's right there. Or better yet, call my mother, and she'll tell you how it's done."

Mr. Ramsey backs into the wall, as if the bullet aimed at me has struck him too. I lower my hands and approach Jett's bed. "I'm *not* your mother."

"No. You're worse." He turns his head toward the wall, blocking me from his sight. "Now get out...CJ."

Of all the emotionally-charged words shared, his calling me CJ hurts the most.

I retreat toward the door. Mr. Ramsey's mouth is curled into a frown. His chest heaves up and down, but the look he's giving me isn't one of hate, but of sadness. Sympathy and gratitude.

"I hope one day you can forgive me, because if sacrificing us is what it takes to keep you alive, that's what I have to do." I pull his ring—the one I took off my necklace earlier in the morning—from my pocket and drop it on the rolling table's laminate top. It hits with a *thunk* that bites me like a slug to the chest. "I'll always care about you, Jett, and that's something you *can* rely on." I spin toward the door, rushing into the corridor before more tears tumble down my cheeks.

Chapter Twenty-Five

The rideshare I called from the hospital dropped me off at the pier per my request. After standing in front of the post for what seemed like hours, metal nail file clenched in my fist, I just couldn't bring myself to scratch off my name. I walked out of his life, but I won't act as though we never existed.

My feet slap the pavement, the thuds playing percussion to the tree frog symphony in the fronds overhead. My sandals, clutched in my right hand, thump against my thigh as I walk down the road. The ocean breeze dies with each inland step, and the stray hairs liberated from last night's braid glue themselves to my forehead.

Mcmaw's car isn't in its space. I whisper a quick thank you to the sky and sprint toward the steps. Diving under the covers and forgetting the sneer painted on Jett's face sounds like an excellent plan, except for an odd stirring in my gut. One I haven't experienced in over a year.

I don't want to hide anymore. I want to hit something. Hard.

Fury swells in me like a tidal wave, gurgling up from my toes and threatening to blow my head off my shoulders. My therapist kept urging me to relinquish control, to let my emotions flow without barrier. She said I'd cry. I'd scream. I might even want to lash out. She never mentioned turning green, busting out of my clothes and morphing into some muscle-riddled monster.

I unlock the front door and slam it behind me as unholy hell erupts like a volcano. Fists clenched at my thighs, I stomp toward my room. My teeth are gritted with such force the back of my neck quivers, and ripples shoot across my ears. I kick the door, which swings open and hits the sheetrock with a *thud*. Papers blow off my desk and flit in front of my dresser before landing on the hardwood floor.

A navy shirt sleeve smooshes out the top of a closed drawer. I grab the silver handles and rip the drawer from its frame, turning it out on the floor. A mountain of long sleeve T-shirts accumulates on the rug, a massive target for a karate kick which sends a rainbow of cotton flying in every direction.

"Damn shirts! Stupid ugly ass shirts!" I ball a yellow one in my fist and hurl it at the wall, where it hits the "Memaw's House" painting she'd hung above the bed. The frame dislodges and skids down the wall, momentarily sticking on my comforter before sliding behind the bed and onto the baseboards with a *thump*.

The flowered Dammit! Doll perches on the foot of my bed. Its "X" eyes stare at me. Taunting. Laughing. I charge forward and grab its skinny legs. "That'll teach you to look at me like that, you little shit!" My voice breaks, surging forth through bouts of raspy breaths as I rail the doll against the mattress. Each strike ushers in a series of ghostly remembrances, memories I want cleansed from my brain for all eternity.

Thwack. The screech of slicing metal. *Thwack.* Noli-Belle's shrieks. *Thwack.* Mama's silence. Her open eyes that didn't see. *Thwack.* Red and blue flashing lights and ear-piercing siren wails. *Thwack.* Dad driving off without looking back. *Thwack.* Jett's car in pieces across the asphalt. *Thwack.* Him in the bed, connected to tubes and machines.

All because of me. Every bit of it.

I'm screaming. I don't even know where it's coming from, but it pours out of me like water from a spigot I can't turn off. My lungs burn. My head swims with little skyrockets and stars glittering in the periphery. I stumble forward onto the mattress, the doll hurtling out of my hands and against the brass lamp on the side table. The lamp tips over and nudges the glass orb with Mama and Noli-Belle's ashes off its walnut stand. It rolls over the table's edge. The ashes swirled inside light up like crystals in the glint of the sunlight bleeding through the blinds.

Bam! It slams the wood floor and rolls about a foot along the rug's edge, bumping into the book I'd been reading, which lays on the floor.

I drop to my knees and scramble to the orb, holding it close to scour the surface. Not broken. I clutch it to my chest as my eyes settle on something poking out from underneath the book jacket. The picture is stiff between my fingers, its front glossy with a sheen from the light that makes his green eyes sparkle more than ever. The inscription in black marker: **To Cami. You Drive Me _____. XO, Jett.**

Away. I drove him away.

It was the only choice.

The rage evaporates, and agony takes over. It's as if a wild beast claws at my insides, begging for escape. I sink into the T-shirt pile, salty tears flowing at will. Rivers of them run toward my ears and drip-drop onto the rug. I clutch the glass orb and Jett's picture to my chest. These are the only parts left of the people I love, people who now seem so unreachable.

Love. My breath catches as the thought races through my mind. Oh my God. Why didn't I see it before? How could I not realize? I curl sideways and draw my knees to my chest, holding his picture close to my face. That square jaw he clenches when I'm trying his patience. The way his full lips flat-line when I meet him snark-for-snark. Those jade eyes that laser through me in a glance and melt all my excuses.

This is more than a summertime fling. More than some trivial distraction.

I'm in love with Jett.

And now, like everyone else, he's gone.

***

Tap. Tap. Tap.

"CJ?" Memaw's voice, softer than usual and about an octave lower, follows behind the three small raps on my bedroom door. "Just a warning. I'm through with this knocking shit. I'm coming in."

It was inevitable. She'd already exercised herculean feats of patience these last few days, giving me the time and space that I needed. She left food trays outside my door, and they'd remained untouched. Each time she brought one—and about a million times in between—she'd stand in the hallway, calling

227

my name outside the door I'd kept shut and locked. But Memaw's not one to be ignored for long, and obviously her patience has worn thin. The lock clicks open, the door creaking as she pushes it in.

My only response is to press my face even farther into the space between my pillow and the wall. My body curls into the fetal position. Her footsteps thump over the hardwood before the mattress depresses behind me, tilting my body ever so slightly closer to hers.

"Jenniston called. Twice. She's worried about you. She's worried about Jett. The boy cares about you, CJ. And you care about him. That accident didn't change anything. It just scared you. Call him. Talk to him. Better yet, go see him."

It's an impossible request. Seeing him, hearing his voice, will only torture us both and make me want to change my mind. I know without a doubt my decision to end this is the best thing for Jett, even if he can't see that right now.

I'm a coiled statue, willing my muscles to remain rigid. Memaw sighs and runs her fingers through my hair. Sad notes tint her voice as she whispers, "You came back to life this summer, CJ. You were resurrected. Don't leave us again."

The mattress groans as she stands, the heft of the coils springing back up behind me. A chill finds me in the absence of her warmth. I refuse to look back at her or acknowledge any of what she's saying. My way is best. I have to believe that or else I've single-handedly destroyed my one fleeting chance at happiness.

Memaw pads back to the door, the tap-tap of her ring against the molding warning me of her frustration. "Silence is our enemy, not our friend. It solves nothing. It only makes things worse. You of all people should know this, CJ. You've lived it before. Don't live it again." She huffs out a breath and continues, "But it's your decision. Make the right one."

The right one. Nothing's a guarantee. You have to do what's best for those you love.

No matter how much it hurts.

My stomach sinks to my toes. There's no other answer, but being in this town, knowing he's so close, is torture. I can't give in and plead for his forgiveness, no matter how the pain slices through my chest. So the only option is to leave—go far away and hope the aching subsides.

And suddenly, it all feels so final. We're over. This summer's over. This whole charade is over. I stand up, drag my suitcases out of the closet, and open them on the floor.

The morning sun peeks over the tops of the palm fronds. Light beams shoot across the front porch, weaving in through the cut-glass panel on the front door and scattering rainbows across the floor. Memaw left a few hours ago—one of her usual volunteer days at the conservation center—and I've been wandering through the house, looking at everything, remembering the good times, committing it to memory so I won't forget when I'm gone.

Which according to my phone should've been ten minutes ago, but the rideshare driver is late.

My room is restored to its original design, only the "Memaw's House" picture, the Dammit! Doll, and the long-forgotten strappy, blue dress Memaw tried to force on me remain as any indicator I've been here this summer. That this had been my home, if even for just a fraction of a lifetime.

The bedroom door clicks shut as a car horn blares from outside, and I rush to the living room windows, sweeping the curtains back to get a better view. A tan Subaru idles in the driveway. I fling open the front door, signaling I'm on my way, and pull my bags across the threshold onto the wooden-slatted porch. When they're safely stacked by the steps, I pause inside the foyer once more. A thousand memories flood in and sting my eyes as I flip the brass handle lock and pull the door closed for the last time.

It's best this way. There is no other choice.

I turn around, not noticing the driver who's made his way to the porch to help with my bags, and slam face-first into his chest.

Hippie James. Mr. Sausage himself.

"Is Bessandra here?"

"What are you—" I start, then realize this must be the second job I overheard James telling Memaw about. Great. Of course I'd end up executing an incognito escape and wind up with Memaw's boyfriend as my getaway driver.

He scrunches his eyebrows together, a look of disappointment clouding his eyes. "I got the call for a ride at this address. I kinda thought Bessandra might be playing a fast one on me."

I don't even want to think about what kind of "fast ones" they've been playing. "Sorry to disappoint, James. It's only me."

He grabs the two large suitcases and starts down the steps as I tote my duffel and laptop case. "Your Memaw didn't tell me you were taking a trip," he hollers back over his shoulder.

"She doesn't know." He stops at the car and whirls around, his mouth hanging wide. "She'll find out soon enough. But not from you." My voice is forceful, strong. "Understand?"

James shakes his head, sitting my bags by the trunk, and scratches the balding patch on his head. "You're putting me in a bad position here. Bessandra and I have gotten closer, and I can't—"

"Take this." I hand him a twenty-dollar bill. He's right, but I'm not asking him to lie outright to Memaw, just to leave out the fact he'd been here today. A lie by omission, I guess. "Get a bottle of wine and come back here tonight. She'll need you."

"Hush money?" he asks, staring at the bill.

"Something like that."

"CJ, I can't." He tries to shove the money back at me, but I cap my palm over his.

Our eyes connect, mine pleading for his understanding or at least his cooperation. "Please, James. I have to get out of here. I have to."

He nods, shoving the money in his pocket, and begins loading my bags in the trunk. I open the door and slide in the backseat. I probably could get away with sitting up front, but forcing conversation isn't tops on my to-do list right now.

James slides behind the wheel, looking at me in his rearview mirror. "Where to?"

I glance at my phone, tapping the map icon on my search return. "The closest Greyhound station, which looks to be in Walterboro."

"Yes, ma'am," he says, throwing it in reverse and backing out of the driveway. I turn around in my seat, watching Memaw's house disappear. When it's gone, I press my face to the side window, and the town slips by in a blur. So many memories, now nothing more than a whir of yesterdays sliding from view.

James stops near the first beach access to let a large group cross the four-lane road. In the grocery store's parking lot ahead, Jett's racing trailer is parked at the curb. Banners extend from it to every light post on the lot while large speakers pump out music for gathered onlookers. In the middle of it all, sitting at a long brown table, is Jett. He's dressed in his racing gear, signing autographs and posing for pictures with Rachel and Trévon at his side. Their cars are parked catty-cornered to the table and fans mill around, checking out the engines underneath the hoods.

Tears spill down my cheeks, streaking toward my chin before dropping off onto my T-shirt in big wet blotches. Watching him disappear from view is an impossible task. The pain rips through me, and I reach for the door handle. Squeezing hard, I fight back the inclination to hurl myself onto the asphalt and run toward him. Right when the battle seems too much to bear, the road clears, and James hits the gas. Jett gets smaller and smaller, fading away from my life and into obscurity.

Up the road, Memaw's Cabriolet is parked out front at the conservation center. She's inside, pursuing her life's devotion to charity work, never realizing she'll be coming home to an empty house. She'll never know how much this summer meant to me—how much *she* meant to me. She'll be disappointed I couldn't dig myself out of this hole and be strong like her.

On the left, the Johnsons' market comes into view. The place where everything started. Bo works out back, unloading big crates from the back of a truck, while Gin sweeps the mat out front. They look happy, smiling and content, and that's when the realization hits me. These people—no more than strangers three short months ago—have become my family. I love them, and the thought of not seeing them, not having them in my life, is another wallop to the chest. I'm in this backseat crying while they're going on with everyday life. For them, nothing's changed this summer. It's like I've never been here at all. But for me—everything's changed, and the deep ache clawing in my chest tells me running away won't be able to counter the effects they've had.

I wrench my earbuds from my pocket, plugging in my music and escaping everything around me. Within a half-hour, James pulls into the Greyhound station, gets out, and opens my door before putting my bags out on the sidewalk.

"How much do I owe you?" I glance between him and my wallet.

He slams the trunk lid, walks over, and gathers me in a huge hug. "The ride's on me, kid. Take care of yourself."

I nod, struggling to hold back the tears yet again, and gather my bags as James slides back behind the wheel. He pauses, staring out at me. "CJ? Call your Memaw when you get where you're going."

"I will. And James?" I swallow hard, taking a deep breath to steady my voice. "You take good care of her, okay? She's a handful, but she'll be the best thing that's happened to you since you got to Edisto."

"Deal." He smiles and slams the door, accelerating away from the curb. I watch until his taillights vanish then make my way to the ticket counter.

A lady in a blue and gray uniform looks up and smiles. "How may I help you today?"

"One, please, on your next bus to Greenville."

I grab my laptop bag and step into the bus's aisle, squeezing myself near the front of the forming line. With a *pshhhh*, the door folds open, and we all move forward. No one touches. No one even acknowledges the existence of others, unless to grumble about how the line's moving too slowly, though it's not directed at anyone personally. Just another pissy observation to set afloat in the world.

The lady in front of me, swathed in a flowy tan cardigan (ridiculous since it's pushing 100 degrees outside) catches the sleeve on the hand grip at the steps. She flails her arm wide and the sweater flows into my face as it comes unhooked. I swat it away, and that's when I see him standing there, waiting with arms folded.

Chapter Twenty-Six

"**D**ad?" The unloading zone turns to quicksand underneath my feet, sucking and gluing them in place. "What are *you* doing here?"

"I might ask you the same thing." He grabs my elbow, shuffling me away from the disembarking passengers, whose not-so-quiet complaints about me holding up the line echo through the terminals. When we're safely out of the way, his eyes dart between me and the others, who stare at our exchange as they walk from the steps to the baggage claim at the side of the bus. Part of me wants to scream—really belt one out—and draw the attention of the whole place, especially the city police officer standing near the ticket counter. It might create the diversion I need to escape from Dad and all his pathetic attempts to be some kind of a parent now.

Problem is, I don't know where I'm headed. Leaving Edisto had been the priority. I hadn't considered all the logistics of my plan. That and, despite my anger, I kind of want to hear what he has to say.

"Memaw called," he continues. "The guy who gave you a ride to the bus station told her where you were headed." Who'd have pegged Hippie James as a big snitch? So much for that hush money I slipped him.

"So she had her people spy on me?" I wiggle my fingers in air quotes for "people."

Dad ignores the question. "You were making progress, CJ. What happened?"

My mouth drops open. Is he seriously standing here like Most-Concerned-Father-of-the-Year? "How would you even know? I haven't heard one damn word from you all summer." The venom-drenched words shoot out with little resistance. I hate we've been reduced to this, but at this point in time, our family's happy memories are barely clinging to life in the farthest recesses of my mind. They're so hazy I've even wondered if they ever really happened at all.

"Language, CJ. I'm still your father, and—"

"You haven't been my father in almost a year! The therapist happens to suggest I 'go away' for the summer, and boom! Bye, CJ!" He raises his hand in protest, but before he can utter a word, I immediately reload and start firing again. "I take that back. There was no good-bye, was there? Just you burning rubber out the driveway at the market. You couldn't wait to get rid of me!"

The crowd's eyes bore into our scene, sending shivers down my spine. The emotional whirlwind wraps me in so many threads of anger and accusation, I scream like a banshee, putting our dirty laundry on blast for the world to see. I glance over my shoulder, connecting with more than ten sets of eyeballs that magically divert to other items of interest in a second. Dad grabs my shoulders and pulls me sideways, physically manipulating my back to the onlookers.

"That's not true, CJ. I never wanted to get rid of you. It's just—"

"It's because I messed up." Tears sting my eyelids, puddling on my lower lashes. "I know I did, Dad, so you can quit blaming me now. Because I blame myself. For everything."

His fingers squeeze hard around my arms. His eyes are shadowed and sullen, like the skies before a storm. "It's nothing like that. You can't see—"

"Then tell me what I missed. You exiled me to Edisto with Memaw, the other person in your life you threw away." Words rolls off my tongue as quickly as they formulate in my brain. No filter, and absolutely no regard for subjects that may or may not be off limits. "And what's with that, by the way? What's Memaw done so wrong that you've shut her out for an entire decade? Explain it to me, because I'm so interested to see how it's all a simple misunderstanding."

"I can't tell you that, because it wasn't a misunderstanding." His voice is calm, almost thoughtful, but I'm so past buying anymore of his excuses. I yank away from his grasp, slide my computer bag back on my shoulder, and turn to walk away when he says something that stops me cold. "It was regret and fear and my own damn foolish pride. You should know all about it, CJ. You inherited that from me."

He might as well have chucked a brick at my back. His words hit me square between the shoulder blades, shooting pain across each limb. I spin back to face him as he stands there, swiping his hand back and forth over his brow.

"I shut Memaw out intentionally. I was mad at her for moving on so quickly after Grandpa. You're probably too young to remember his funeral, but—"

"I remember everything." My eyes lock with Dad's. "Memaw and Grandpa, his funeral, when you called Memaw crazy and said she should be committed."

"Oh. I never realized you heard all that." For the first time, shame crosses his face as he pinches his lips and glances at his shoes. "It's just, the damn thing was more like a party than a funeral for a well-respected Charleston businessman. I mean, what did all of Grandpa's colleagues think when they arrived at a cocktail party instead of a conservative time to focus on—"

"On what, Dad? The grief? The loss? You and I both know how that works out. But that's not Memaw. And it wasn't Grandpa, either." I step closer to Dad, leaning my head to the side to catch his gaze. "The party was his request and so was her selling the house and moving out to the island so soon afterwards. Did you even talk to her about it?"

"No. I didn't." He spits the words out, but then quickly retracts the angry edge of his words to a more somber tone. "I felt disrespected, and I reacted by shutting her out. The same way I shut you out, CJ, when the anger consumed me after the accident."

Tears sting my eyelids at his admission. I'd been right all along. "I know you hate me because I killed Mama and Noli-Belle."

237

His eyes snap to mine, narrowed and stormy, and his jaw drops ever so slightly as he shakes his head. "I've never thought that. I was mad at myself. I sent you to Memaw's so I wouldn't hurt you anymore."

His words are like a puzzle I can't piece together. Why would he ever be mad at himself? He wasn't even there when the accident happened. "I don't get it," I mumble as a slight tremble courses over my skin in response to my frayed nerves.

He walks over and grabs both my shoulders, his fingertips pressing into my skin with enough force to keep my attention firmly grounded on him. "We're too much alike, CJ."

My anger coils inside. The hurt from his absence over the past year tastes bitter in my mouth. "I'm nothing like you."

Dad throws his head back, laughing. The sound of it makes me want to lash out. Slap him. Push him away the way he did to me. "There's a reason Mama always called you my clone. Same auburn hair. Same freckles. Same piss-poor attitude." He tilts his head toward me and arches his eyebrows as if to say *amiright?* before continuing. "We're runners. We don't face things head-on. Instead, we absorb them, bury our heads in the sand, strap the blame on our own backs, and shut everyone else out."

There's validity in his words, even if I can't admit that to him. I shove his hands off my shoulders and readjust the strap of my duffel across my chest, stepping backward. "Whatever."

"Time to quit running."

"Like you have any right to say that to me!"

"I didn't before, but I've changed this summer. I thought you had too."

I did change—in some respects—but I'm not ready to face my part in my mama's and sister's deaths. "Guess not. Nothing's changed."

Dad grabs my suitcases with each hand then leans in close, his nose nearly touching mine. "Everything's changed, CJ, and we have a lot to talk about. Mama'd want us to figure this out, and that's what we're gonna do. Right now."

Okay, so he's right. Everything *has* changed. But it's a bitter-sweet truth, because the people responsible for that change are no longer part of my life.

Up ahead, on the right, the green street sign glints in the fad-ing afternoon sun. Oak-lined Kensington Avenue—with all its southern charms and wrap-around porches and neighborhood block parties and backyard barbecues—was an idyllic place to grow up and call home.

Only it doesn't feel like home anymore.

Instead of slowing down to turn, Dad accelerates past our street toward the rural stretches of highway beyond the city lim-its.

"Where are we going?" My voice trembles as I eyeball Dad, who keeps his focus glued to the road. He doesn't answer, only kneads the steering wheel. His chin tucks back to his throat and his forehead angles toward the windshield as if he's running headlong into something. The Explorer jolts ahead, the engine purring louder as the speedometer needle progresses.

"Dad," I ask again through gritted teeth. "Where are we go-ing?"

"You *know* where we're going."

No. I don't take this route anymore. Ever.

Oh God. He's taking me to that grassy pasture where I'd hung upside-down, still strapped in my seatbelt while Mama and Noli-Belle died in front of me. I promised myself that night when the firemen finally cut me free that I'd never, ever go back there. Now, he has the audacity to drag me here against my will. My fingers clasp the door handle as I consider tucking and rolling out the side of the car. But that won't happen. He knows it, and I know it. Fear pins me to the seat.

That is until the familiar stretch of road comes into sight, and my switch flips. Paralyzing fear gives way to explosive anger. My hands grapple with the seatbelt as a high-pitched whirring crams in my brain. I can't come back here. I won't. And the only way to stop that is by stopping Dad. I unstrap myself and reach to-ward him—to choke him or knock him out of the way, I have no idea—but his arm slams against my chest, trapping me against the vinyl interior.

"This is for your own good!"

"I hate you! I really hate you!"

The Explorer pulls slowly onto the shoulder, gravel crunching beneath the tires. My fingers rake over his skin, leaving red raised streaks in their wake. He's unfazed, his hold strong and unrelenting, while I squirm like a worm on a fishhook.

He shifts to park, then leans across the console to finagle his grip securely on my shoulders. "You don't hate me. You're scared."

"I do hate you...for bringing me here!" My fingers once again wrap around the door handle, and with a sharp pull, the door flails open. Halfway dumped onto the grass, I wrench away from his grip and scramble to my feet in a full sprint toward the tree line opposite the accident scene. But Dad, whose legs are twice as long as mine, catches up easily, grabs my arm, and jerks me back to his chest. I pummel my fists against his shirt with an endless stream of profanities and garbled words, but as the urgency burning in my chest dissolves, the screams morph into uncontrollable sobs. My shoulders heave under the heft of his arms. My face smooshes into the cottony folds of his polo, wet with tears.

In the background, a vague recognition registers in my brain that he's moving me somewhere, maneuvering toward another location, and my feet fumble along at his guidance. It's betrayal at every step. When we stop, the quiet blankets us as if we're in a vacuum. The only sound being my own heartbeat echoing in my head, a hollow *thump-thump-thump* against my eardrums.

Dad pushes me back but keeps his fingers thrust firmly into my biceps. He puts some space between us, and the hot August breeze filters through the gap. "Open your eyes."

The sobs subside, but tears continue to squeeze out the corners of my tightly-clamped eyes. After spending the last year trying to purge my brain of the memories of this place, there is no way in hell I am going to open them up and usher all the pain back in.

"No." The word doesn't come out right. It's quiet and breathy, as if there's not enough air in my lungs to actually formulate the sound. I clamp my hands over my face, vigorously shaking my head from side to side the way I did as a child in the throes of a tantrum. "I can't."

"Can't? Or won't?"

A shudder tears up my spine. Never mind the fact we're standing on cursed ground, the very place half our family died. Sure, let's play semantics instead. That makes perfect sense.

"There's a difference, CJ," he continues. His voice is heavy, and every word comes out deliberately, as if there's supposed to be a period after each one.

"You brought me here for an English lesson?" My weak voice is strong and loud again, until I'm screaming at him through clenched teeth. My fists are balled at my temples.

But despite my teeter-totter walk along the thin edge of falling the freak apart, Dad remains calm. Too calm. Too patient. He's so unlike the man who left me behind a few months ago. "You won't open your eyes because the reality scares you. But you have to. You can only move on when you acknowledge the truth...and then accept it."

Accept it. He's says it like it's synonymous with coming to terms with a failing grade or one of those über-horrible haircuts where they totally do the opposite of what you're expecting. But how can I accept the fact Mama and Noli-Belle are dead—and even worse, that I killed them?

I quit writhing in his grip. His fingers relax as he moves one hand to my chin, cupping it and tilting my face towards his. "Look at me."

A little peek and the waning sunlight floods in, swathing Dad's face in coppery softness. It's like looking in a mirror. We're so much alike, more than the golden-brown freckles dotting the bridge of our noses or the knotted wisps of auburn hair. More than I've ever realized before.

"I'm sorry. If only I'd done things different, they might still be here."

"You have to stop this—"

"I read the accident report," I mumble, looking at the ground. "I overcorrected. We wouldn't have flipped into that tree if—"

"See?" He shakes his finger in my face. When I glance up, his lips spread into a grin. "That right there tells me all I need to know."

Grief has completely consumed his rational brain, which explains the changes I sense in him—the weird calm then and the illogical exuberance now. His gaze locks on mine. His eyes spread so wide I'm nervous. A maniacal smile is plastered on his face.

"I don't underst—"

"If."

"If what?"

"You said 'we wouldn't have flipped if.' That's wrong thinking, CJ. There is no if. There's only what actually happened. The rest is conjecture we can't possibly know."

This all sounds too familiar. It's the same old song-and-dance, only this time it's coming from Dad's mouth and not my shrink-extraordinaire, Dr. Zhou. "That's therapy talk, Dad. The truth is if I hadn't overcorrected, then we wouldn't have flipped into that tree."

"So that's what this all boils down to in your mind?" He tilts his head and threads his arms across his chest. "Well then, think about this: If I wasn't tired from work, then I would've been driving, and this would be a non-issue." He pauses and shrugs. "And for that matter, if my boss hadn't been a real jerk that day, then maybe I wouldn't have been so worn out. And if he hadn't been in the throes of a bitter divorce, then maybe he wouldn't have been in such a bad mood. So, if I'm calculating this right, my boss's ex-wife is the one who's really responsible for the wreck, right?"

"Quit being ridiculous, Dad."

"Don't you get it? You and I have spent nearly a year blaming ourselves for what happened when the honest-to-God truth is no one's to blame. It was an accident, and sometimes an accident is just that—an elaborate concoction of events that converge into tragedy. No one ever wanted this to happen. Not you. Not me." He hesitates, clearing his throat, before he tacks on one last name. "Not even Jacob Lanford."

The mention of his name, the way Dad casually drops it into the conversation, is a bomb ready to detonate. An involuntary scowl crimps the edges of my lips as I spit out his name. "Jacob? You mean Mr. Lanford, the one who ran us off the road?"

The first time I'd seen him had been the only time. He knelt on the ground outside my shattered window, yelling about how he'd called for help and telling me everything would be okay. He was wrong, and I never saw him again. The police arrived and ushered him away. Two days later, when he was officially charged with vehicular homicide, I refused to watch the local broadcasts or look at the online news, terrified of seeing his face again. Looking into the eyes of the man whose carelessness set the entire tragedy in motion and not physically imploding was an impossibility for me. If there's anyone I hate more than myself for what happened, it's him.

"It was an accident."

Seriously? Dad is making excuses for him? "Yeah, he accidentally texted while he was driving. Oops, the phone fell right into his hand. I wonder how many times that'd happened before?"

"Never, actually."

I snort, shaking my head. "Yeah...right."

"No, really. He'd never done it before."

"And how would you know?"

"Because I talked to him. I went to see him."

His words ignite in me like a firecracker, exploding sparks in every direction. I'm sure they'll shoot from my eyes and burn Dad to a crisp. "You *what*?"

"I had to. I needed to hear what he had to say, and believe me, it changed things."

"It changes nothing!" I lunge at him, pounding my fists into his chest, until a dizzying array of stars swirl through my line of sight. I have to squat to keep my balance.

A shiver crawls through me as the memories filter in. The bright set of headlights in our lane as we entered the curve. The complete sense of slow motion when the awful realization hit just a split-second before the crunch of the fender. The weird quiet when the car was flipping that allowed me to concentrate on minute details, like how a lipstick tube from Mama's purse bounced on the dash or the exact number of rollovers we endured. I just kept repeating to myself the entire time: dirt, dirt, dirt, sky, sky, sky. Three times, ending with a deafening crunch of metal slicing through the silence. My life never flashed before my eyes.

But maybe that's because I wasn't the one dying.

Dad continues, his voice still easy and measured. "Jacob has two daughters, four years apart like you and your sister were. The youngest one has a lot of health problems, and on the night of the accident, his wife had called him in a panic because she was having a seizure. He was on his way home when he sideswiped y'all."

Well, he sounds like the world's-greatest-father-material for sure. Imagine his poor wife having to track him down to update him on their sick daughter. "If she was so sick, why wasn't he at home? And why was a stupid text more important than his family?"

Dad squats beside me and runs his hand down my arm with a chuckle. "You sound like I did a couple months ago, but it's not fair to make assumptions. Medical bills were piling up, so he took on a second job. The text was from his wife telling him the paramedics had arrived."

So maybe Jacob Lanford *was* a good father—a great one—who made a bad decision. But I can't accept fate for what it is. My mind can't understand how bad things happen to good people, and it's only too easy to believe it must all be the result of something nefarious.

But it's not.

Mama was right all those years ago when I caught her in the bathroom, tissues smashed over her face as she sobbed into them. As a pediatric nurse, she'd taken care of hundreds of kids, but every time one got a terminal diagnosis, she'd hole herself away for a few hours. Occupational hazards of a woman who cared too much for those around her. It was her best and worst feature all rolled into one. We knew to let her have her space, but that night I walked in and put my arms around her. That's when she said it, the very piece of wisdom running through my head now. "You can't make sense of the senseless, CJ. Bad things happen, and we may never know why. It's how we move forward that matters."

I stare at Dad, the tears pooling in my eyes a mirror to what I see in his.

"It was an accident," he says. "But now, like our family, the Lanfords are faced with losing a critical part of theirs."

The thought of another kid losing their parent, to know the heartbreak I'd faced in the past year, rips at my insides. But the situation's bigger than us. "I hate it for his family, but the lawyers have to sort it out."

"Not necessarily," he says. "We still have to testify next Friday."

A lump grows in my throat as Dad's eyes bore into me. "What are you asking me to do?"

"It's not what I'm asking. It's what Mama and Noli-Belle are trying to show us."

He pulls me to standing and turns my body toward the accident site, forcing me to look at the place I'd been so careful to avoid. Until now.

One look steals my breath. There, in front of the deeply-gashed pecan tree, two makeshift memorials stand in the grass, wooden crosses with Mama's and Noli-Belle's names crudely carved in the horizontal piece. And all around them, so thick the grass is blocked out, is a stand of orange daylilies, tall, proud and waving in the breeze—beauty disrupting the somber scene.

I walk over and run my fingers across the rubbery-smooth petals. The spicy-sweet aroma swirls in the air around me. "Where did these come from?"

"They appeared and kept multiplying all summer." Dad steps beside me and links his arm through mine. "You think maybe they're trying to tell us something?"

A strange warmth encircles me, like a blanket around my shoulders, and I realize Mama and Noli-Belle are here hand-delivering a message. I've lost too much this past year—my family, my friends, my first love—to let this cycle continue. I can be the change. I can be the one who makes sense of the senseless.

With a smile, I lean into his arm. "Yeah, Dad. I do."

Chapter Twenty-Seven

Maybe it *is* noble, but the whole "making sense of the senseless" thing obviously doesn't come with a handy instruction guide. Translating everything from earlier into some tangible sort of action has me stumped. All the thoughts and feelings refuse to bend into elegant words. Instead, they pile up like a set of clunky Legos whose holes don't align.

Maybe it's because being in my own bedroom again reminds me of how it used to be. Maybe it's because every five seconds I have to remind myself to focus and stop wondering about Jett or if he's thinking of me.

"I give up," I grumble, ripping the notebook paper from my spiral binder, then wad it into a crinkly ball. I chuck it at the trashcan beside my desk.

Her fingers land on my shoulder with so little pressure I barely sense them through my shirt. "That's why I'm here. To make sure that doesn't happen."

"Em?" We've been talking again for weeks, through late-night phone calls and texts, but seeing her face to face, being able to reach out and physically touch her, my heart flutters in my chest.

A pillow sticks out from under her left arm, and there's a duffel bag on her right shoulder. "Your dad called. He thought you might need a friend tonight."

Score another one for Dad and all his recent Yoda-like wisdom. He's backing up this new leaf he turned over with some serious momentum. If anyone can get me through this day, it's the one friend who's been by my side since first grade. Even when I didn't deserve her.

"I know today's been pretty emotional. We don't have to talk," she says, sitting on the corner of my bed. "We can just hang out or watch TV."

But suddenly I do want to talk. About anything but the accident. Her life, my life, and everything we've missed. "Tell me," I whisper.

"Tell you what?"

"Everything."

We fall back into our old patterns with ease. I relax against my upholstered headboard, pillow clutched to my chest, and she lies across my bedspread, describing how Trent showed up at her door the morning after he left Edisto with a dozen purple (Em's favorite color) roses in hand and officially asked her to be his girlfriend. She pulls at her necklace, and Trent's class ring bobs in the lamp light. I force a smile, instinctively fiddling with my own chain, now naked against my skin. When Jett's ring was on it, there was a heft to it, a constant reminder of him. Now, I tend to forget it's even there. It feels so empty.

Em's gaze burns holes through me. She cocks her head and gnaws the inside of her cheek.

"What?"

"You were daydreaming. Anything...or anyone...you'd like to talk about?"

"What's there to say?"

"Oh, I think you have a lot to say." She scoots forward on the covers and grabs my hand. "You shared things with him this summer. He revived you, and even though you haven't said it, I think you love him."

And there it is. The exact thing that's been circulating in my thoughts since I left Edisto. I did love Jett. My heart butterflies its beat. I still love him. But I never told him.

Tears well along my lower lashes, threatening to spill over.

"Have y'all talked?"

I shake my head. Five days have passed since I dropped his ring on that bed table and ended things. I was the one who'd slammed the door on us, but it stings so much when his silence verifies it.

"Have you at least stalked his social media?"

"The opposite actually." Seeing him will only twist the knife in my gut. Jett and I aren't over because I *wanted* to lose him; we're over because I was *afraid* of losing him. The logic is all messed up, but there's a thread of rationality in there somewhere. "I can't."

"What if he's posting about how much he's missing you?"

What if he's not?

"Nah, he's got a big race coming up. Too much other stuff to focus on."

"You're totally underestimating yourself." She leans over me to retrieve my phone from the nightstand and drops it in my lap. "Just check. Get it over with. You know you want to."

I blow out a breath, clicking open the app, then tap on his name. Four new posts. The first three are tagged from Rachel's page. Jett's wearing sunglasses, propped against his racecar with a deadly sneer and the entourage in tow—Jett's dad, Rachel, Trévon, and even Dani. Her passive aggressive post comment hurts. *It takes more than THAT to keep this boy down. #winning #champions #RamseyRacing*

My stomach sinks like an elevator plunging ten floors. Em reads over my shoulder. She clicks her tongue, then mutters under her breath, "Bitch."

"You have no idea." I manage a giggle, despite the nagging urge to vomit all over my bed. It's bad enough for Jett to be pissed at me for ending things. It's worse to know Rachel's in his ear, poisoning everything we once had.

Em points to the fourth picture. "So that's Gin and Bo?"

I stare at the picture of Jett sitting on the Johnsons' rec room sofa. Gin and Bo are squeezed on either side of him. What I wouldn't give to jump back in time and be there with them. With Em along for the ride, of course.

"That's them...the gang." I nearly choke on the words.

"I know you miss your friends."

"I do. They're great. You'd totally like Gin, she's..." Beside me, Em's silent, gnawing her lip and looking off into space. "Em?"

She sighs. "I'm a tad jealous, okay? I mean, that tone in your voice? That used to be how you described us."

"It's still us. No one can take your place, Em." I nudge her. "You and me, we know everything there is to know about each other. Maybe that was the problem."

"Huh?"

"Gin didn't know much about me, so when I was messed up, she didn't have any expectations about how I should be. It was like having a blank slate. I thought I could erase the past. Start fresh. But it turns out the closer Gin and I got, the more I missed you. The more I realized I couldn't erase us. And I didn't want to."

A smile creeps over her lips. "Aw, you big mushy baby." Em playfully shoves my arm. "Well then, I guess this Gin's a pretty good girl. I'd love to meet her someday."

Someday is a day that'll never come. I've burned all the bridges in Edisto, left my friends without any sort of good-bye, deserted Memaw, and drove away the one I fell in love with. And now, looking at their posts, it's easy to see, at least for them, life goes on.

Without me.

I shrug. "Y'all would've hit it off."

"Have you talked to her? At least sent an email?"

I wouldn't even know where to start.

Em lips curled in that pitiful puppy dog way. "How 'bout I help with that?" she offers. I don't know how to explain that co-herent, eloquent words are not my forte today, but before I can, Em hops off the bed and grabs my notebook from the desk. "Use this to write a rough draft," she says, tossing it to me. A folded piece of paper falls out and flits to the rug. She picks it up and the paper crinkles as she unfolds it. An image of wild camellias dance across a leafy vine. "What's this?"

"Nothing." I grimace and drop my eyes to my hands. These unexpected reminders are bullets.

"I can tell by your face it's not nothing."

"Jett drew it." It's the first time I've said his name out loud today. What used to roll off my tongue so freely now lumbers off in a bitter, stinging mess.

"Flowers on some kind of a twisted branch?" She scrunches her nose; it was the same look she always had in Trig class when she tried to understand secants and cosecants.

"They're camellias on a vine. It's a tattoo design."

"It's kind of weird shape for a tattoo, right?" She presses the paper against her abdomen as if trying to imagine how it'd look flowing across her belly button.

"No...it's actually kinda perfect. But not for there. It was designed for a specific location."

"Oh...kay." She drags it out, her way of saying *tell me more.*

"There's something I need to show you. Then you'll understand." I stand up, and in one quick move, pull my T-shirt over my head and toss it on the desk chair. Em's bewildered gaze turns to wide-eyed awareness when she spots the silvery-pink scar. She reaches toward it, but her fingers never actually make contact. Instead, they hover in the air above it. "My reminder of the accident. Jett said if I dressed it up a bit, maybe it'd be therapeutic."

Silence. Em says nothing, just continues to stare. I'm not used to showing people this part of myself. Dad refused to look at it for any length of time, and Memaw and Jett were surprisingly chill about the whole mess. But this—whatever this is from Em—is one step from torture. "Em...what is it?"

"I think..." She begins nodding, her smile returning. "You should do it. In fact, I'll take you myself. Next Thursday, the day before the trial, you're getting your tattoo, CJ."

"You think?"

"I know." She steps forward, lining up the paper with the scar. "What Jett did for you is perfect."

Beside me, Em snores, a slight breathy gurgling against the pillow sham. After hours of talking, she finally passed out facedown. But I can't sleep. Instead, I think about Mama and Noli-Belle, about Em and how we found our way back to each

251

other, but mostly, I think about Jett and how he gave me the courage to love again. How he made me believe there was more life to live. I lost sight of that, let fear creep back in, and it'd cost me everything. But if there's one thing I can do to ensure my love for Jett isn't in vain, it's learn from my mistakes and go forward with an eager, unafraid heart.

Without waking her, I ease from the sheets and pad across the rug to my desk. The click of the lamp sends an orange warmth across my notebook and the flowery tattoo design. I unzip my purse and shove the paper inside, then pick up a fresh pen from the stainless-steel holder on the desktop. Important documents should always be written with crisp, flowing ink. And this might be the most important thing I ever put on paper.

Chapter Twenty-Eight

The inside looks like I thought it would. Lots of granite columns in the lobby, marble floors and oversized dark-stained wooden doors, way taller than any normal human. It's like everything has been expertly designed to make you feel insignificant. But despite the grandiose building, nothing makes me feel quite as small as comprehending the gravity of what I have to do and the implications it will have for everyone.

I thought I had at least another day to prepare, but when the lawyer contacted us and said the judge had called a special session one day early, my meager confidence shriveled. Sleep eluded me last night as I stared at the ceiling, begging Mama and Noli Belle for strength.

The courtroom door squeaks open, and Dad, Em, and I walk down the middle row in single file and take the first three seats on the right. Jacob Lanford is already seated at the defendant's table, hunched together with his lawyer. He sneaks a few quick glances at us over his shoulder. Behind them, in the row immediately to our left, a middle-aged woman with salt-and-pepper hair pulled back in a messy bun and two girls, the oldest looking to be about twelve, sit with their hands folded in their laps, eyes glued to the floor. The courtroom is no place for kids, but when the youngest girl gets up, kisses her fingers, and plants them against Jacob's cheek, I get it. Family. Love. Support. The eight-year-old is well versed in what's taken me a year to understand.

The door swings wide again and the prosecutor walks in, stopping to shake Dad's hand and give a slight nod, an affirmation everything's a-go. He slides behind the mahogany desk and eases his briefcase onto the top.

When the bailiff requests we all rise, my knees buckle, and I grab hold of the wooden railing like a crutch. Sensing my anxiety, Em interlaces her fingers with mine, physically assisting me to stay upright. The judge takes the bench, signals for everyone to sit, then clears his throat and looks at the jury.

"Early yesterday morning, I met with the prosecution and defense in my chambers to discuss a highly unusual request. It is the nature of this request that inspired me to call this special session. I appreciate everyone rearranging their schedules accordingly."

The judge glances up from the bench, but no one moves. The atmosphere is heavy as he continues. "The prosecution presented a letter written by the key witness, Miss Camelia Ainsworth, that addresses the court. She has requested to read it aloud. The letter has now been read and reviewed by both myself and the defense, and upon doing so, it has been decided to grant said request. With that being said, the court recognizes Miss Camelia Jayne Ainsworth."

The judge nods in my direction and holds the folded white paper over the front of his bench. I will my legs not to give way as a *clack-clack-clacking* echoes around the room. I'm unsure if the noise is coming from the hard bottoms of my sandals or my wobbly knees knocking together.

The paper unfolds easily in my fingers. The black type stares back at me, representing my innermost thoughts and feelings soon to become public record. I take a deep breath and run my tongue along my teeth, trying to generate some degree of moisture in my cotton-dry mouth. With a shaky voice, I begin reading.

To Whom It May Concern:

Eleven months ago, my life changed in the blink of an eye on a twisty two-lane road. What started out as a night of fun family time ended in a terrible tragedy that still haunts me to this day. Closing my eyes each night only means one more opportunity to hear my sister's screams or see my mama's lifeless stare. They echo in the quiet moments of rest and even in my waking thoughts when sleep's elusive.

That day changed me. It changed my dad, my family, my relationships. And not just in our family, but in Mr. Lanford's as well. But something—or someone—didn't change. Two people will remain forever frozen in time. Consistent, steady, true in life, and now in death.

Eleanor Kate Ainsworth and Magnolia Belle Ainsworth. The people they were, the passions they had, the love in their souls still linger here. When I need direction, they are my compass, my true north. And they are the reason I'm here today.

But for you to understand my request, you must first understand these people, because without them—who they were—I wouldn't be standing before you the person I am now. So, on behalf of the new Camelia Jayne "Cami" Ainsworth, let me enlighten you.

Eleanor Kate Ainsworth—always Mama to me and my sister, Ellie to my dad, and Wonder Woman to the hundreds of people she touched during her years as a pediatric nurse—was my hero. She had an incredible heart for all people. She loved gardenias and baking three-layer cakes and being a wife and mother. She used to tell me to fight hard and love harder. Always forgive and be free. Stand for something or fall for anything. But mostly, she just told me to live, because the ride is awesome but all too short. She had no idea how short hers would be.

But compared to Noli-Belle, she lived a hundred lives. Twelve years. One hundred forty-four months to be exact. That's all she got. But man, she made them count. My sister was thirsty—for knowledge, understanding, and her place in this world. So many hours she'd lay on her back outside

255

in the grass with that astronomy book, searching the skies for star patterns and mysteries of the great beyond. She noticed everything. She marveled at everything. She questioned everything. She wanted to be the first woman on Mars. Fearless. Brave. Believing. Four years younger than me, she stood head and shoulders above me. The world has surely missed out on the best she still had to offer.

I could be mad they're gone. Angry, bitter, and belligerent. I could shake my fist at God and everyone around me, curse fate and point fingers about why these two incredible people were taken away. I could do that. I have done that. But no more.

There's been a lot of talk about who's to blame. The truth? We can twist, fold and scrutinize every detail and only discover the blame lies with everyone and no one. It's a whirlwind of circumstances and decisions that mishmashed together in what became the worst day of my life, my dad's life, even Mr. Lanford's life. I've spent the last year wondering what if. What if we'd never left home in the first place? What if we'd taken a different route? What if I hadn't been the one driving the car? It's an endless, maddening stream that's terrorized me, while outwardly, I've shoved everyone away.

But then this summer happened, and I found out love can't fix our problems, but it can heal our souls. I learned to love again, open my heart, let people in despite my pain and loss. Sure, I'm different now—we all are—but that doesn't mean I'm shattered and no good. And if I keep letting fear and guilt dictate my life, then I might as well have died along with them.

Mama and Noli-Belle wouldn't want that. On the roadside where they died, amidst the memorials built in their honor, lilies are blooming. In the aftermath of tragedy, there's beauty. After the worst days of our lives, come the most joyful ones if we are open to the possibilities. I believe that now.

This was an accident—a terrible culmination of decisions, actions, and circumstances, and we'd give anything for a do-over. But that's the one thing about life, right? There are no do-overs, and living in the past or cramming ourselves into a shell of who we used to be only creates more heartache from tragedy.

This isn't the answer. Love is the answer. Forgiveness is the answer.

That is why I come before the court, imploring the powers that be to grant leniency to Mr. Lanford. He has a beautiful family at home waiting for a husband and daddy to return. My mama and sister will never come home, but theirs can.

Please choose to create beauty in the aftermath of this tragedy and restore the Lanford family. It's what I want. It's what Dad wants. It's what my mama and sister would want, too.

Sincerely,

Camelia Jayne Ainsworth

There's no sound in the courtroom, not even the shuffle of people shifting in their chairs. I lift my eyes to the crowd and immediately land on the oldest Lanford daughter. She reminds me so much of Noli-Belle. Her squared shoulders and strong chin tremble ever so slightly. She doesn't cry, obstinate in the face of a family crisis. Our connection is magnetic. I don't move until she does; a small grin breaches her lips, and without a sound, she mouths two simple words: *Thank you.*

After a few blank seconds, the judge breaks the silence.

"Miss Ainsworth, are you finished?" His stern grimace from earlier fades, replaced by a new tenderness that also resonates in his tone. But not from pity. No; if I'm reading him correctly, he almost seems proud.

"Yes, Your Honor."

"Very well then. The court has heard what you have to say. With that, let's take a ten-minute recess."

The pounding gavel cues my feet to move, and I take off down the aisle, through the gigantic doors, and all the way to the gray stone steps out front. Dad and Em catch up, hot on my heels.

"CJ!" Dad grabs my arm, turning me toward him. "Are you okay?"

There are some things in my life that'll never be *okay*. I'll never get over the loss of Mama and Noli-Belle. I'll never forget my summer with Memaw, and Jett will always be my first love. I don't know how to forget those things, but now I know I don't have to. They're all a part of what makes me who I am, and they're all parts of who I'll become. There's no way of knowing the future, but maybe that's the point. All we can do is put our-selves out there, be willing to lay our hearts on the line, and see where it goes.

Dad and Em crowd around me, their eyes big and searching mine as if waiting on the coming meltdown. Only there isn't one. I wrap my arms around them, tugging them both close to me, and laugh. "I'm good."

"Suddenly she's got it all figured out," Dad laughs. "What do you think, Em? Is she good?"

Em looks over at me and winks. "She's getting there."

"I just need a little time," I say, giving them another squeeze. "And the people I love most."

"Exactly!" Dad wags his finger in my face. "So, let's get you home."

Chapter Twenty-Nine

The *dink-doonk, dink-doonk, dink-doonk* of Dad's blinker signals our arrival. As the engine's hum dies away, I stare up at my bedroom window. Life here used to be so good. Can it ever be that way again? I don't know, but it won't be for a lack of trying.

After court, Dad dropped Em off at her house. She'd been with me nearly every moment since arriving back in Greenville, and as I watched her wave good-bye, a pang of nerves clawed my insides. Dad said this was something we needed to do together. Just the two of us. There was also a long lecture where he mentioned something about a prodigal son, but I sort of zoned out after five minutes.

Dad eyes me from the driver's seat. "Now that everything's over, are you glad to be home?"

"You have no idea. Turns out this is exactly what I needed all along."

"Then what are we waiting for?" I half-expect another speech, but he only smiles and steps out of the car. I meet him at the bottom of the steps as he reaches for my hand. We can't predict how all this will go, but at least we're facing it together.

What I don't expect is the front door swinging open before we even get to the steps. Memaw struts out onto the porch, hands on her hips. "Like father, like daughter. So, what're you two hooligans doing in Edisto?"

"I came to apologize, Memaw."

Dad lets go of my hand and wraps his arm around my shoulder, hauling me in tight to his side. "We both did…Mom."

At first, she's expressionless, which in itself is a rarity for a woman whose emotions plaster themselves across her face with no filter, but then a smile creeps around the corners of her lips.

"'Bout damn time. Come on in, my pain-in-the-ass, prodigal children."

Thirty minutes later, Memaw and Dad are actually talking like civilized human beings, so I sneak away to my room. Everything's the same as when I left, including the "Memaw's House" artwork. How true that stupid picture is. Everything I needed to know I definitely learned at Memaw's this summer. How to trust. How to live. How to love.

I hold my breath and walk to the closet door, opening it slowly to peek inside. When I see it's still there, I exhale. The slinky blue dress hangs there with a purpose. It's what I want to wear when I see Jett again. I undress and toss my clothes on the bed, then swipe the dress from its hanger and slip it over my head. The gauzy fabric skims my body, its feather-lite touch flowy and summery. And there, under the spaghetti strap and above the low neckline, my camellia-covered scar is out for the world to see.

And for the first time, I'm proud of it.

In the den, Memaw and Dad are still talking and shuffling through some papers. I clear my throat as I walk into the room. Both of them stop to stare. Memaw crosses the room and runs her finger along the strap with a smile. "This dress looks just like I thought it would."

"Thank you, Memaw," I whisper, quickly pulling her in for a hug. She doesn't answer, just squeezes me harder. Dad gets up from the couch and joins us, his arms circling around both our shoulders. Somehow my grade-A dysfunctional family finally got its shit together.

Now that's settled, other things need my attention. "Guys, I hate to break up this happy family moment, but can someone give me a ride? There's somewhere I need to be."

"You mean someone you need to see." Memaw winks and walks to the foyer table, grabs her purse, then looks at Dad. "Pierce, take your old mom out to dinner, and on the way, drop CJ off at the racetrack."

Dad drops me off at the front gate and I head out to the track to see if I can find Jett and salvage any part of what we started this summer. I'm not even into the thick of the crowds when two familiar figures catch my attention.

My stomach is lead when I walk behind them and tap her on the shoulder. "Gin?"

It takes a second for recognition to register on her face. When it does, her mouth drops open wide. "CJ? Oh my God, CJ!" She lunges forward and wraps me into her arms, nearly choking me with her blond ponytail. "I missed you. Don't you ever leave me like that again!"

"I missed you, too." Through the wild strands of her hair stuck across my face, Bo leans in and smiles. "Hey Bo," I mumble to him over Gin's shoulder.

This kind of reception is not anything like I anticipated. I'd left them high and dry like I did Memaw and Jett. But Memaw'd forgiven me without a hitch, and now Gin and Bo are smiling and hugging me without a second thought. As happy as I am, I can't help cringing over the twisting in my gut. Will Jett be so excited to see me?

"It's about time you got your ass back here. Where'd you go?" Bo laughs. He steps in closer and fixes his eyes on my bare shoulder. "You look different, and...you got a weird tattoo?"

"It's not weird," Gin protests. "They're camellias. Like her name."

Before the usual brother-sister banter commences, I cut to the chase. "I'll explain it later. Right now, I—"

Before I can finish the question, a shrill voice yells my name out in the crowd. It doesn't take long to figure out who it is. To my left, a flash of bubble-gum-pink hair breaks out from the fans. Rachel charges at me, her shoes slapping the pavement with loud thuds.

"What the hell are you doing here? This is the last thing Jett needs, for you to come slinking back in here like—"

Someone standing behind me—someone I didn't know was there—steps around me and reaches out to grab her arm, holding it steady. Rachel's eyes widen as she shrinks like a scolded cat.

Mr. Ramsey clears his throat, and not in the *I've-got-a-cold* sort of way. More like an *I-mean-business* kind of throat clearing. "Rachel, stop." His voice is hard, but as she begins to protest, he throws in the final shot. "You're not needed here. Leave."

As Rachel runs, disappearing into the crowd, I grab Mr. Ramsey's arm.

He stares at me. "You're back in Edisto." It's not a question. It's almost like he's not even surprised, and I can't help wondering if he's happy to see me or if he'd rather I'd never come back.

I swallow hard. "Mr. Ramsey, may I see Jett?"

"No. You can't."

My breath catches in my throat at his words, and I have to stare at the ground in order not to lose my balance. Everything spins. He hates me, and that means Jett hates me. Just when vomiting seems inevitable, Mr. Ramsey tips my chin up with his finger. His stern glare melts into a soft smile. "He's not here."

"But...the qualifications?" I glance back at a car lapping the track.

"As last year's champion, he's assured a spot in the race. Might not be a good one, but that's a chance he's willing to take." He reaches out and pats my shoulder. "Besides, he had somewhere else to be."

None of this makes sense. It's not like Jett to blow off racing for just anything— especially for the championship. This is what he's been working toward all summer.

"He's gone to see you, CJ. But the real question is, why are *you* here?" The voice is unfamiliar, but when I turn around, I immediately recognize the face. She walks toward me, flanked on one side by Jenniston as if they're the best of friends.

"My court date was moved up. It's over," I mumble, the words barely slipping through the confusion muddling my brain. "Wait...you're Jett's mom...Janice." I bob my finger in her direction as a teenage boy steps out from behind her, waving shyly at me. "Hey, Buck."

What the hell has gone on these last two weeks? Janice must notice my furrowed brow because she reaches out and pats my shoulder, her voice soft and full of honey. "I'm back in his life...because of you. He sent the email you convinced him to write," she says as Jenniston strokes her arm. "You changed him—you changed our family—and Jett's not willing to give you up. Not anymore. He knew tomorrow would be hard for you, so he was willing to sacrifice this to be there for you."

Mr. Ramsey shares a knowing smile with Janice. "The boy's smarter than I ever was. He takes care of the important things. It took me years to understand that." He brings Jenniston's hand to his lips. "I realized I'd been too hard on him, guilting him for not putting all of his attention into racing, when it's you, CJ, who taught him life is about more than this track. I apologized for not seeing him for who he really is."

The implication of their words soak in. Jett still cares about me, so much he'd gamble on the championship to stand by me without even knowing how I'd react. My body aches to wrap my arms around him and swear never to leave again. "I have to see him."

Jenniston nods, her rosy lips smiling wide. "He's at the house getting his things, so you better get going if you're gonna catch him."

I glance at my watch. "Bo, can you give me a ride?"

He frowns, shaking his head. "I can't...I'm working the pits today. Just call him and tell him you're on the way."

Gin snaps her head toward him, eyes flaming and hands clenched on her hips. "Call him? CALL HIM! These two are making all these romantic gestures and you want them to reunite over a piece of freakin' plastic? This is exactly why you only date online. No. Just no." She stabs her finger with a firm order. "Give her your keys, Bo."

Gin's dreamy, romantic, made-in-the-movies scenario makes sense. If this isn't the time for a grand gesture, I don't know what is.

"Do what?"

263

"You heard her. Hand 'em over." I stretch out my hand, palm up and fingers wiggling.

Bo huffs out a loud breath, pulls his keys from his pocket, and slams them into my hand. "I must really like y'all."

I clutch them in my fingers, the metal cold against my skin, and lean forward to kiss his cheek. "We like you, too, Bo. Y'all wish me luck," I yell over my shoulder as I take off toward the parking lot.

Bo's Bronco looks more like a tank parked in its corner space. The top's off, so other than the windshield, it's completely open-air. Baptism by fire, all right. *You can do this, CJ. For Jett.*

I hoist myself into the driver's seat, heart thumping a mile a minute, insert the key, and turn before I can think about it too much. The engine rumbles to life, vibrating the steering wheel as I shift into drive and drop the accelerator with so much force, the tires squeal as I peel out onto the main road. In the rearview mirror, I catch a brief glimpse of Bo's face. It's possible he's regretting this decision already.

The coastal breeze wafts in all around me, and compared to Jett's car, super tight and cramped on the inside, Bo's is much wider and open. It's uncomfortable how I have to lean forward and stretch out my leg super far to keep it pressed firmly on the gas. My therapist's words loop through my head. Being uncomfortable means adaptation, which leads to growth. I was never willing to grow beyond the grief before. Jett gave me a reason.

Love. For him. For life. For myself.

And love can do a lot of things, but it can't solve problems. It was stupid to expect it should. It's not a magic potion. I had to decide to move past the pain and make logical, rational choices about my future. Maybe love gives me the strength to do that. It makes me believe in myself, in others. It gives me something to fight for, live for. Love is the motivator, but I...I am in charge. And I'm tired of throwing my future away. Loving Jett brought happiness back to my life. Loving him made sense of the senseless.

The twelve miles back to the island go surprisingly easy with little traffic and no major freak-outs on my part. Up ahead, the

Ramsey compound springs into view, along with a quick glimpse of Jett before he ducks into his car. As it starts to reverse down the drive, I stomp on the gas, sprinting to the gate's edge, and park perpendicular to the drive.

His Challenger screeches to a halt, and Jett jumps out, waving his arms. "What the hell, Bo? Get outta my—" His eyes land on me and he drops his arms, standing there in shocked silence before he mutters, "Cami?"

Butterflies. It's been two weeks since I've heard it, and it still gets me.

I open the door and jump out onto the sand-laden street, and he meets me at the front fender. "Hey, Jett."

Standing this close to him, launching myself into his arms seems the natural inclination. But Gin's right. This is our romantic movie moment, complete with the oceany breeze rippling through his hair. We stare at each other, barely blinking, while the delicious tension charges like electricity bouncing between us.

"You drove?"

"Yeah, I did."

"Why? How?"

"Because of you. I had to get to you, Jett."

"I…I knew you could do it, but…you were still so scared."

"I quit being afraid. Of everything. The fear cost me too much. Including you."

It's the first time he breaks eye contact and stares at his feet. "When you left…"

I take the cue and step forward, so close our bodies are only inches apart, and take his hand. His palms are sweaty like mine, and our skin slides across each other's in a reunion that shoots chills through my veins. Chill bumps pop up, head to toe, despite the summer heat. "I know. I don't expect things to be like they were or for you to feel the same. But I have something to say, so let me get it out while I still can."

Jett brings his gaze back to me, and for a minute, I'm lost, distracted by his lips and the intense desire to press mine against his. I swallow hard, refocusing, and continue. "I thought I could walk away, save myself from more scars. It turns out, the worst pain came from not being with you."

Jett narrows his eyes and shakes his head. His fingers squeeze mine harder than before. "I never wanted that."

My heart sinks to my stomach. I've been such a fool. "I know, and I'm sorry. For everything."

"I'm not." His words and sly smile catch me off guard. He continues, "I couldn't fix you any more than you could fix me. It took you leaving for me to realize that, and so I decided it was time to figure some shit out."

So that's what Janice meant. "I heard. I ran into your mom and Buck at the track when I went there looking for you. I still can't believe you're missing the qualifiers."

"I tried to go. I sat there all morning, but all I could think about was you, alone and upset in a courtroom tomorrow. I just...I couldn't do it. So what if I'll have a sucky position for the race? Who cares? You needed me more." He shrugs and then narrows his eyes. "But, why are you here when court is tomorrow?"

"Turns out we both did some soul-searching while I was gone. The judge called a special session this morning, and he dismissed the case on account of a letter I wrote requesting leniency. People deserve second chances, right?"

I know I want one—a second chance with Jett.

"I'm big on second chances."

"I was hoping you'd say that."

He leans in close. Is he about to kiss me? I stand waiting with puckered lips and shallow breath, but instead, he asks another question. "Is this a replica of the drawing?" Jett swipes his finger over the tattooed scar. His eyes widen. "Wait, this is permanent."

"Turns out you were kinda permanent, Jett. What I really want to say is...I love you."

His eyes soften as he stands here looking at me. The chills from his touch spill over every surface of my skin, and all I can think is how much this summer brought me, how much more I understand.

He eases me toward the Bronco's fender and leans in to crush his mouth to mine.

"I love you, too, Cami," he mumbles in the breaths between each kiss.

Chapter Thirty

E m picks up my threadbare stuffed rabbit from the box in the U-Haul and clutches it to her chest. "I still can't believe you're leaving me."

She's in a state of denial about Dad's decision to move us to Edisto. He's transferring jobs to the Charleston office, and I'll finish out school with Jett, Bo, and Gin as part of the island homeschool group. I'm not gonna lie. It's been bittersweet saying good-bye to my childhood home, the place I lived with Mama and Noli-Belle. And then telling Em we were relocating 250 miles away when we just got our friendship back on track was brutal. But it's for that reason I know we'll be okay. The limits of our friendship have been pushed to the brink, and we survived and came back stronger than ever. This isn't a hurdle. It's just a daytrip.

"I'm not leaving you. We're going to talk all the time." I snatch the stuffed animal from her hands and toss it at Trent, who's unloading boxes from the back. "Besides, you have Trent, and next year we'll all be together at college."

"Yeah, all of us," Jett says. He walks out from the floor-to-ceiling clutter in the trailer and jumps down on the sand.

Trent elbows him in the side. "I still can't believe you're giving up the dream, man."

"I'm not. I'll still be racing. Just making time to do other stuff, too." Jett winks at me, a look that melts me faster than the 98-degree summer heat. "I won't be the first racer to get a college degree."

To say Jett's dad was blown away by his son's artistic skills is an understatement. It was something Jett had kept close to the cuff, but when he produced the portfolio of home plans, Mr. Ramsey stood there slack-jawed as he flipped from page to page.

Soon, there was a stack of print-outs on the Ramsey dining room table about statewide arts programs and some impressive statistics on the "growth corridors in eco-friendly, sustainable design."

Meanwhile, I'm considering pursuing a nursing degree—maybe picking up where Mama left off. And I'm not complaining that Em, Trent, Jett and I have all ended up with plans to attend the same college.

I grab a small stack of boxes on the hand truck and wheel them to the steps where Gin and Buck sit. She's twirling her hair around her finger, laughing and touching Buck on the arm. When she sees me, I motion her over.

"You and Buck are getting awfully chummy, huh? Anything you want to tell me?" I tease.

Her cheeks flush crimson. "CJ!" She glances back over her shoulder at Buck, who's staring at a hangnail. Then she leans in close to my ear and whispers, "I'll fill you in later."

Gin trots back over to him and immediately falls back into her flirting dance. Good for her. She's waited a long time for the right guy to show up, and if Buck's anything like his brother, then she's a lucky girl.

Dad steps out on the porch and whistles for everyone's attention. Memaw comes out behind him with a broom in one hand and a bottle of window cleaner in the other. Once everyone gathers in the yard, Dad yells down, "How 'bout we all go eat at Something's Fishy? My treat since all of you helped me and CJ get moved in."

Something's Fishy is Dad's favorite new food addiction. Memaw had taken him to meet Hippie James last week. I was skeptical. The old Dad would've had no part of it. But to my surprise, Dad and James clicked immediately. So much so, he and James caught a baseball game over a couple of beers at the bar after his shift ended.

As everyone begins to clean up and leave, Bo steps between me and Jett and drapes his arms over our shoulders. "Afterwards, we're taking Trent, Em, and Buck to the pier and making them Edisto-official. Y'all coming?"

"Give us about five minutes, and we'll meet y'all at the restaurant." Jett glances at his watch and shoots me a conspiratorial gaze.

We sit on the top porch step watching everyone load in their cars. Memaw's the last out of the house, dodging us on her way. "Hey Memaw!" I holler, and she turns around. "For the love of all things holy, stay away from the shrimp and grits with all that extra sausage!"

A wicked grin creeps over her face, and she flips me the bird before going to Dad's car.

When everyone drives away, Jett pulls me to standing, and we head around the house, up a flight of stairs, and then another to the raised deck. It's the same deck where Jett and I shared our first kiss. And since Dad and I have taken a long-term lease on Mr. Ramsey's rental house, there'll be plenty more starry nights like that one.

But the view in the daytime is just as amazing, stretching out for miles of sandy beaches and blue-green Atlantic waters. This time, I'm not even terrified of being so high above the palmettos. Jett leans against the railing and pulls me in close, nuzzling my neck.

Oh yes, many more nights up here, for sure.

But right now, everyone's waiting on us. "You know, they're all gonna start wondering where we are."

"Let 'em," he mumbles, his lips exploring the slope of my neck.

"Including my dad? He's not as understanding as Memaw." A look of panic crosses Jett's face, as though he's a criminal and the police rolled into town. I laugh and hold out my hand. "Besides, it's my turn to drive."

"I teach you how to drive a stick and suddenly you know everything."

"Not everything." Jett gives me the *you're-full-of-crap* eyebrow, and I concede. "Ok, most things."

"Do you know how much I love you?"

"Lots. Tons. More than the gallons of water in the ocean. More than the—"

271

"Ok, smartass. Now how much do you love me?"

"As much as I ever could…but…"

He frowns, eyes narrowed. "But? There's a but?"

"*But* not as much as I ever will. Because every day, I love you more than the day before." I roll my eyes and throw my hands in the air. "I know, I'm hopeless. I'm smothering myself in my own sap."

"I like your sap," Jett teases. I press myself against him and run my hands down his shoulders, over his chest, his stomach, to his hips, and then slip them deep in his pockets. He lets out a small sigh, his breathing accelerating as he whispers, "I thought you said we needed to go."

"We do." I yank the car keys from his pocket and dangle them in the air. "Race you."

The End

Acknowledgements

How do I even begin to say thank you to all the people who have helped with AS MUCH AS I EVER COULD or my continued development as an author along this journey? It would be impossible to convey just how much each of you has meant to the process, so please accept this as my meager attempt to do so.

First, a huge thank you goes out to my readers. Y'all amaze me and humble me and remind me of what this process is really about. It's about creating characters that y'all can love and relate to on a human level and then want to bring them into your life. You first loved Rayne and Gage in MEANT TO BE BROKEN, and likewise, I hope CJ and Jett also plant themselves into your heart. Every time you purchase a copy, refer it to a friend, or leave a review, you help them gain new life in another reader's heart, and for that, I could never thank you enough.

To God, I simply lift up Psalm 37:4. You have truly provided a path for the desires of my heart. I am so grateful...for everything. I only hope I do You proud.

To the "green girls" of Filles Vertes Publishing who once again took a chance on another emotional Southern romance: Thank you for giving me the platform to bring CJ and Jett and their wonderful coastal town of Edisto Beach, SC to life in these pages. Myra, Jess, Carla, Milly, and so many others diligently working behind the scenes in this crazy publishing biz—y'all are awesome!

To my critique partners, Carla and Jena: I wouldn't be here without y'all. Your tough love and critical eyes made a difference in this book; your warmth and friendship has made a difference in me. And can I just say, Jena, that you rocked the cover design. I mean, y'all...have you seen all that attention to detail?! I love you both, my sisters.

To my tribe: From reading early drafts to simply being there for support (which is not always such a simple task! LOL), I treasure each of you, and from the bottom of my heart, please know how much I appreciate and adore you all! All my love and gratitude to The Writing Bootcamp Buds, Sarah Barkoff, Haleigh Wenger, Krystle Brantzeg, Stuart White (and the WriteMentor program), Khadijah VanBrakle, Katy Upperman, Atina Atwood, and so many others in the Twitter and Instagram writing communities.

To the contests along the way that saw the value in the manuscript and gave me the always-needed moral support to "keep at it," I want to say a huge thanks to the NEORWA Cleveland Rocks Romance contest, The Music City RWA Melody of Love contest, and the Sun versus Snow contest.

To my kiddos, Maddox, Hayden, and Colton: Don't ever let fear rob you of living life to the fullest. Explore, Excel, Exemplify. Learn by example, and be the example. And always remember that Mama is in your corner! I love y'all!

And finally, to my forever "love interest," Gene: I spend a lot of time concocting "book boyfriends" but the best in each of them comes directly from you. Like CJ tells Jett, "You're the good in my world." If not for your sacrifice and your devotion to my words, I'd never be where I am today. Thank you for being my husband, my best friend, my #1 fan, and the inspiration for many more books. All my love to you…always.

ABOUT THE AUTHOR

Brandy Woods Snow is a Young Adult author, journalist, wife, mama of three, Christian, and proud Southerner.

When Brandy's not writing, reading or driving carpool for her kids, she enjoys kayaking, family hikes, yelling "Go Tigers!" as loud as she can, playing the piano and taking "naked" Jeep Wrangler cruises on twisty, country roads.

Brandy's debut novel, *Meant To Be Broken* was released in 2018 with Filles Vertes Publishing.

Check out our full catalog at FVPub.com

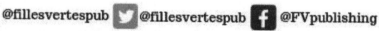

FILLES VERTES
PUBLISHING

and follow us for more!

More from the author...

Available at FVPub.com
and major online retailers

Brandy Woods Snow

Want more from our incredible authors?

F V P

VISIT OUR WEBSITE FOR ADDITIONAL CONTENT, EXCLUSIVE NEWS, BOOK TRAILERS, AND MORE!

Filles Vertes

www.FillesVertesPublishing.com